THE MAN WHO MURDERED HIS STAG

STEFAN LE ROY

HADDOCK
MANOR

Published in the UK in 2022 by Haddock Manor

www.StefanLeRoy.com

Paperback ISBN: 978-17396251-3-9
Hardback ISBN: 978-1-7396251-2-2
.epub eBook ISBN: 978-1-7396251-1-5

FOR MATTY

THANK YOU

Binny, for your endless love and support.
Kimberley Miller, for your sublime wordsmithery.
and above all
HaShem, my rock and refuge.

Prologue

1994, SOHO

Unsure of the outcome fate would hand him, his lungs heaved, and the muscles in his legs burned as he sprinted. The fact he was even on foot had not been the plan, but spotting the officers snooping around his car he had been left with little choice. Had they seen him? He was unsure. But his instant decision had been to flee.

And she? She was all that mattered now, for the moment at least. It was for her he would run; for her he would risk whatever came next. He could barely stand the thought of being apart from her, but if there was a glimmer of hope for them to be reunited again, he knew, beyond doubt, that he must hide her as quickly as he could.

As he tore through London's back streets, he made snap decisions at each juncture, twisting and turning in random directions in a bid to prolong the inevitability of his capture. But time may have already run out. The echoing clatter of footsteps from his pursuer was unmistakable. Was it just the one cop? Or maybe both? He couldn't tell. But if he didn't take action now, it would be over for him and her.

He lurched left. This street was narrower, shadowed by five- and six-storey buildings. Up ahead he spotted an old pub on a junction, a row of overflowing bins against one wall under a billboard. There! He threw himself behind the metal containers and risked a look. Good. Just the one.

The footsteps halted. His pursuer was no doubt debating whether his quarry had turned left or right. The decision must have been swift. He heard the officer move closer, breathing hard, as indeed he was. Time was up.

"Enough," he whispered, and reached into his jacket. If they found him, they'd find her. He couldn't let that happen. Better he was alone.

The lone police officer was unaware he was being watched, unaware of the pistol aimed at his back as he turned to locate the man he had been chasing. One bullet and his legs crumpled.

The shooter watched the officer go still, impassive.

"This is simply a delay, my beauty," he whispered, hearing the sirens and sliding her to safety. "Will you wait for me?"

Chapter One

2003, VENICE

Standing for a moment, motionless aside from blinking in the midday sunlight, Tom felt a little like the living statue he'd seen that morning outside the Doge's Palace, minus the silver paint and the pose. He was immobilised by the disbelief of what he'd just done.

It had come as no surprise to Tom that Venice in February was one of the most beautiful places in the world to find oneself. His *Guide to Historic European Cities* had suggested it; his presence here had confirmed it. Prior to arriving, and in his typically unromantic way, he had joked that it was probably the only time of year cold enough to subdue the stench of the canals that meandered through the heart of the city. Yet here, from the veranda of the Grand Canal Hotel, the spectacular panorama silenced his sarcasm, and across a table laid for two, the small leather-bound box he had just presented had silenced his girlfriend.

He sat down. All sound had distorted like it does at the deep end of a pool.

"Didn't you hear me, silly?"

He studied her pale and pretty face. What had he missed?

"I said yes! Yes, yes, yes! I will marry you. Unless ..." She raised her eyebrows, knowing him. "...you've gone right off the idea in the last ten seconds?"

"Yes ..." he exhaled, slumping in his seat. "I mean, no! I haven't gone off the idea. It's just ... I wasn't sure what you'd say. I ..."

He was on his feet again, pondering a monologue about her making him the happiest man in the world, when a sharp *"Cretino Inglese!"* made him swing around: he was face to face with an impeccably dressed lady soaked in an expensive Chianti.

On any other occasion, Tom would have been apologetic, but Jenny had just agreed to be his – *his!* – and it was the vigilant Jenny who intervened with the apology and then hissed, "I've put the money for our drinks on the table, so let's leave. Now."

Later that day, the newly affianced Tom and Jenny strolled around the bustling alleyways of San Marco, animated by the prospect of their forthcoming marriage. Arriving at the main square, they gazed across the historic flagstone piazza, the dying light of the afternoon sun shimmering in gold relief across the Basilica's facia.

Tom looked up at the famous Campanile bell tower, an imposing landmark at more than three hundred feet high. That day, he felt as tall. Venice. What a place. And what a place to take the step of commitment. He was twenty-nine years old. He was arm in arm with his fiancée. He was determined. *Tom, it's a life of risk and ... and action now for you.* He turned to kiss his bride-to-be. *No more hiding. No more endless weighing up of damage limitation. Yes, things are going to be different now.*

* * *

A week later, back to their daily routines and individual houses, they continued to make plans for their wedding. Jenny maintained they should keep their own homes until something more binding occurred, but the reality was they'd barely spent more than a few days apart. On a daily basis, the only major decision to be made over breakfast was whose home they would end up at that evening after work. Jenny lived across the village from him in her tiny two-bedroomed terraced house, which she shared with her Danish housemate, and would walk across to see him in his flat next to the train station, which he shared with Tom the Second, his cat with the missing front left leg. He had found Tom the Second two years ago by the side of the road directly outside the flat, his leg badly broken. No one claimed him in the weeks of his recovery, which had pleased Tom, accustomed as he had become to having the animal as company. "Tom treats that three-legged furball like a son, you know," Jenny had said to mutual friends on numerous occasions, so 'Tom the Second' the cat became – not his preferred Nelson, on account of the leg – and stayed, all of his needs and veterinary bills met by his new father.

Jenny. He still cringed when he thought about the first sentence that had spluttered from his lips when he had first met her. A BA undergraduate in Philosophy and Literature, she had been working lunchtimes and evenings at the dreary student bar at Essex University – imaginatively named the S U Bar. On a rare day off work, he'd been visiting his cousin Mike, who had just started a job as a chef in one of the university's canteens, and they'd made a beeline for the bar for a quick half and some lunch. "What's a pretty girl like you doing in a place like this, then?" he'd said. She'd said, "I'm here to serve you beer so I can make a few extra pennies, therefore allowing me to continue my studies of a wide-ranging and flexible philosophy curriculum that embraces both analytic and Continental philosophical thought."

Almost three years later, Jenny still relished telling this story, and Tom's embarrassment had not faded. It made him sound like some kind of clichéd serial womaniser when, in actual fact, it was the first (and last) time he'd ever made a verbal pass at a girl in his entire life. These days, though, there was a sort of pride coupled to it, for having the guts to speak to her at all. He still shuddered when he recalled the utter helplessness of that moment, however. How this petite, rather pale girl, with long blonde hair and astonishing blue eyes, had put a beer in front of him and had him captivated in a second. But they spoke again, and again, and now here they were. Looking back, he could only feel grateful that fate had dealt him such a providential and unexpected hand, or else he was sure he would still be single!

* * *

The day had seemed long, and Tom was tired. Yet again another suspected bomb alert had hampered his return from Liverpool Road, London N1. BrightTech Media, the website development company he worked for, had taken police advice and allowed staff to leave early. Tom made his way to Angel, his nearest Tube station, only to find it was temporarily closed to the public. Londoners had become not so much expectant, but certainly resigned to these interruptions to their daily routine, and he had (passively) observed a definite reduction in the brief eye-to-eye combat among fellow Tube travellers, and the familiar compliance with the unwritten Underground rule of aimless stares while listening to the tuneless clatter from the track below, heads nodding in time, had been restored.

He opted not to take the advice of the armed police officer

standing outside Angel, who had ventured that Tom's best bet was to jump in a cab to Liverpool Street station, and instead made the quick stroll back to King's Cross St Pancras. There he joined the jostling queue before finally using the Circle line to Liverpool Street.

Wedged between two large women, he imagined how his life might look without Jenny. He didn't like the look of it at all and congratulated himself once more for his horrendous first sentence. It had got them talking, hadn't it? How bizarre life was, in that she had been in that bar, and he had gone to the same bar ... the randomness of it all. And yet was it? *Are we really masters of our own destiny or, by some trickery, do we just imagine we are?* He thought about that short break in Venice when he'd asked that question, and a weird grin smiled back at him from his distorted reflection in the window opposite. His had been such a calculated life until he'd met Jenny. Jenny had changed that. Well, to a certain extent.

The train slowed, the Barbican sign slid in and out of view, and then it rumbled to a stop. An undeniably attractive girl boarded and made a dash for the vacant seat directly opposite him, obscuring his reflection. Immediately he looked down at the floor, as was common practice. How, in a city of over seven million people, did people meet people and then actually get to know them? Although he didn't socialise much outside of office hours, he did know people through work. In fact, quite a number of them had become friends. *Actually, I have quite a number of friends through work*, he thought, trying to bolster his flailing ego. But did he know them? He was known as 'the techie geek' from programming. The one who bought the first round of drinks when he was occasionally invited to join the lunchtime clique ... there was only ever time for one round of drinks at lunchtime ... They were friends, weren't they? But did they know him?

The train rumbled to one stop from Liverpool Street.

He might still make the 6.08pm train bound for Wivenhoe and be home before 7.30pm. If only people understood that programming was a huge part of any designed website and needed proper scheduling. Why did they expect everything to be done in a heartbeat? He looked up.

Experience life on the internet as it was meant to be. www.GamezMatez.com. Unique, interactive 3D gaming and live video chat. Log on today and make some playmatez!

The poster reminded him of Mike, who was always gloating about having dozens of mates – online – who he would play multiplayer games with into the night, chatting to each other via their headsets while they played. "And the best bit, Tommy," Mike assured him, "is that we can all get pissed, right, cos nobody has to drive home!" No amount of persuasion from Mike had led Tom to "join the clan", as he put it. No amount of teasing about 'geekiness' would see him throw himself into a cyber pool of activity, the last bastion of male camaraderie as he saw it.

Premier Online Dating London – online dating with a focus on friendship. Live chatting, dating, and above all … making friends!

"Good grief," Tom blurted out at this poster, blatantly breaking one of the other prime laws of the Underground: no speaking.

The large lady sitting to his right startled. "I beg your pardon?"

"It must be harder to make friends than I thought." Past all self-consciousness, he added, "I know it's 2003, but how can people be that desperate?"

The lady stared into the side of his head and then back at the floor, and he almost laughed out loud at the causticness – was that the word? – of her 'I beg your pardon?'. What a world.

* * *

The lights were already on in his flat, so he guessed Jenny had let herself in. A shriek of laughter confirmed that was true. He placed, not lobbed, his keys into an irregular-shaped, glazed bowl – the result of one of Jenny's many discontinued evening classes – and listened.

"Oh, Ali, that would be excellent. D'you think she'd want to come?" Jenny said. "Wow, I haven't seen Sharon for years ... well, not properly anyway. I did bump into her in town about six months ago, but I told you about that, didn't I. Didn't I? Well, let's just say she was having trouble shifting the pounds after sprog *numero deux*. Still, I bet she looks as good as she always did. Anyway, must dash. Tom's back ... not the cat ... the man. See you Sunday. Let me know who's up for it and who's not ... love to John ... see ya!" She jumped up as Tom stepped into the doorway. "That was Ali. We've just concocted the most wonderful plan!"

"Really?" Tom was pretty sure that any plan Jenny had concocted with her friend Alison was probably not going to be that wonderful; but then it may not even be a plan that got anywhere near out of the starting blocks of that conversation, so he would do some listening and then they could get on with their lives. "Let me grab a beer. Do you want anything? And then you can tell me all about it." He headed for the kitchen.

"How was your day?" he called.

"There's no need to shout!"

He turned. She was right behind him.

"Sorry." He groped around inside the fridge for a can.

"It's okay," she said. "I've got a glass of wine on the go. How was your day?"

"Well, there was the bomb scare I phoned you about, for starters."

"Oh, yes, I forgot to say. Oh, and you are late home. I was just watching the news before Ali rang. Luckily it was just a hoax in the end."

"What a bloody waste of time. Somebody needs to string these toerags up and shoot the lot of 'em."

"Who? The hoaxers, the police or the actual bombers?"

"I'm being grumpy, aren't I? What a crap day." He opened the can and drank.

"Was work the other reason your day was crap?"

"Yep. Us programmers will never be understood, Jen. But, hey, I'm home now." He looked all the way down from his six-foot-two to her five-foot-two and pulled her into a hug. "Go on, tell me what you and Scatty Ali have concocted."

Jenny leaned out of the hug and looked up at him. "We're organising a hen weekend!"

"A hen weekend."

"Yes–"

"So you can flaunt your singledom for one last–"

"Tom! It's a getaway with all the girls to celebrate the fact I'm getting married to you. Don't tell me you don't trust me!"

"With Alison, of all people!" Ouch, he was grumpy. He took a long drink of his beer. "Sorry, but you know what she's put poor old John through ... Anyway, sorry, again, please carry on."

"So we reckon we'll do it about a week or two before the wedding." She looked up at him, obviously excited. "I told Ali I'd check when you're planning on having your stag do. We may as well have them at the same time."

"Stag do," Tom repeated, the thought as alien to him as Jenny's hen do.

"Yes. You must have given it some thought?"

"Well, yes ... I mean no, not yet anyway." He frowned. "Where will this hen night be?"

"It's a hen weekend, and at the moment, we're thinking of Prague. It's meant to be almost as beautiful as Venice," Jen replied, smiling at the memory, "only a lot cheaper."

"Prague."

Prague?

"So, come on, why haven't you thought about your stag do?"

"I don't know, really. It's been hectic at work, and, anyway, who would feed the cat if I went away?"

"We'll find someone to take good care of him. Why are you avoiding the issue, Tom? Why wouldn't you want to have a stag do?"

"Oh, I don't know, sweetheart," he sighed. "I just don't think it's me, and I can't really see who'd want to come."

"Well, I think that's crazy. You've got to have a stag do, Tom, even if it's just for one evening. You've got plenty of friends at work, haven't you? And there's your cousin Mike, Ali's John, Dave at the pub. You have plenty of friends."

That word again. Friends.

"I'll have a miserable time in Prague if I know you're sitting at home on your own."

"I've got Tom the Second."

"Oh, Tom, don't be so ... so ..."

Over dinner, he promised he would plan something, and her face lit up in the way it always did when she only ever wanted the best for him. But her best for him was his risk management and, lying in bed that night, he saw Jenny dancing in a Prague nightclub, pressed up against a handsome Czech, and fighting among drunken stag friends, and he cursed the man who'd come up with the concept of bloody prenuptial getaways.

Chapter Two

INTERESTED PARTIES

Chief Superintendent David Blakney was not a man given to public outbursts of anger, but his fist hit the desk before his exiting duty sergeant had firmly closed the office door behind her. His long-held position as a Metropolitan Police Service chief had equipped him with the ability to speed read, and the paperwork that had just been dropped onto his desk had instantly caused his normally cool temperament to boil over.

"Lawson, you bastard ..." he seethed through gritted teeth.

The object of his vehemence was a convicted felon by the name of Mickey Lawson, and the paperwork he had just received was a report that the man was to be released from prison the very next morning. The news of Mickey's early release on parole wasn't necessarily a surprise to Blakney – in fact, he had long been hoping for an expedited discharge – but the precise timing was all wrong, according to the plans he had in place. Now he would have to adapt these plans, and quickly.

With little grace, the chief superintendent dropped his large frame into the chair behind his desk and drummed his fingers on the fading green leather. Although he was reaching the end of his illustrious career, the ageing man's mind was still sharp. His ability to be cunning was almost as agile as the day he had become an officer of the Met ... despite the regularly replaced bottles of fine Scotch he kept in the right-hand bottom drawer. Blakney knew he would now have to make his move early in order to get this last play right.

"I'm bringing you straight back in, Lawson," he muttered. "And I'll bring the Lady in with you."

Mickey Lawson was the single dirty stain on the chief superintendent's almost spotless reputation in a career that had spanned nearly forty-five years. He had always been hungry for success and had matched his hunger with relentless determination. Because of this doggedness, he had risen through the ranks and into the prized position he held today. But there had been one non-result that had infuriated him for almost a decade; a failure, as he saw it, that mocked his hard-won status as the Metropolitan Police's safe pair of hands.

Nine years ago, the chief superintendent had been given the responsibility of overseeing a highly secretive transfer of priceless jewels from London City Airport to an unprecedented exhibition at the National Gallery. Among the precious cargo was a fabulous pink diamond, on loan from the Dutch royal family and the largest of its kind ever recorded. So large was the jewel that experts, after its theft, could not agree if its worth on the black market would be ten, fifteen or even twenty million pounds. Blakney's reputation had been dragged through a media circus for many months. His commissioner had even pressed for him to give a public account and apology in full glare of the TV cameras and onlookers. To make matters worse, during the robbery, one of Blakney's men had been severely injured by a single gunshot wound to his back, leaving him paralysed for life. And the man responsible had been Mickey Lawson.

Despite Mickey's daring and calculated raid, where he successfully made off with the priceless gem, he was discovered by armed officers shortly after, hunkered down in a shed at the side of one of London's many rejuvenation building sites. But Mickey had somehow managed to part company with his prize, and the chief superintendent and his men were unable to extract any information whatsoever as to the whereabouts of the diamond, known by then as the Pink Lady. Lawson was still sent down for a lengthy stretch in a high-security prison, and Blakney was left to rue his infamous cock-up, a source of embarrassment and anger that had eaten away at him ever since.

Blakney knew, of course, beyond all certainty, that Lawson would not have discarded the diamond during the police pursuit. He also felt sure that the thief would not have had time to have met with an accomplice in order to pass the gem off. No, he believed Mickey must have stashed it somewhere safe just in case he had been caught. In fact, for weeks after the theft, many officers at the chief superintendent's disposal were tasked with a meticulous street-by-street search for the stolen diamond, retracing the estimated route that Lawson had likely taken from the crime scene up until the moment he was caught. But it was to no avail, and Blakney's pride in his work had suffered a near-mortal blow, he felt, until now.

The chief superintendent regained his composure. Leaning forward, he reached for his phone and made the call he'd now been forced into making far earlier than planned. An officer picked up the call at the receiving end without saying a word.

"Michaels," Blakney said quietly. "Lawson is out tomorrow. We need to move now. Listen carefully and make sure you do everything exactly as I say."

* * *

Donnie Sykes was a bull of a man. Even at the age of sixty-two, his six-foot four-inch bulk was enough to intimidate the most commanding characters. Although from humble beginnings, the East Ender always attempted to bear the grace of a man born into money. In truth, those who spent just a few moments in his presence were left with no uncertainty that this was a man who had always taken whatever he wanted from whomever he had chosen to take it from.

Known to the law establishment for decades, Sykes had built a small empire on a criminal career that existed and survived purely because its foundation was rooted in fear. Since his early years, growing up in the back streets of Walthamstow, Donnie's name had grown in infamy due to his increasing taste for extreme violence. For him, this had ensured not just the loyalty of his growing firm but also the savage suppression of his criminal rivals. His long career had seen him hone his talents in extortion, racketeering, prostitution, money laundering and, in more recent years, the organised theft of precious stones and their resale on the black market.

Although Donnie had always hated the established rule of law, recent years had caused his vilification of the police to wane as his wealth became a tool that could corrupt officers at seemingly any level. His elevated status as a crime lord and, more importantly, his vast wealth and articulate manner of speech had meant there were few echelons of power he could not exploit. Like Chief Superintendent David Blakney, Donnie Sykes had a vested interest in Mickey Lawson's movements, and after an inside tip from a paid informant, he too was about to make his own play to intercept the notorious jewel thief. Like Blakney, Sykes' objective was to obtain the Pink Lady. However, unlike the chief superintendent, his dual purpose was not to see Mickey Lawson serve more time to restore Blakney's damaged reputation. No. As far as Donnie was concerned, a dead Mickey Lawson would do just fine.

It was now Sykes' turn to make a phone call. Opening the top drawer of his desk, he selected one of four secure mobile phones and hit the only speed dial stored in the contacts list. Seconds later, a man with a heavy Serbian accent answered.

"Why you call me?" the man said, with an edge of venom.

"I know this is irregular," Donnie answered calmly, "but your current operation needs to be put on hold. I have a new target who needs to be taken care of immediately."

"This is more than irregular. Our agreement is I contact you when job is done. I do not like changes to agreement."

"Trust me, Doković, I have no choice. Your current contract will be honoured, but for now, I have a more pressing matter that will make both of us very rich men. In fact, once this is done, you may not be that concerned about completing your current contract."

There was a pause. "I very much doubt that, Mr Sykes. I have never once not completed a task I have commit to. This is why you hired me, is it no? Nevertheless, give the details and I will make sure is taken care of."

"Thank you, Doković," Sykes said, restraining his anger at being questioned by a hired gun. "The new target is a Mickey Lawson, and he has something that is very precious to me. You will have to move quickly, so listen carefully ..."

Chapter Three

PRENUPTIAL IMPASSE

The pristine double glass doors at the entrance of BrightTech Media belied the rather drab interior of the fledgling web development company operating on three floors. Like so many companies in London, a great deal of notability was given to having an address 'in the city', but beyond the double doors and shiny signage, the working experience was distinctly average.

It was Monday morning, and Tom, arriving slightly late, pushed his way through the doors into the dimly lit reception and collided with a row of boxes obstructing his path. He sprawled inelegantly across the budget brown carpet-tile floor, mouth open in protest and cheeks flushed partly with anger and partly with embarrassment. He glared at the boxes and then looked around for someone to blame. It clearly wasn't anything to do with the two reps who had turned to snigger at his misfortune. Getting to his feet, he spotted a heavyset, shaven-headed delivery man in dark green overalls. Under his chin were wedged two large computer equipment boxes which, despite their obvious weight, did not hamper his cheerful whistling.

Stacking the boxes with the others, he noticed Tom's disgruntled stare. "Alwite, mate?"

"No, actually, I'm not alright. Some berk nearly broke my

neck by leaving boxes right inside the door. It's not very well lit in here, and ..."

The man's previously cheerful demeanour vanished. Conscious that he was still being watched by the reps and noting the size of the man, Tom opted to backtrack. "Yes, well, it's just that ... it's not really the most sensible place to leave a load of boxes, is it?"

Nodding to himself in a self-assured, I've-dealt-with-plenty-of-your-sort-before-and-you-won't-be-the-last-mate kind of way, the delivery man got right up in Tom's face.

"Two fings, pal."

"Sorry?"

Tom flinched as the man held two large fingers up in front of his nose. "Two fings before you apologise an' I fawget you called me a berk." Tom nodded, wishing the reps would just go to wherever it was they were supposed to be going. "One," he continued, gesturing over his shoulder. "On me van it sez free delivery door-to-door, right? It don't say nuffink about luggin' boxes up and daan stairs. Geddit?"

"Absolutely, quite right," Tom nodded rapidly.

"An' two. Wever your office 'ere is in the dark or lit up like Blackpool bleedin' illuminations, it ain't got nuffink to do wiv me if you ain't lookin' where yer goin'."

"True, very true," Tom agreed hastily, "and I'm sorry for calling you a–"

"An' free–"

"What? Sorry. I thought there were only two."

The man stared him down. "She told me to put 'em 'ere," he said, pointing towards the reception desk.

"Okay, look, this is really just a misunderstanding. I'm sorry, I–"

The delivery man smiled. "Apology 'ccepted, squire." And he

resumed his whistling and left.

With a sigh of relief, Tom headed over to speak to Avril at the reception desk. She had headphones on and was transcribing a letter or something. He thanked God, or whoever that she hadn't been eavesdropping. He liked Avril, but she wouldn't win any competitions for discretion. The reps had gone, thankfully.

Leaning over the desk, he tapped her on the shoulder. She jumped slightly, turned and removed her headphones. "Morning, Tom. Running a bit late, aren't you?"

"Yeah, just a little."

"Seen the new goodies, then?"

Tom looked at her for a moment and then realised. "Oh, the computer boxes blocking the entrance. Yes. They won't be for us, though. New toys for the design department, no doubt. Our programming department hasn't had an upgrade in years. Those damn designers only have to click their fingers as soon as they're a single operating system behind, and him upstairs is straight on to MacsForYou."

Avril smiled blankly at him, clearly not understanding. "You met Alfie, then?"

"Who?"

"Alfie, the delivery guy?" Avril pointed at the boxes. "He's lovely," she continued. "I just love a man what's polite and happy at work, not to mention the muscles," she said with a giggle.

"Oh, him. Alfie his name, is it? Yes, we met briefly," Tom replied. "How's your boyfriend David?" he then asked, changing the subject.

"It's Daniel. And he's fine, thanks. Oh, Tom, he's so lovely, you know. On Saturday he told me we're going away for a romantic weekend in two weeks' time. He said, 'Don't make any plans, babe, cos I've got everything organised.' He won't tell me where we're going, though. It's so exciting. I just love a man what takes the initiative. He's so masterful. He even insisted I throw a sickie on the Friday so we get a long weekend of it."

"Great, that sounds really great," Tom said with slight impatience. "Any mail for me, Avril?"

"Er ..." She shuffled through the mail on her desk. "No, not today, Tom."

"Okay, thanks. I'll catch you later, yeah?"

"Okay. Oh, how was your weekend?" she called after him.

"Yeah, great, thanks."

Tom's weekend had certainly not been great. In fact, it had been far from the relaxing time he and Jenny usually enjoyed together. He had barely slept on Friday night for thinking about his potential stag do, and on Saturday, he had been tired and tetchy all day. On Sunday, Alison had come up from Kent. This had been the final straw. Alison, Jenny's long-time friend, seemed to detest him, and the feeling was certainly mutual. He often found himself biting his tongue in her company as she picked holes in his appearance, his mannerisms, and his comments. Amazingly, the mild-mannered Jenny never appeared to be aware of their mutual distaste for one another. Tom put it down to the fact that Jenny always saw the best in people and ignored the worst. Perhaps this was one of the reasons she was with him.

What is it with women? Tom thought as he climbed the stairs to the second floor. How could one woman love him so much and another despise him so completely without ever having bothered to get to know him? Why were perfectly nice girls like Avril physically attracted to thugs like Alfie, the delivery man? And then there was Dick, or Daniel, or whatever his name was. Tom had never met Avril's boyfriend, but he was sure if he ever did, he would no doubt find him loathsome. Avril had droned on to Tom about her boyfriend for the best part of a year now, often expounding, in lurid detail, of his many marvellous qualities. Why did every bloke have to be so bloody marvellous, take the initiative, be 'masterful'? "Why can't we just be normal?" he muttered.

Tom arrived at his workstation, dumped his bag on the floor and slumped into his chair, turning on his computer as he did so.

"Morning, T."

"Morning, Miles," Tom replied without turning.

Miles, the new boy in programming, slid himself over on the casters of his swivel chair.

"Wha'sup, man?" Miles drawled. "You late, and you iz never late, bro!"

Tom leaned away. Miles was practically jammed up against him. He couldn't abide people who didn't have a handle on the rules of personal space, but with spectacles as thick as Miles', Tom probably appeared as if he was ten feet away.

"I've had a bad weekend, and I'm having an even worse start to the week."

"Woman troubles?" Miles said with a grin. "Word to muvva, bro."

"Miles. One, I'm not your brother. Two, stop talking like that. You're a white, middle-class schoolboy, not a dude from south central LA. And three, you wouldn't recognise woman troubles as you barely spend any time with the female sex."

"Wrong, actually," Miles objected. "I was with three lovely ladies just last night. Till the early hours as it happens."

"Really?" Tom said, trying to sound sarcastic but, irritatingly, slightly interested.

"Yeah, really. I joined an online thing a couple of weeks ago and chatted with some girls I used to go to school with. We meet up most nights and–"

"Oh, not you as well," Tom groaned. "You must be desperate, Miles. Get lost and leave me to get on with my work, okay?"

"One, don't be rude," Miles retorted as he wheeled himself away. "And two, it's not desperate, actually. I'm taking one of the girls out on Friday."

"Yeah, yeah, whatever," Tom replied, turning back to his computer.

He checked his workload for the day and turned the page of his wiro-bound BrightTech Media company calendar. It was the first day of June, and his eyes were instantly drawn to a date that had been circled with a red pen. A date at the end of the month. Good grief! It was less than a month before the wedding! How the heck had that come around so fast?

With his workload forgotten, his head was suddenly swamped with images of wedding dresses, reception halls, catering brochures, photograph albums and ... damn ... that bloody stag do he promised he'd have. What was he going to do? He might have made the promise to keep her happy, but he'd not really considered he would actually have to go ahead with it. Memories of Venice came flooding back, and the vow he had made to himself that he was going to take a few more risks and start living. But that was just 'enthusiasm of the moment' stuff, wasn't it? He had put his heart on the line by proposing to Jenny, and she'd said yes. That was a risk, wasn't it? And that had worked out better than he could ever have imagined. So what was holding him back? Did he think no one would want to come? No, it wasn't that. He was sure he could get enough people interested. So what was it?

His eyes strayed to the desktop calendar again. Each month featured a so-called Word of Wisdom intended to 'inspire creative inspiration' as some pillock from the design department had put it to him one lunchtime. Tom had nodded in polite agreement while thinking that if January through to May's quotes were anything to go by, he might end up a monotonous, faceless, voiceless automaton who'd forgotten his own name come December; such was the effect of such drivel on his life. However, June's words of wisdom were penned by some twentieth-century philosopher named Tillich. The quote read: 'Decision is a risk rooted in the courage of being free.' Tom pondered these weighty words for a moment until suddenly, it dawned on him. "Decision is the key!" he said, slapping his hand hard on his desk. A couple of colleagues looked up from their work. "Sorry," he smiled, "something wrong with my keyboard."

For the next half an hour, Tom's mind was racing. He was going to go for it and throw a stag do. And not just an evening. Oh no. He was going to have the whole shebang: a weekend away!

He felt a strange but agreeable sense of liberation for the rest of the day. For the first time, just like Tillich had written, he'd realised that even making a decision was a risk. That, he concluded, was why he had been holding back all his life. Taking no risks meant he had always avoided making life-changing decisions. With one sentence from the distant past, he'd understood he'd been living a life of boredom, decided he was bored of being bored and found out there was only one way to change things: *Make the decision to take a few risks and experience freedom!*

That evening over dinner, he announced he was going to organise a stag do. Jenny dropped her fork. She then bounced around the table and gave him a hug. "I knew you could do it, darling," she said. "I'm so, so glad you're going for it. I'll be so much more relaxed knowing you're having fun too!"

Later, in front of the TV, he noticed the similarity between the look in Jenny's eyes that evening and the one he had seen in Avril's that morning. He again considered the words of Tillich and the fact that taking the odd risk was indeed a way in which to feel free. Had Daniel ... Damien ... taken a risk when he'd booked that surprise weekend for Avril? It had certainly paid off. Yes, taking risks was good. And then Jenny turned to him and said, "So where are you going to have your stag do?" His pleasant thoughts were stalled.

"Erm, well, I haven't got that far yet."

"You need to book something, Tom. It's the first of June today, and we are getting married on the 27th. If you're going to have the stag do the week before the wedding, then it gives you less than three weeks to organise things."

Less than three weeks. "Wow, I guess you're right," he managed, grappling with Tillich.

Jenny appeared not to notice the struggle. "What about Dublin?" she asked, excited.

"No. I don't think so. I've heard it's not really very Irish anymore. Probably ruined by too many stag dos and hen parties, I imagine."

"What about Spain? Mallorca or something like that?"

"You know I don't like clubbing."

"Scotland?"

"Too cold."

"Well, you're not going to Prague!"

"Don't worry," he laughed. "I wouldn't dream of cramping your style." He glanced at the TV. "Hey, I know!" he exclaimed, pointing at the screen.

Jenny looked over at the TV and saw footage of a cruise ship. "A cruise?" she said, baffled. "You haven't time to go on a cruise or the money ... you've lost the plot!"

"Not a cruise ship, Jen, but a boat – a canal boat. It's

something I've always fancied doing."

"Really?" She looked unconvinced. "Are you sure?"

"Yes, it'll be great fun. The camaraderie, cooking on a little stove, sitting on the roof in the sun and enjoying a beer ..."

"Well, it's your stag do, love. If you've always wanted to do it, then do it now because you won't be getting me on a canal boat."

"I should probably start to look into it," said the new, decisive Tom. "I'm sure I'll be able to find something online."

"Oh, not now, Tom. Can't you do it tomorrow?"

"No, no," said Tom, standing up and trying to sound masterful. "No time like the present. I'm going to be more Tillich!"

"Tillich?"

"Never mind."

Within a few minutes, he'd managed to find at least ten reputable-looking boating holiday websites. He was sure at least one would fit the bill. He jotted down contact numbers and decided he would start phoning around the next day. He fell asleep thinking about who he was going to ask to join him for his prenuptial celebrations.

* * *

During his lunch break the next day, a frustrated Tom put down the phone on the seventh contact from his boating websites list. "Damn, damn and damn," he muttered. Most of the contacts offered the weekend break he was looking for, but they were fully booked. In fact, the last person he had spoken to had been quite scornful of Tom's lack of foresight, considering he was to have a stag do in only three weeks' time. Tom put a line through the company's phone number. "Right, who's next?"

He got lucky with Blakes Boat Hire. There was a boat available due to a cancellation. It was a twelve-berth narrowboat called *May* and available for pickup from Beccles. The small market town in Suffolk, set on the banks of the Waveney River, was, as the old guy – Bill Blakes – who'd answered the phone had said, "The perfect starting point for exploring the whole of the Norfolk Broads." Tom was happy with that.

"A twelve-berth, you say?" he asked.

"That's right, me lad," the man continued in his Norfolk drawl. "But believe you me, you won't want twelve blokes on a narrowboat for a long weekend. I reckon eight people on a boat that size would be ample."

"Perfect," smiled Tom when the booking had been confirmed, and he'd hung up. "Wow! I'm having a stag do! Now for stage two."

Earlier that morning, when he'd been buying a newspaper, he'd noticed an advert on the front promoting a special offer for the Complete Set of Roald Dahl's Works. He'd loved lying in bed listening to his mother read those fantastic stories. His favourite, by a long way, had been *Charlie and the Chocolate Factory*, and that's when the idea for stage two had hit him. He would take a leaf out of Willy Wonka's book and give special tickets to those he was going to invite along to the stag do. It was a bit cheesy, but it might get a few laughs from the seven lucky recipients!

Tom didn't have any friends in the design department, but what he did have on his computer system was a 'borrowed' copy of Photoshop. In the remaining twenty minutes of his lunch hour, he quickly set to work designing a stag do invitation ticket. He put the dates, a picture of a narrowboat on a canal (downloaded from the Blakes Boat Hire website), an RSVP email address and, across the top right corner, a flash which read, 'Only £100 to cover all hiring costs'. He quickly printed the tickets before anyone noticed.

Four of the lucky recipients were BrightTech Media employees, so, during the afternoon, with a degree of both excitement and apprehension, Tom made visits to their respective departments for bogus reasons. As he secretively handed over the tickets, he was pleasantly surprised by their warm responses: "Cheers, Tom, count me in!"; "Nice one, mate. I'm definitely up for it!"; "My missus owes me a weekend out; looking forward to it!"; "Sound, bro! I've always wanted to do the canals ... wicked!" So that was Lawrence in Finance, Kevin in Administration, Steve in Maintenance and Miles in Programming, even though he could be bloody annoying. On the way to the station, he posted the remaining three tickets to his cousin Mike, Martin (an old school friend) and Scatty Ali's John. He couldn't help but feel rather pleased with himself for being so organised and decisive, and boarded the train with an unaccustomed lightness of step.

Chapter Four

AN UNLIKELY PARTNERSHIP

For the past nine years, Mickey Lawson had served time at Her Majesty's pleasure within the confines of London's Category B men's prison, Wormwood Scrubs. The prison itself was infamous for holding notable former inmates such as Charles Bronson and George Blake, the double agent and KGB operative.

Because of the nature of Lawson's crime and the level of violence that had been used, the majority of his sentence had been served in the prison's notorious D Wing, reserved almost exclusively for high-risk prisoners who mostly require single cells. In some ways, his confinement to a single cell seemed, initially at least, to be a godsend for Mickey, as very few prisoners enter Wormwood Scrubs as potential multimillionaires. Jealousy, in confined spaces, does not make for a good bedfellow.

News of the jewel thief's daring raid had spread like wildfire among the prison's inmates. However, as the early weeks of his incarceration passed, rather than make Mickey a target among the other inmates, news of 'his' priceless diamond resulted in almost a decade of goodwill and, at times, even a reverence for his criminal prowess. Throughout his sentence, numerous inmates attempted to curry favour with the Scrubs' most famous resident in the vain hope he might show them reciprocal favour were he to become truly rich once his stint inside was over. Mickey, however, had no interest in forming partnerships. Since his early years as a swindling confidence man, and before escalating to more serious criminal activities, he had always worked alone. That said, there was one connection Lawson knew he would have to make on the inside, but it wouldn't be easy.

It didn't take Mickey long to realise he would have a very serious problem on his hands once he had served his time: the Metropolitan Police and half of the criminal fraternity in London would be considering what his first move would be the moment he was released from prison. Would he head straight for the hidden Lady? Or would he lay low and bide his time? Either way, Mickey knew he could not take the risk of picking up a tail from the police. Worse, he could not risk being bundled into the back of a rival's car at gunpoint and forced to reveal the whereabouts of the priceless gem, after which he knew he would be expendable. But nine years inside was enough time to construct the master plan that would ensure his precise release date would be altered on the official records that were open to the public domain. How? His plan was to corrupt the prison governor himself.

* * *

At the start of Lawson's sentence, Prison Governor Stephen Riley was ten years from retirement, but his long-serving and varied career in prison security and management had left him tired and somewhat disillusioned with his lot. When he looked back, there were very few held positions, or even occasions, that he recalled with any degree of warmth. Over the years, his increasing responsibilities had become harder and harder to manage and, as far as he was concerned, he had reaped very little reward for all his efforts. At fifty-five, his daily routine, which started each day at 7.15am, had become brutally demanding within an environment of overcrowded, often violent inmates and constantly understaffed rotas performed by officers who were frequently unfit for duty. In a sense, Riley had come to identify more with his inmates than his colleagues, as his vocation had come to represent an interminable sentence. Too old to change careers now, the best he could hope for was that the next ten years would pass as quickly as possible.

* * *

Three years of Mickey Lawson's sentence had passed before he was allowed the opportunity to come face to face with the governor, but it was another eighteen months before he would meet him again without Riley's officers being within earshot of their conversation.

Lawson had been summoned to the governor's office for a halfway review of his nine-year sentence. He knew this might be his only chance to change the potentially disastrous fate that awaited him on the outside. However, he also knew he was about to deploy a high-risk strategy that could result in extending his sentence if the plan backfired. But if Mickey was good at one thing, it was reading people. Since his early days as a swindling conman, he had quickly learned the art of recognising facial expressions, understanding body movements and reading between the lines of what was spoken. This talent had helped him gain the upper hand in any given conversation, enabling him to manipulate his quarry into producing a result that almost always favoured Mickey's desired outcome.

As the two men sat on either side of the governor's oversized desk, it was Riley who spoke first. He leaned forward with a half-smile on his face and said, "So ... you're our diamond thief, then? Mr Lawson, is it? Well, Mr Lawson, are you going to tell me where you hid the diamond?"

"No, sir, I'm afraid I can't do that," Mickey replied respectfully.

"Well, it's worth a lot of money – millions, it is said – so I hope you're not able to tell because you can't remember where you stashed it?" The governor chuckled at his own remark and leaned back, linking his hands behind his head.

"Absolutely not, sir. I know exactly where it is. But I'm afraid it is not worth millions unless the holder knows how to sell it."

Riley shuffled slightly in his seat. He had meant his opening comments to be merely an icebreaker, but now he was intrigued at Lawson's unexpectedly honest response. He leaned forward again. "And do you, Lawson? Do you know how to sell it?"

Mickey took a deep breath. "Yes, sir, I do," he replied, again respectfully, watching the other man's face without making it appear obvious that every twitch and flicker was being scrutinised. "But I will not have the opportunity to sell it. The moment I step out of this prison, I will be forcibly 'picked up' by those who would seek to extract the information I alone know. I'll most likely be tortured until I reveal the whereabouts of the diamond, so they can retrieve it and sell it for themselves." Mickey waited. Yes. He had the man's attention. "You see, sir, the whole of London wants to know where the diamond is, and half of them would kill me in order to get it. As you know, my release will be on public record, so if anyone really wants to discover where the diamond is, then I believe you and I both know it's inevitable I will be picked up the moment I leave here."

Riley was deep in thought, processing Mickey's words, his chin on his knuckles.

Mickey stayed quiet. Watching.

"And if you could depart from here in secret ... where would that leave you?"

It was Lawson's turn to lean forward, and he looked the governor directly in the eyes. "That would leave me grateful, sir. Very grateful indeed."

For a long moment, the two of them remained locked eye to eye. Neither diverting their gaze. Neither showed a flicker of emotion. For a nanosecond, Mickey thought he may have overstepped the mark, that he may have misjudged the governor's corruptibility. Perhaps this was a man not hateful of his own lot in life? A man truly above temptation? But Lawson was wrong to doubt his gut feeling about the governor.

A second later, Riley rose to his feet, strode over to the door and quietly closed it. He returned purposefully to his side of the scruffy desk but appeared to resist the urge to sit down. Instead, he placed his palms on the desk and said, "What is it you need, Mr Lawson? And what are you prepared to give in return in order to make it happen?"

What Mickey Lawson needed was very simple: he needed to ensure that whoever might want to intercept him upon his release would end up disappointed.

"Sir, perhaps we can assume I will be on best behaviour for the rest of my stay here. And perhaps, for the sake of argument, you would look very favourably on my obvious rehabilitated character and obvious remorse–"

"You do understand, Mr Lawson," interjected the governor, "that your crime was not only theft, but also violence, and violence of extreme brutality? This aspect, coupled with the fact you will not give up the location of the stolen diamond, means it would be very hard to see an early release of anything more than a few months at best."

"I understand both points very clearly, sir, and I fully understand I will regrettably be seeing out virtually my entire sentence. However, all I am asking is that you oversee the final official release date to be given out on public record."

Riley seemed confused. "But I thought you wanted to walk out of here free from the risk of being picked up?"

"That is exactly what I want, sir. What we both want, in fact, if we are both to benefit. But I would like to suggest a slight clerical 'error' on the release date paperwork and that my actual release date, the day I walk free, will be twenty-four hours earlier. That would give me the time I need to retrieve the diamond and be safely away."

"In order to sell the diamond, yes?"

Lawson resisted the urge to laugh at the stupidity of Riley's question. "Unfortunately, a little patience will be required, sir. This is where I will need you to trust me, as I do have a fair bit of experience in these matters." Noting that Riley seemed prepared to accept this comment, Mickey continued. "If I try to make an immediate move in selling the diamond, I may as well have thrown it into the Thames. Therefore there will need to be a cooling-off period, as such, while I lay low... for a short while."

"How long?"

"At least a few weeks. After that, I can make a few tentative enquiries with some 'warm' contacts."

"Warm contacts?"

"People I have dealt with before, sir."

"And will they buy the diamond?"

"No."

"No?"

"No. These contacts are not buyers; they are people who facilitate the sale of precious stones onto the black market. They are our link to interested parties who, as well as having vast wealth, know how to remain anonymous when buying hot property such as a priceless diamond."

Mickey was sticking as close to the truth as possible in order to keep the governor completely focused. He knew from experience this was the best way to ensure a potential 'partner' would not get cold feet, so to speak.

"But how can you know for sure the diamond will sell?" Riley asked, dropping his voice.

"Sir, this is a once-in-a-lifetime purchase. The word 'priceless', in this particular case, is a complete farce. A jewel as famous as the Dutch royal family's Pink Lady will be worth tens of millions on the black market. It simply has no rival in terms of value, which means it becomes invaluable to a multitude of anonymous collectors."

Using the name Pink Lady stirred an almost imperceptible – to most – reaction; a rise in heart rate that showed up in the brief, sharp smell of sweat and dilation of Riley's pupils.

"And my cut?" Riley ventured, his voice even lower than before.

"Sir, without your help, I cannot leave here safely and make this sale happen. But if we can agree now that you will arrange for me to leave without anyone knowing, I will guarantee you five million pounds from the sale."

"Oh my good lord above." The response was involuntary, and the governor exhaled and then slumped into his chair. "That would make for some retirement. Not to mention the shock I will have to prepare Mrs Riley for." Mickey had him in the sweet spot. The rest was just a formality. "Okay, Mr Lawson, I think we have an accord. Let's go over this one more time so

I can make sure we get every detail correct."

"Thank you, sir. This is exactly what we'll need to do ..."

Chapter Five

FRIENDS?

When Tom got home, Jenny was cooking pasta, and he kissed her cheek. "So, I hear you've been busy with your stag do plans, even designing your own invite tickets," she said with a smile.

"What? How did you find that out?"

Her face fell a little. "Well, I found out in a bad way, really ..." she said. "A guy called Kevin from your work rang and said he was very sorry, but when he got home this evening, he realised the dates for your stag do clash with some golf society match he has planned that he can't get out of."

"What? Golf ... bloody golf? That's just ... well, unbelievable!"

"I know, I'm sorry. He was very apologetic and said he'll bring the ticket back into work tomorrow so you can give it to someone else."

"Well, he needn't bother. I wasn't sure about inviting him in the first place, to be honest. I think seven blokes on a narrowboat will be enough."

"I hope you're not too disappointed?" Jenny drained the pasta shells.

Tom was disappointed but didn't make a big deal out of it. He mentally crossed Kevin off the list. One less body on the narrowboat.

The following morning, Miles failed to greet him with the usual gusto, and when Tom looked over, he saw him sitting at his workstation, fumbling with his ticket.

"Morning, Miles. What's up?"

"Tom, bro. It's the stag do," he groaned. "My mum won't let me go."

"Yeah, right!" Tom said and rolled his eyes and laughed. He looked back at Miles. "Good grief, Miles, you're not serious? You're twenty years old! What are you talking about?"

"You don't understand, bro."

"I'm not your bro, and no, I don't, so let's hear it."

"Well, it's my grandmother," Miles explained, clearly not happy. "She lives in France, yeah, and she's about a hundred years old or something, and apparently she's dying. My mum reckons she hasn't got long, bro, and she wants the whole family to visit."

"And you're off to France on the weekend of my stag do, I suppose?"

Miles nodded.

"Well," Tom sighed, "you're doing the right thing, mate. I'd do the same myself. It's a shame, but don't worry, I'm not annoyed or anything."

He sat down and started up his computer, mentally crossing Miles off the list. Two less bodies.

A short time later, while engrossed in coding some HTML, a pop-up informed him he had new mail on his personal email account. Despite the fact that company protocol dictated all employees wait until lunchtime to deal with their personal email, Tom had a quick look. He was pleased to see two new emails, both with 'Stag do' in the subject field. "Excellent," he whispered. "Now we're getting somewhere."

The first was from Martin Storey, his old school pal:

Hello Tom, trust you're well. Sorry I couldn't take your call last night. I was in, but I couldn't face talking to anyone ... sorry. Had a bad day. The doctor is signing me off again this week. The depression is the worst it's ever been. Re the stag do – really flattered you'd want the likes of me there. Anyhow, it's going to have to be a no for now, unless something major happens. I just can't face being around people at the moment, especially people I don't know. So, sorry again, and hope you understand, Tom. Maybe we could get together for a drink sometime soon? Just the two of us?

Take care, Martin.

"Oh, man. That makes it three." Tom really felt for Martin and understood, but he was still disappointed. He clicked to open the following message. It was from Scatty Ali's John:

Awite Bud, how's it hanging? Lookin' forward to it and all that, only here's the thing – is it possible to make the 'do' the weekend after? It's just that I'm working on those dates and I definitely can't get the time off ...

"The weekend after is my wedding, you prat. Your half-witted wife is a flippin' bridesmaid," Tom seethed before reading on:

Work have already been moaning about the amount of time I've been taking off. Trust that's gonna be OK? If not then have a top time without me, you lucky devil. Let me know, big guy!!!!

Chopper John

P.S. Watching the game tonight? C'mon Ing-er-land! Yeah Baby!!!

"Moron." He closed his email.

That afternoon he brooded. If they couldn't even be bothered to show up to a mate's stag do, what the hell would they do if he actually needed them for something serious? They weren't mates at all. Real friends didn't let you down in the run-up to the biggest day of your life. John hadn't even remembered when he was getting married! He may as well forfeit the deposit and cancel the whole damn thing. So much for taking risks.

"I may as well quit before the others get a chance to stick the knife in, too," he later said to Jenny, the brooding having become a morose mood. "I knew from the start this was a bad idea."

"Nonsense," Jenny said. "Come on, silly, you can't give up now. The four of you can still have a great time. It might even be better with four?" She was trying to sound convincing, well aware this was akin to telling certain men that football is 'just a game' immediately after the final whistle has been blown and theirs was the losing side. "It's not like we don't have a large enough wedding fund," she continued. "We can cover the cost of the missing places easily. I still think you should go for it. You'll regret it if you don't."

Tom considered this. Regret wasn't something he particularly wanted to take into the early stages of his marriage, so by the end of the evening, he had reluctantly agreed to keep the booking for the remaining four. Dammit.

* * *

"Oh, Tom, just the man."

Tom turned away from the coffee machine to see Steve

from Maintenance coming up the stairs. He was clutching his invitation, and the look on his face informed Tom, without the aid of words, what was coming.

"Not you as well, Steve?"

"Sorry?"

"The stag do. Please don't tell me you're not coming either?"

"Either?" Steve had the cheek to look anguished.

"Yes, flaming either. I just can't believe this. You're the fifth to pull out!"

"The fifth? I'm so sorry, mate, I didn't know." Steve looked genuinely embarrassed. "It's a real pain, I know, but I do have a valid reason–"

"Really," Tom said coldly.

"Yes. My wife, Crystal, she ... she had a miscarriage last night. Pretty serious actually, an ectopic, the doctors called it. We're devastated, and she's got to stay in hospital for a few days. I've only popped in today to speak to my manager before getting back to her, and when she gets out, I want to be there for her, you know. You understand, don't you–"

"Listen, Steve ..." It was now Tom's turn to look embarrassed. "I am so sorry for getting narky, and I'm so sorry for your loss. How is Crystal? She'll be okay, won't she?"

Tom passed his untouched coffee over to Steve and poured himself another as his colleague finished telling him about the sad events of the previous evening.

His list was now down to two, and Tom felt aggrieved. Steve was the only one who'd discounted himself because he absolutely had to; as for the rest of them ... *Steve's a good mate, really,* he told himself. He made a mental note to send Crystal some flowers from him and Jenny. He did, however, decide that a list of two was far too short to warrant the hire of the narrowboat. But he'd give it until the end of the week, just in case one or two of them could change their plans and come after all.

"I'll probably just have a night on the town with Mike and Lawrence," he said to Jenny over pizza that night.

But it was obvious even she was feeling slightly embarrassed on his behalf, and her "I'm sure whatever you end up doing, the three of you will have a great time" seemed forced for his usually loquacious fiancée.

* * *

By 5.30pm the next day, Tom was grateful not to have received any further cancellations. No regretful calls about golf, no sick grandmas, and thankfully no conversations with sad news. He shut down his computer and made his way down the stairs. After calling goodbye to Avril, he had very nearly made it to the exit when there was a clatter of footsteps behind him.

"Tom! Hang on, mate!"

As the plump, red-faced Lawrence (from Finance) approached, Tom eyed him dubiously. At the exact moment, his mobile phone went off in his pocket. "Just a sec, Lawrence. Hi, Mike ... yeah, fine, you? Oh, the stag do ... yep ... What do you mean? You are joking, right?"

Lawrence waited, gathering his breath from his little trot across the reception area.

"Oh great, Mike, that's just great!" Tom barked, no longer able to keep his cool. "Thanks for nothing, mate. You're supposed to be the one person I can rely on! You're my cousin, for crying out loud! Fine. Okay ... sorry? Are you still the best man? Well, I guess I'll have to have a think about that one, won't I!"

Tom snapped his phone shut. For a second, he stood still, staring at the floor. Then he glared at Lawrence. "Un-believable ..." he exhaled, shaking his head. And with that, he turned and headed for the double doors.

"Err, Tom?" Lawrence raised his hand, index finger extended as if answering a question in class.

Without turning, Tom raised a hand to silence his 'friend'. "There's no need, Lawrence. You're off the hook, fellah! Save your excuse. The stag do is well and truly off. Goodnight!" He kicked open one of the double doors and stormed off to get his train.

Lawrence stood in reception for a few moments, his finger still in the air and a perplexed look on his face. "I only wanted to know if I needed to bring my sleeping bag," he said.

* * *

Four cans of strong lager in the homeward train's buffet bar failed to improve Tom's mood and, crashing through his front door, the uncharacteristic argument he picked with Jenny put her into one, so he took refuge at the Black Buoy pub close to the local quay, just a couple of minutes' walk from the flat.

By around 9pm, Tom finally began to cool down, and his anger gave way to despondency. Still in his work clothes, he'd let rip at the landlord with the whole sorry tale. Roger, a middle-aged, balding man, was a good listener. He'd spent twenty years honing the art of agony aunt or devil's advocate while diligently towelling beer and wine glasses dry. He had seen all sorts, and heard more, and was quite accustomed to translating slurred speech. Tom was not a heavy drinker at the best of times, and as the evening wore on, this became increasingly evident as he added three pints to the four cans he'd drunk on the train.

"Where's Jen tonight?" Roger asked after Tom's monologue of stag do woe.

"I-I, well, I caused a bit of a ... a bit of a row."

"Really? Nothing serious, I hope? Less than a month to go now till the big day," Roger ventured, holding up and inspecting a glass.

"Naah, nothing serioushh. Hey, I don't s'pose you wanna go on a stag do, do you? Weekend on a narrowboat?"

"Ha!" Leaning forward, Roger aimed a thumb over his shoulder towards the kitchen area and winked. "You reckon she'd let me out for a whole weekend on a stag do. Not flamin' likely. I'm flattered, Tom, I really am, but you've got to remember, mate, I've been married for over twenty years. The leash gets tighter every year, I'll tell you that. Besides, I'm getting a bit long in the tooth for all that malarkey."

"Can't believe they all pulled out, the ... the ..."

"Little shysters," came an impassioned voice.

Tom swivelled a bit on his stool and saw an elderly man at the other end of the bar. The wrinkled old fellow had not looked up and continued twirling his pint from its base, staring down into it.

"Yes, yes, quite right," Tom agreed, swivelling back to Roger. "They let me down, Rog. All of 'em. I made up my mind to take a rishk. I made up my mind to trust in the friendssship of those so-called mates of mine. P-probably why I took it out on poor old Jen tonight. She kind of encouraged me to do something I wouldn't normally do, you know, take a rishk, I guess. Part of me really shtill wants to do something a little rishkier than I would normally do, you know? I shouldn't have taken things out on her, though. I'll have to make it up to her tomorrow. To tell you the truth, I feel a bit guilty about it. I think I've been a bit of a ... a ..."

"Little shyster," the old man said again, equally as impassioned.

Tom leaned over the bar. "What's hish problem?"

"Who? Bob? Oh, don't worry about him. He lost his job over at the dockyard on Monday. He's been on a bit of a binge ever since. They finally told him he was too old for manual work." Roger leaned toward Tom. "He's seventy-one, they reckon. If that's true, I wouldn't have wanted to piss him off when he was twenty-one, eh?"

"Hmmm," was all Tom could manage. His head was spinning, and he decided he ought to start sobering up before he went home. He slid his glass over the bar to Roger. "Juss an orange juice, I think, Rog."

"No problem, Tom. So what are you going to do about the stag weekend? Maybe you should just make it a one-nighter? I'm sure all your friends would be up for it then, don't you think?"

"Oh, I don't know. It's all a bit depresshing, really. And that rubbissh doesn't help," he said, suddenly noticing a musical backdrop that was unfamiliar to the Black Buoy. "What is that crap, and where's it coming from?"

"It's folk music, don't you like it?" Roger gestured to a jukebox in the far corner of the pub.

"No, I don't. I've never heard music in here before."

"No, you haven't. That's my latest acquisition," Roger said proudly, planting a pint of orange juice under Tom's nose. "A real old-fashioned Wurlitzer-style jukebox. I won it on eBay last week for three hundred and fifty quid. I know the music's not your taste, but what d'you think of the machine?"

Tom turned to look. "On eBay, huh? I useshd to be a bit of an eBay addict myself. Picked up all sorts of things for my flat."

"Yeah, me too. There really is nothing you can't get on eBay."

"Or get rid of," Tom chuckled, thinking about the lucky sod who'd managed to get rid of the awful jukebox. And then an idea hit him, just as he took a gulp of his orange juice.

"Crikey! You alright, Tom?" asked a startled Roger as Tom froze mid-gulp. "Mate? What's happening? You still in there?"

But Tom was not listening. He'd just had the most amazing, original, brilliant idea.

"That's it, Rog!" he eventually said, plonking the glass heavily on the bar. "It's a bit rishky, but what the hell ... I'm up for a rishk!"

"What on earth are you on about, Tom?"

"Sorry, Rog, no time. Got to do it now ... thanks ... fantasshic idea."

Tom, unsteady on his feet, made a rolling dash for the door.

"Tom! Just be careful on your way, okay!" a bewildered Roger called after him.

"Little shyster," grunted the voice from the other end of the bar, but Tom was already out of the door.

* * *

Fifteen minutes later, Tom had safely staggered the two-minute walk to his front door. After two more minutes fiddling with his key and several more clumsily tiptoeing around trying not to wake Jenny up, he slumped into his chair and switched on his computer. He winced at the ridiculously loud start up bonging and whirring noises and glanced over his shoulder to see if it had disturbed Jenny. There was no sound from the bedroom. He turned back to the screen. "Right, Thomassh my old son, here we go ..."

Selecting 'Tickets and Travel', with a subcategory of 'Experiences', on his eBay account, he forced his beer-addled brain and fingers to type:

Title: Mystry Stag Do Tickits

Subtitle: Seven tickets availble for a top stag weekend on a canal boat!!

Item Description: One time offr

He was feeling dizzy now as the mixture of alcohol and tiredness came in waves.

Item description: One time offr, not tobe repeated! Anominous pre-married guy seeks seven wouldbe shpmates to join him for long weekend stag do in the sun on a naarow boat on the Northolk Broads. You have until Sunday eveng to bid for your tickit. Once you have sucsefsfully bidded for your lucky ticket, you can join me for the ride of your life.

Tom sat back and considered the last sentence. "A bit cocky, I reckon," he decided. He deleted the end and rewrote it:

Once you have sucsefsfully bidded for your lucky ticket, smply make your online payment. On reciept I will email you all the details and then get ready for a corking weekend! The steg do will take place at the end of this month from Friday 19th to Monday 22nd June! There is no resereve on these tickets, so get

bidding boys. Erm, when i say boys, imean boys. Sorry girls.

God luck.

P.S. No shysters ;-) !!!

And there it was. Job done. That would teach 'em, his 'friends'. The auction would end just after midnight on Sunday. He clicked the button to submit the listing, leaned back in his chair and yawned, wondering if he should have added a photo of one of the tickets. "Naah," he told himself. "It'll add to the intrigue."

All he wanted to do now was sleep. He switched off the computer and managed to manoeuvre himself, still fully clothed, into bed. Jenny still didn't stir.

* * *

After what seemed like several minutes, Tom was shaken awake by Jenny. "Come on, Tom. I've already called you three times. What's the matter with you? What time did you come to bed last night?

"Eh? I'm not sure," Tom replied, pulling the duvet back over his face. His head was throbbing, his mouth felt like cardboard, and his eyelids seemed glued shut.

"Come on!" Jenny snapped, obviously irritated. "You're going to be late. It's almost nine o'clock. I've got coffee and toast on the table, but it's getting cold."

Tom was beginning to come around. "Hang on a minute ... it's Saturday," he mumbled. He stuck his head out. "It's Saturday!"

"Yes, well done. It is Saturday! But you have to be at

Birmingham NEC by one o'clock for the BTM exhibition, remember?" Jenny peered at him. "Good gracious, Tom, are you drunk?"

Tom groaned at the horrible realisation that he probably still was and at the equally horrible realisation that this weekend was a working weekend for him. The dreaded annual BrightTech Media exhibition. He dragged himself out of bed and groaned while showering, shaving, drinking cold coffee and promising Jenny he would buy her dinner the Monday night he was back from the exhibition. And then he made it to the station. Just.

About an hour into his journey, the man opposite him on the train pulled a laptop from his case and opened it up on the table. And suddenly, through his horrendous hangover, Tom had a flashback.

"Oh, crap."

The man looked over the top of the laptop at him.

"Oh no."

He stared out of the mud-flecked window at the passing fields. Perhaps he hadn't done what he thought he might have done. Or perhaps he had. Without access to a computer, there was no way of knowing. He eyed the laptop. And the sullen man typing into it. No. He had no choice but to wait until Monday to find out whether he had been sober enough or drunk enough to pull off something as stupid as putting tickets for his stag do up for auction on eBay. But who in their right mind would buy a ticket online for the stag do of a person they didn't even know? Nobody, that's who. Satisfied with his analysis, he fell asleep.

* * *

Jenny was at work when he returned on Monday, but Tom the Second greeted him with much circling and purring. Heading straight for his computer, he railed as it whined and limped through starting up. "Come on! It's 2003, for goodness' sake!" he said, jiggling a leg nervously as eBay eventually opened. He hardly dared look.

Even in his drunken stupor, it appeared he had managed to submit his listing correctly.

"Oh no."

The spelling! And grammar!

"Oh, crap."

Worse than that, the bidding history showed there had been a frenzied interest in the tickets and each one of the seven had been claimed. Indeed, a small bidding war had ensued, which ensured he would more than recoup his costs, but that was the least of his worries. Seven complete strangers would now be joining him, on a narrowboat, for his stag weekend. He'd absolutely gone and done it now. He'd wanted to take a few more risks, but this? This was insane. Bonkers.

"You plonker," he said and sat back in his chair, his hands clamped to his head. "You absolute plonker."

Chapter Six

A WOLF IN STAG'S CLOTHING

If Mickey Lawson was in possession of any sort of emotion, he did not show it. His demeanour revealed no signs of wariness but equally no apparent delight at the prospect of becoming a free man once again. Although his final moments as an imprisoned man would soon be behind him, he knew the days that lay ahead were uncertain, and he would need to be vigilant. This was no time to relax; this was a time to move fast and then lay low to ensure his future as a very rich man.

Mickey was confident of one thing: the governor had kept his end of the agreement by ensuring his official release date had been doctored, allowing him time to get away unhindered. Two days earlier, he had been summoned to Riley's office, and the two of them had gone over proceedings one last time. They had not seen each other for a long while, but in the final year before Lawson's release, they had exchanged the occasional private letter. Most of the correspondence was to clarify a few minor details of the release plan, but a couple of Mickey's letters had included requests for certain privileges, such as a current map of London and its surrounding counties, and for weekly use of a computer with access to the internet. The sanctioning of these privileges had been an encouraging sign for Lawson that the prison governor was committed to their pact. But on seeing the governor for the final time, Mickey noted with interest how quickly Riley had aged. The governor looked tired. Rather than feel sorry for him, though, he had taken this as further encouragement that the man would not renege on their agreement. It was clear Riley wanted out and that he was just as keen as Lawson to leave Wormwood Scrubs behind and start a new life ... the 'good' life. After Mickey's earnest assurances that he would keep his end of the bargain once the diamond had been sold, the two men parted. But when the door of his cell had been closed behind him, Mickey sat down on his bunk and whispered, "Fat fool." Once he was back on the outside, his maxim would be reinstated. "Like I would share my money with an idiot like you," he muttered. "I work alone. I've always worked alone."

An hour before his release, Mickey was led out of his cell in order to be processed. After the requisite amount of paperwork had been cleared, he was then reunited with the items that had been removed from his person more than nine years earlier. In truth, there were very few possessions to return: his original clothes, a small roll of twenty-pound notes, some loose change and a few other items. After being ordered to change out of his prison attire and back into his old clothes, he was led through the prison's cavernous hallways. As they went, the officer in front unlocked and relocked the paint-peeled iron gates before finally reaching a large wooden door with huge steel bolts at its top and base. Once unbolted, it swung open, and Mickey was motioned through. As he stepped onto a sunlit pavement, a warm June breeze encircled the freed man. But rather than stand and take stock of his freedom, Lawson chose to move quickly. Glancing right and then left, he started to jog across the road, hailing an oncoming black cab as he went.

"Where to, guv?"

Mickey slammed the door. "Fourteen Chancery Court, and step on it."

* * *

Donnie Sykes was fuming. Slamming the telephone receiver down, he grabbed one of the mobile phones from his top drawer and hit the usual speed dial.

"What?"

Was the Serbian incapable of even basic civility?

"Doković, you need to listen carefully. I have a prison informant on the inside at Scrubs. The screw just called to say Lawson was released this morning."

"What? Why early?"

"It doesn't matter why; what matters is we need to find him. Fast. Obviously, we can't tail him from the prison now, so we need to anticipate his next move."

"But how we do that? If half of police in London were not able to locate the diamond, then where do we start with the whole man?"

"We may have a possible lead. My screw doubts Lawson will go for the diamond straight away and says he's obliged to report to his parole officer immediately after release. Given he's had nine years inside, I doubt even a little scrote like Mickey would be stupid enough to risk any unwanted attention so quickly. But even if he isn't planning on visiting his parole officer, the man might have some clue as to how Mickey can be tracked down. If that's the case, I'm sure you have the talent to extract any necessary information from him. But my best guess is that he'll meet with his parole officer in order to appease him, then make a move on the diamond before 'disappearing' for a while. That would be my move, and that's all we've got to go on for the moment."

"Where can I find this parole officer?"

"Fourteen Chancery Court. His name's Colin Sturgeon. If this doesn't work out, we may have one more lead. The same screw found out that Lawson had been given weekly access to the internet. He's going to check the computer he'd been using and see if there's anything in the browsing history that could hint at where he may be heading. But this could take time, so, for now, Sturgeon is our best bet, so get moving."

Sykes sat motionless, staring out of his window. "When I get you, Mickey, I'm gonna gut you like a fuckin' animal," he growled.

* * *

Fourteen Chancery Court. A decrepit Victorian townhouse that contained various offices, each one spread out across four spacious floors. The friendly receptionist directed him up to the second floor. He sat on one of six orange plastic chairs lining the drab hallway directly outside Colin Sturgeon's office. Despite the annoyance at having to meet with the man, Mickey kept up a deliberate calm, something he was well practised at. The wait was beginning to irritate him, though, and he was genuinely considering leaving when the parole officer's door was flung open. A skinny man with beige cords and a thin grey roll-neck jumper stepped into the hallway. He had chunky, round-framed glasses that completed an attire more akin, in Mickey's mind at least, to a science teacher rather than a parole officer.

"Mr Lawson? Mr Michael Lawson?" he said, peering at Mickey, and held out a hand.

"Yes. I'm Mickey," Lawson replied, deadpan.

Sturgeon smiled warmly. "Okay, Mickey, it is. Would you like to come through and sit down? This really shouldn't take too long."

Ten minutes later, after Sturgeon had been through the procedures and formalities that ingratiate prison leavers back into society, the thin little man stood to indicate that the meeting was ending. As he walked Mickey to the door, he held out his hand once more, and the two men shook. As they did so, Sturgeon cocked his head slightly and asked, "So, Mickey, what are your immediate plans after you leave here, may I ask?"

Mickey, admittedly vaguely flummoxed by the unexpected question, didn't have time to fabricate a complete lie. As a result, he sifted through his plans for the next few days. He got imaginative with the information, just enough so it would appear truthful. After all, all good lies are grounded in truth. "I have a few bits to pick up this afternoon, essentials, then I'll be heading north from Liverpool Street as I've been offered a short-term job with my cousin."

"A job already! Wow, Mickey, that's great news," replied Sturgeon with genuine warmth. "Well, I do hope it all works out for you, I really do. But remember, you will need to stay in touch."

With that, the two men parted, and three minutes later, Mickey was in a taxi once again, heading for his second destination with a mixture of apprehension and delicious excitement. After almost a decade, he was about to be reunited with his Lady.

* * *

Less than an hour after Mickey Lawson's departure from Colin Sturgeon's office, a black five-series BMW with darkened windows pulled illegally into a permit-only parking space opposite the parole officer's workplace. After about a minute, a man in a black suit, black shirt and long black leather coat exited the car and checked left and right, front and back of where he stood. At six foot and five inches, Dusan Doković may have been large and muscular, but his pale complexion and overly long arms gave him the look of something Dr Frankenstein might have created. He also looked like the sort of man most people would not choose to impede. Sally Jameson, the same receptionist who had earlier given directions to Mickey, was certainly not going to try and delay the man who offered a short, plausible explanation for a visit to Sturgeon's office.

Even if Dusan Doković had found Mickey present in Sturgeon's stuffy room, the unfortunate outcome for the genial parole officer would have likely been the same. With Lawson having already fled, Sturgeon was now Doković's only hope of finding the jewel thief. The initial shock of having this enormous brute burst into his office and demand to know of Mickey Lawson's whereabouts instantly gave way to pure fear after Sturgeon had threatened to call the police if Dusan did not leave immediately. The intruder instantly launched himself at the man, grabbing him firmly by the throat before spinning him in his office chair and slamming the back of his head down onto his own desk.

The next few minutes for the parole officer were unpleasant as Doković extracted every single piece of information, eye to eye, before tightening his grip until the life had almost faded from the man's terrified face. And then Dusan smiled, reached into his coat pocket for a gun and delivered a single muffled shot into the man's pounding heart. The sad truth was that despite the very little information Colin Sturgeon had been able to give, no amount of cooperation would have saved his life. Dusan Doković was not new to his chosen profession and once the hitman had been seen, he was never going to leave a witness alive who could incriminate him. Although Sturgeon's last revelations had been less than hoped for, Doković now had at least one potential lead. He glanced at his watch. He still had time to make it across Central London. Luckily for Sally Jameson, the friendly receptionist was nowhere to be found when Doković returned to the ground floor. Leaving her alive was an irritation, but a considerable payout was now forefront of his mind. If he stood any chance of claiming it, he needed to get to Liverpool Street.

* * *

On the street, Mickey covertly scanned the faces of passers-by for some sort of recognition of his own but saw none. He was unimpressed by how much the area had changed over the past nine years. The local borough's fervent rejuvenation of the area had evidently seen no bounds nor had it met with any apparent restrictions. So many of the landmarks that had been recognisable to him had either been removed, replaced or altered beyond his recognition. And then he had an awful thought: what if the Lady's hiding place no longer existed? His mind raced back to almost a decade previous. Had he been clever enough to envisage such a remarkable change to surroundings in only nine years? The answer was undoubtedly no. But had he been lucky enough for the diamond's hiding place not to have been revealed or even destroyed? He turned and strolled casually towards the place where he hoped his treasure was still hidden, a nervous sweat beginning to run down his back.

Minutes after his daring jewel theft, he had been seen jumping into a silver Audi. Whether Lawson had been alone or had had accomplices, was still unknown to the Metropolitan Police. A decade ago, there had not been surveillance cameras hovering over every street corner, making it impossible to piece together the route the thief had taken. It took a further twenty minutes before the police had managed to track his car down, parked behind a strip club called Peanuts. No link had been found, however, of a connection between the club and the theft. In fact, the police had come to the conclusion that the perpetrator of the crime had possibly sought to implicate the club in the theft before taking off on foot to make his getaway.

Unfortunately for Mickey, however, his getaway had been unsuccessful. It had taken fewer than another thirty minutes for a crack team of armed officers to triangulate his whereabouts and locate him hiding in a building-site shed. Sensing – correctly – that he may well be picked up, thirty minutes had been more than enough time for Mickey to stash his stolen prize.

Nine years on, Lawson was now approaching the site, his heart pounding. He checked around him and crossed the road to where the White Hart pub, in mock Tudor with weed-filled hanging baskets, had provided him with a hasty hideaway for the jewel. Anticipation gave way to concern as the location came into view. The previously detached pub now had a high-rise building attached to its east side. The side that had held an old wooden billboard advertising cigarettes; the side where he had rammed the jewel between the billboard and the wall.

Taking another quick look around him, he circled the building around the south-facing front, along the west side and the north-facing rear. Perhaps there was a gap? Some kind of building regulation? There was a foul smell and piles of rotting crates and other junk. Still checking, moving carefully, he manoeuvred around the rubbish. He stopped at the furthest point on the wall, on the northeast corner where the high-rise blocked out almost all the light and peered into the gloom. His breath stopped in his chest. Clearly, neither the developers, the pub owners, nor the owners of the billboard had felt it worthwhile to remove the now-decaying frame.

Mickey wasted no time. He squeezed into the gap and slid his fingers behind the base of the frame, stinking rotten wood crumbling as he moved them along. It had to be there. He inched a bit further, one ear listening out for unwelcome company. And then he felt it: a rough, damp piece of cloth. Wriggling his fingers until he could grasp it, he pulled at it, but the wood was swollen, pinning it to the pub wall. "Come on," he grunted, trying again, finally feeling it shift. Pulling it free, he smiled as he unfolded the dirty black cloth. And there she was. The Pink Lady, briefly glimmering in the dim light. Rewrapping her, he zipped her safely into the interior pocket of the green backpack he'd grabbed from a Blacks outdoor gear shop after leaving Sturgeon's office. He then reached back in, pretty sure he would find what else he was looking for, successfully reacquainted with the diamond as he was. Good. His gun was still there too.

Ten minutes later, Mickey was in the back of a cab heading for Liverpool Street. "We're going to have some R&R, me and you," he muttered to his backpack, "while we work out our next move."

In the same pocket, next to his Lady, was the folded printout of an eBay transaction. On it were the words: 'Mystry Stag Do Tickits'. He smiled. This guy was clearly not the whole ticket. And neither had Riley been when he agreed to let him use a computer with internet access. A weekend on some idiot's stag do, off grid on a narrowboat on the Norfolk Broads, was the perfect hideout.

Chapter Seven

RAGTAG BUT READY

The following morning, as Tom approached Blakes Boat Hire, he was still struggling with feelings of doubt concerning the potentially awkward weekend ahead. He'd never been the most sociable of people, so the thought of meeting seven new characters – complete strangers – all at once had raised his fear levels with each mile of his three-hour drive to the waterside village of Beccles. Situated next to the River Waveney, he had discovered Beccles was indeed a popular starting point throughout the year for narrowboaters exploring the Norfolk Broads – as Bill Blakes himself had said. The Broads, as it was more commonly known, was a beautiful rural network of connected canals and rivers.

Tom drove slowly over a small stone bridge, guiding his sixteen-year-old Volvo 340 down onto a grassy patch that passed for a parking area, directly in front of what appeared to be various storage and reception huts. A small, faded sign in one of the hut's windows confirmed he had arrived at his destination, and he turned off the engine. As the car spluttered to a halt, he heard a cockerel through his half-opened window, perhaps trying to compete with the sound of church bells in the distance.

"Well, Tom," he muttered, "you really are out in the sticks

now, mate."

He had purposefully arrived a good deal earlier than the time arranged with the ticket purchasers so he could find a pub or café from which to get a good look at each member of the group. But it was quite clear that Blakes Boat Hire was a fairly rundown establishment that had invested no effort in providing its customers with such amenities. As he approached the door, there appeared to be no activity inside. He was beginning to wonder if he had arrived too early for even the proprietor to be onsite. But as he raised his fist to knock, the door opened, leaving Tom standing with his arm raised in the air staring at an old, white-bearded man with a wide grin on his craggy face. He must have been well into his eighties and was dressed in all-in-one long johns and an oversized pair of black wellington boots. The clipboard he was holding was briskly shoved under his left arm, and he held his right hand out towards Tom. "Well, if he ain't Tom, then maybe you are, me lad."

"I'm sorry?"

"Him in there," replied the man and pointed a thumb over his shoulder. "He says he ain't Tom, so I'm guessing you are!"

"Oh yes, that's right. I'm Tom. Tom Marshall. But, sorry, who's the other chap you're referring to?"

"One of your lads. Didn't catch his name, though. Anyways, I'm Bill Blakes. We spoke on the phone. Come on in, and we'll get the paperwork started." And Bill turned and strode into the hut, his wellies flapping at his skinny calves.

Tom was surprised to see that the inside of the hut was quite tidy. In fact, as it could almost pass as organised, as well as homely, he suspected the old man might actually live in the decrepit structure. As his eyes adjusted to the dim light, he saw a man to his right in a worn armchair next to a blackened wood burner. Tom observed him for a moment, unsure if he was here as part of the group. At face value, it appeared to him the man seemed a little too old to have bought into a stag do. Tom guessed he was in his late forties and pale and thin, but he had a certain tough persona that warned he was not to be messed with.

"I'm Tom Marshall. I'm the chap who organised this trip," he said, eyeing the stranger.

"Mickey," the man replied, without standing to greet him.

Although Tom detected no particular rudeness in Mickey, he was a little taken aback by the abrupt response.

"Ah, Mickey. Brilliant." Tom laughed nervously. "Well, I'm pleased to meet you, Mickey, and I'm looking forward to the weekend ahead."

"Do you want the printout of the auction transaction? I'm guessing it acts as my ticket."

"Erm. No. That's okay. You hold onto it. I got your email confirmation. The whole ticket thing was a bit of fun, really, when I was a bit, well, tipsy, which is why I forgot to put a picture of the actual ticket on eBay."

"Fun?"

"Yes. I was a bit of a Willy Wonka fan as a kid if you know what I mean."

"Not really," replied Mickey. But then his face moved into a strange grin. "But fun sounds good to me. I'm up for a laugh."

Tom relaxed a little and returned an awkward smile before turning back to Bill. The old man had a perplexed look on his face. "Don't you boys know each other, lad?" he asked.

"Erm, no," Tom admitted, slightly embarrassed. "That's kind of the whole point of this weekend. The truth is, none of us know each other at all. That is if the others actually turn up."

"On a stag do?" the old man continued, frowning. "What kind of stag do is that, lad? Doesn't make a whole lot of sense to me."

"Well, no. I guess it is a little unusual, but the thing is–"

"But nothing," the old man chuckled. "Your business is no concern of mine, me lad. You youngsters … I gave up long ago trying to keep up."

"Erm, quite."

"Right," Bill continued. "Let's have all your names, then, and after we get you all logged in, we'll go and take a look over *May*." He held out a battered clipboard with a booking form attached.

"May?" Tom replied.

"Your boat, me lad. You ain't gonna go far without her, and not much further unless you know how to handle her!"

"Ah, yes, of course, the boat," Tom said. "Absolutely. I imagine we'll need to know how to treat her right." He took the clipboard and completed his own details before adding the names of his seven guests from memory. He'd always been good at remembering data like names and numbers but could always double-check the names when everyone arrived if the old man needed him to. "Here you go. That's us. All eight of us."

After a quick glance, Bill placed the clipboard on his desk and invited the two men to follow him. As he passed the table, Mickey unclipped the list, folded it and slid it into his jacket pocket. Although he'd used a false surname to purchase his 'ticket' online, he had kept the name Mickey, something he'd chastised himself for afterwards. Despite the fact there must be tens of thousands of Mickeys in the UK, there would be very few who were being hunted, and he was not going to leave any chances as to his whereabouts.

In the next hour, the remaining six members of Tom's unusual gathering descended on Blakes Boat Hire. First to arrive was Dennis Slaughter, a six-foot three heavily built mechanic from Bolton. Dennis was dressed in black jeans and a white T-shirt under a sleeveless denim jacket, which had an array of motorbike enthusiast badges sown over virtually every inch. Although he looked as though he was a member of some hardened Hell's Angels chapter, complete with multiple tattoos, his soft voice and gentle demeanour quickly put Tom at ease as they introduced themselves.

Next to arrive, and simultaneously, were Dave, Gavin and Sherwin. It transpired that the three strangers had met in a café outside Beccles train station before getting a taxi for the final part of their journey. The three had got into a conversation that quickly revealed they were fellow ticket bearers. It hadn't taken long for the men to hit it off, and each had agreed that the forthcoming trip – a stag do for total strangers – was possibly the maddest idea anyone could have come up with. As they each introduced themselves to Tom, who was resigning himself to his fate, there was the realisation that perhaps this weekend was going to be a game-changer, after all. Maybe this was the catalyst that would finally shake up his calculated life of mediocrity.

Tom warmed to Dave Alpar immediately. The polite young chap, who he estimated was probably still in his early twenties, was not only genial but also sickeningly handsome. A quick introduction revealed that Dave was Australian, originating from Sydney, and was nearing the final stint of a working visa in the UK. When he had happened upon Tom's auctioned stag do ticket online, the well-toned and tanned young man had jumped at the chance of a final hurrah before heading back to Oz.

Next was Gavin Davies. Fiercely Welsh and, as confirmed by his gleaming white football shirt, a devoted follower of Swansea City AFC. Tom suspected Gavin's devotion might be more of a fanaticism judging by the large swan tattooed on the side of his neck. As far as Tom was concerned, anyone who was prepared to have their favourite team's emblem permanently inscribed on any part of their body would normally be given a wide berth. But despite the man's overly enthusiastic handshake and slightly crazed stare, it was hard for Tom not to take an instant liking to Gavin.

"How's it going, Tommo? Gav's the name. Marvellous this is, boyo, and I would never have thought of it myself. Must be the first ever bloody stag do when nobody knows nobody, in my view!"

"Yes, well, thanks," was all Tom could muster as his hand was being wrenched up and down.

The final member of the trio was Sherwin Aitken. What the Jamaican lacked in stature was more than made up for by a laidback cool and a huge friendly grin. As they shook hands, Tom, once again, couldn't help but take a real liking to the man, and was sure he was going to be great fun to have around, even if he didn't quite understand all his new acquaintance was saying.

"Thomas, mon. Gav is totally on the money. Dis is going to be one sick weekend. You is the craziest fool I've ever witnessed, mon, but we'll make dis a stag do to beat 'em all. Righteous!"

The last two members of the party arrived within ten minutes of each other. First was Neville Chambers, and swiftly after came Gaston Chevalier. Neville, who had made his way down from Liverpool, seemed a slightly odd character to Tom. With a feeble handshake, he squeakily introduced himself to Tom before greeting each of the other members. It seemed clear to Tom that Neville was unsure he'd made the right decision to come here. He knew the feeling!

If Neville was the nervy sort, then Gaston Chevalier was his polar opposite. The proud Frenchman, a trainee chef for the past two years at a very posh Leeds restaurant, arrived in a maelstrom. As his speeding taxi screeched onto Blakes' grassy parking area, the rear door was thrown open, and a number of bags were thrown from the vehicle. A lanky figure, impeccably dressed in a white shirt and black pressed trousers, leapt out of the car shouting obscenities in French at its driver. As the cabbie rolled his eyes and hit the accelerator, the final arrivee turned and shook his fist vehemently in the direction of the fleeing car. In a cloud of dust, the man brushed himself down, stood upright and slicked back his jet-black hair. Then, as if the last few seconds had not occurred, the Frenchman simply picked up his expensive leather holdalls and nonchalantly sauntered over to the group, who were staring on in complete silence. When they asked what had happened, he simply muttered "Imbecile" and lit a cigarette, so they didn't ask again.

"Well, Tom, me lad," chuckled Bill. "You've gathered yourself the scurviest bunch of sea dogs here as I have ever seen! Come on, let's go and meet *May*!"

* * *

Undercover officer Phil Michaels sat down in the small office at Norwich station and felt for the extremely tender bump on the back of his head. In the early hours of the morning, Michaels had been discovered by cleaners in one of the toilets on the last train from Liverpool Street the previous evening. Judging by the dried blood on the back of his neck, he had clearly taken a blow to the head. To add insult to injury, Michaels had also had his hands bound behind his back with his own necktie and a gag tied tightly over his mouth. The cleaners freed the shaky officer and escorted him to the station's office, where the duty manager brought him a hot cup of tea and some wet paper towels to clean up with. The confused manager kindly offered to call for an ambulance and inform the local police, both of which Michaels flatly refused. After identifying himself as a police officer, he had thanked the manager, asking him not to mention anything of what had happened. He'd said he was part of an undercover operation, and would contact his superior directly, organise being picked up, and seek medical care if he needed it. The manager agreed to Michaels' requests and left the officer to drink his tea in peace and make his call in private.

If he was honest, Michaels was dreading making the call to his superior. He knew the chief was going to be furious when he learned he'd failed to engage with Mickey. Only twenty-four hours earlier, Michaels, who had been on standby for information of Mickey's whereabouts, got the call he needed from Blakney. It transpired that the impatient chief superintendent had made a wholly unprofessional phone call to Colin Sturgeon. After finding that Mickey had just left the parole officer's premises, he had demanded Sturgeon reveal any details from the brief meeting between the two, lying that it was of utmost importance to a national security issue. Naturally, the parole officer had not withheld anything – not that he considered the meagre information to be of any possible value – but less than half an hour after Blakney had rung off, the unfortunate Colin Sturgeon was about to realise just how valuable the knowledge of Mickey's whereabouts actually was.

After the call from Blakney, Michaels quickly made his way over to Liverpool Street. Armed with a printed image of Mickey Lawson, which he hoped was relatively recent, Michaels had set about roaming the entrance gates to the station's eighteen platforms. Although Colin Sturgeon had freely passed on the information to Blakney that Lawson had intimated a late departure from the station in order to head north, the lack of a specific destination made the officer's task a challenge. For almost an hour, he strolled around, getting a coffee, then a paper, constantly scanning faces, before he received another call from his superior. Blakney phoned him to warn him to be vigilant, as he had learned that Mickey Lawson's parole officer had not long ago been murdered and that the newly released convict could well have been involved.

After a further two hours of trying to intercept Lawson, Michaels was beginning to lose hope. And then he spotted a lithe figure in a navy bomber jacket, a green backpack slung across his shoulder, striding across the station floor toward Platform 13. The trained undercover officer did not need to glance at his printed photograph to be sure. Within an instant, he knew the pale, tough-looking man crossing his path, only thirty feet ahead of him was his man.

Before making a move, Michaels allowed Lawson to pass through the platform gate, and head for his waiting train, which the officer noted was bound for Norwich. Only when he had seen his man board the train did he begin to follow. After flashing his police identification at a disinterested gate attendant, Michaels passed through unhindered and boarded the train at the first available carriage. Although he had watched Mickey Lawson board at least six carriages ahead of him, he was not going to take any chances. Conscious that the former conman might be aware enough to slip a potential tail by alighting from the train as it began to depart, Michaels' plan was to make his way up through the carriages until he got a clear view of Mickey. In light of Blakney's new information about Sturgeon's murder, the undercover officer also needed to ensure he wasn't walking into a potential trap. For all Michaels knew, Lawson could potentially be meeting with unsavoury connections, which would result in his being outnumbered if things became nasty. Unfortunately, although the officer never did get to see his assailant, things did get nasty, rendering him bloodied, bound and dumped in a most undignified fashion in a most undignified place.

Michaels reluctantly put his cup of tea down and drew his mobile phone from his jacket pocket.

"Where the hell have you been, Michaels?" Blakney had picked up the officer's call within a single ring, so it was evident to Michaels that the chief superintendent was on edge, angry even, and desperate for news.

"Sir, please, I can explain–"

"Where's Mickey? Do you have him? More importantly, do you have the diamond?"

"No, sir, that's what I need to explain. I'm in Norwich."

"Norwich?"

"Yes, sir, Norwich. I managed to spot Lawson last night at Liverpool Street and followed him onto a train bound for Norwich."

"Hardly up bloody north, Michaels!"

"No, sir, I guess not, but like I say ... I got onto the train and made my way up through the carriages to get a visual on Lawson before confronting him."

"And?" Blakney was clearly furious.

"And nothing. I only managed to get through four carriages before someone smashed the back of my head in, pushed me into a toilet and gagged and bound me."

"So Mickey is back to his violent ways ..." said the chief superintendent, half to himself.

"Well, that's just it, sir. I know I hadn't passed him on my way up through the carriages, so ..."

"So?"

"So it means one of two things. Either he now has an accomplice ..."

"Or?"

"Or, worse, he has pursuers, other than us, who want to get hold of the diamond."

"Right." There was a long pause. "Then you stay there, and

I'll get more officers up to you. You can't scour the whole of bloody Norwich on your own."

"Well, there's the problem, sir. Just because Mickey Lawson boarded the train to Norwich, it doesn't mean this is where he got off. He could have got off or changed lines at a number of stops. He could be anywhere by now. But there's also another problem ..."

"And what precisely is *that?*"

Michaels winced at the acute pain that pounded at the back of his head. "I'm afraid I am going to have to withdraw from this case, sir, for now, sir."

"What? *Why?*"

"Sir, I believe the bastard may have fractured my skull. I ... well, I need to get to a hospital. Again, I'm sorry, but I'm going to have to ask that you replace me for the moment, and I will do my best to get back to the case just a soon as I can, sir."

Blakney huffed. "Understood. I will pass proceedings over to DI Williamson. But Michaels, he does not know what we know, and I am trusting you to keep particulars between us. Is that understood?"

"Sir, you know that you can count on me. And I hope you are able to track Mickey down quickly."

"Get yourself to a hospital, man," the chief said dispassionately. "I'll take it from here."

Chapter Eight

NOT SETTING SAIL

Old Bill led the way, with Tom and his party of seven following behind. The seventy-foot *May*, dark grey with red stripes running along her steel hull, looked a little antiquated, but not a single member of the party could help but be impressed by her charm.

"Crikey," Tom mused, thinking of the narrow, twisting waterways they might have to encounter. How would they ever turn around to come back? "She's a bit ... well, she's a bit long."

"Long?" Bill looked at him with genuine incomprehension.

"Well, I mean, will she actually fit? And what about locks?"

"Fit?" Bill roared with laughter. "My boy, these boats were designed for these waters. Trust me, lad, she's been up and down here more times than you've looked at one of your fancy modern phones. And there aren't any locks in these parts for miles."

The introductory tour included just about everything Tom hoped they would need to know in order to return the charming *May* unscathed. "One last thing, Tom, me lad ..." the old man said, "though I doubt you'll be needin' it."

"What's that?"

"The windlass, lad."

"I'm sorry, the ...?" Tom replied.

"The lock gate key I showed you how to use earlier." He pointed to the L-shaped steel bar Gavin was still holding.

"Why's that then?" Gavin asked.

"Because if you get out as far as Oulton or Walsham, which I don't imagine you will, but nonetheless, you'll need it for the locks, lad, and to get her back. So if you lads go out that way and lose it on the other side, well then, you're buggered!" Bill laughed out loud. Then, satisfied that his job was done, he shook Tom's hand again. "Mind yourself, lads, and good luck! I have a feeling you're gonna need it!" Still chuckling, he shuffled off the way they had come.

"What a strange old boyo," Gavin said, looking at Tom. "Right, boss, what do we do now?"

Aware this was probably the first of many questions that would be aimed in his direction in the next few days, Tom thought for a second before saying, "Erm, well, I guess we ought to get our stuff on board, work out where we are all going to sleep, and then set sail."

"Push off, mon," Sherwin said.

"Excuse me?"

"Old Bill said it's pushing off, not setting sail."

"Oh. I see, yes. Quite right. Great, let's get the stuff onboard."

May, an old-fashioned canal boat, was divided into various sections with sleeping quarters on either side of a galley kitchen, which was surprisingly well equipped with a full-sized oven and hob, a bathroom tucked between the bunks in the stern and the kitchen, and a cosy living/dining area. Mickey was the first to step down into the boat, pushing past Tom and Gavin and ducking under the hatch to head straight for the bow end, his backpack in his right hand. Thinking Mickey had picked up his own green backpack by mistake,

Tom opened his mouth to call after him but then realised they were identical. His had been a gift from Jenny a couple of days before the trip; Mickey must have bought his from the same shop. He decided to remain in the stern and dumped his backpack on one of the bunks.

An hour later, once they'd all selected bunks and found their way around the kitchen, Gavin and Sherwin took charge of the tiller while Dave, Neville and Dennis sat in the bow and planned a route they could take through the waterways and directed them. With the noticeable absence of Mickey, who had spent the entire time below deck, they started to relax, getting a feel for how to manoeuvre *May*, enjoying the sunny afternoon and getting to know each other.

Tom startled slightly when his phone rang. "Hello, my darling."

"Hello yourself," Jenny said. "How are you? How's it going? I've been trying to reach you all afternoon!"

"I've barely had a signal," Tom said. "But we're all fine. Been having a few beers and chatting."

"Really?"

"Yes, really." Tom ducked inside the boat and lowered his voice to a whisper. "Actually, I'm really enjoying it so far. The guys seem really nice, well, most of them, and I think we're going to have fun."

"Most?"

"A couple of them are a bit, you know, quiet or odd, but then we are complete strangers." He was thinking of Mickey in the bow and Neville's nervousness.

"Well, I'm glad to hear you're all enjoying yourself. Well, mostly all of you. You know what you need, don't you?"

"What's that?"

"An icebreaker."

"An icebreaker?"

"Yes. Have you stopped anywhere yet?"

"No."

"Well, there you go. Find one of those riverside pubs and stop to eat. That way, you can all sit around a table and really get to know one another ... including the ones who seem a little odd!"

"We had planned to eat on the boat from some of the supplies I brought with me."

"What, sausages and beans? Tom, you need to treat them to a nice meal. Trust me, if they see you're a generous guy, that will break the ice and be the perfect way to get everyone on the best of terms."

"Hmm, okay. I think you're probably right, as ever."

"Naturally. Right, I'll let you get back to it. I love you, but please take care!"

"Take care? Careful is my middle name! I love you too, and I'll call you tomorrow."

"Oh, oh, Tom! Wait. I almost forgot."

"Forgot what?"

"I put a present in the new backpack I bought for you."

"Did you?" Tom asked. "But I've already been in my bag, and I didn't find anything."

"Ah-ha! That's because it has a hidden compartment. It's why I bought that particular backpack! I thought it would be fun for you to find."

"Wow, I'd never have known. Where is the compartment?"

"That's for you to find out. It took me ten minutes to find, even though I knew it had one. But, Tom, don't open it in front of the others. It's a private gift from me to you. It's only something small and silly, but I hope you like it."

"Well, I look forward to finding it later. Thank you, and speak tomorrow."

Tom put his phone in his pocket and returned to the stern. "Dave? Dennis?" he called. "Can you see a pub up ahead on that map? Shall we stop for some food? My treat!"

"Fair dinkum," Dennis called back with a smile on his face.

"Ha!" Dave laughed, aiming a thumb at Dennis. "Get him. He's picking up Ozzie already!"

According to the map, the Woolpack Inn sat beside the riverbank just under a mile ahead and had plenty of mooring, it seemed the ideal place to stop. Grabbing sweaters and coats in the cooler evening air, the group gathered around one of the large tables in the garden, and Tom opened a tab and ordered a round of beers.

"Speech!" a couple of the guys said, and most of the rest laughed and agreed. Mickey observed.

"Why are we here? Where are your own mates, and who are you marrying, boyo? Tell us everything!" Gavin laughed.

"Yeah, this is some kind of crazy stag do!" Dave added.

"You're not wrong, like," Neville agreed.

"Well," Tom began, realising he was now speaking to the group as a whole for the first time. "The truth is, this weekend probably shouldn't really have happened."

"You got dat right, you crazy fool mon," Sherwin laughed.

"Yep," continued Tom. "It was actually my future wife Jenny who suggested I have a stag do. But all the, erm, mates I asked ... well, one by one they sort of dropped out, due to various reasons, so that's when, when I was a bit drunk–" Several raised their pint glasses at that. "I had the crazy idea to auction off the tickets on eBay and see what happened–"

"You crazy fool, mon," Sherwin repeated, and they all laughed again.

"Yes, indeed!" Tom had to admit. "And here we all are, so, well, let's enjoy this unexpected trip and the food. In fact, it was also Jenny who suggested we stop somewhere and I buy you all dinner."

"Your Jenny iz obviously a very fine woman!" Gaston said. "Unlike zis ghastly establishment!" he added, with a look of pomposity on his face.

"Enough!" Dennis countered. "It's great!"

"Jen is, yes, a very fine woman. But she is also, generally, always right, and I think she was right about stopping to eat. So ... I'd like to make a toast to us, and my unexpected stag do. I'm hoping we'll all get on together, even make good friendships, but, most of all, have a weekend to remember!"

"You English are all crazy, you know zat, right?" Gaston mocked but then raised his glass and cigarette. "To Thomas and iz Jenny! May you both be 'appy and alwayz in lurve!"

The rest of the party raised their glasses. "To Tom and Jen!"

* * *

Donnie Sykes picked up the call instantly. "What's the news, Doković?"

"I am closing in on the target," replied the hired gun.

"Where are you? Is Mickey alone?" This was the news he had been hoping for, so desperately in fact that he was positively hungry for it.

"Where is not important. I have been tailing from a distance but have not had clear opportunity to get to him yet ... too many people about. This is only small delay. I will get him. But he is no longer alone. It looks as though he has joined with a group of men. Nobody I know, but do not look like professionals."

"This will not be a problem, though?"

Doković was insulted. "Not once have I had problem in past ... you know this. There is one concern–"

"What? What concern is this?"

"When I pick up Lawson's tail there was undercover police officer already follow him. A pathetic man. Easy to spot from mile off."

"A police officer? Did you kill him?"

"Do you think I am this stupid?" Doković sneered. "Do you want the whole of Met breathing down our necks? No, I did not kill him, but he may have wish for death when he awoke."

"This will be one of Blakney's men, no doubt," seethed Sykes. "I should have guessed that pompous idiot would be out to get the diamond for himself, and I reckon he'd do just about anything to get to Mickey before we do. You must not let that happen, Doković. You must finish this!"

"I understand. They have been on the move, but has been easy to keep up with them. I am watching them now and I will finish. I will call again soon."

Sykes ended the call, poured himself a Scotch and leaned back in his chair. "Mickey Lawson. Got you, you little shit ..."

Chapter Nine

A JAILBIRD AND A GIANT

Tom started searching through his pockets. "Excuse me, chaps, I'm just going to go and get my wallet. I think I left it in my backpack ... won't be long."

Carefully navigating the two hundred metres back to *May* in the dark, Tom lowered himself into the boat. Spotting his backpack, he quickly undid the two buckles and began tipping the contents onto his bunk. He heard something fall but didn't see what it was. "Bugger," he said, looking at the unfamiliar items. He then realised he'd entered the boat from the bow end, not the stern, and this backpack was not his own but Mickey's. He started shoving the contents back inside.

"What the hell do you think you're doing?"

Tom span around to see Mickey standing halfway down the short set of steps, leaning in. He froze. Even though Mickey was silhouetted against the dark sky, it was clear the man had a gun in his right hand, and it was directly pointed at his chest.

Instinctively Tom raised his hands and blurted out, "No! Mickey, wait! I've just realised I'm in the wrong end of the boat and this isn't my bag. I–"

"You're bloody right it isn't, pal," Mickey spat back. "But you knew that, didn't you, you liar. That feeble excuse about leaving your wallet. Who the hell are you? And how the hell did you know about the Lady? More importantly, who the hell else knows? You have three seconds to tell me, or I will kill you right where you stand."

"Mickey, please! I don't know what–" Tom gasped.

"Three ..."

"You're talking–"

"Two ..."

"About!"

Tom saw a shadow appear behind Mickey, followed by a sickening cracking sound that reverberated through the hull of the boat. A split second later, Mickey crumpled and fell the final couple of steps and onto the floor, the gun dropping from his hand and landing with a dull thump on the oak boards. In horror, Tom looked up to see Gavin, the large metal lock key in his hand.

"Wow, that was close eh, Tommo? Looks like I got here just in time! If it weren't for this little puppy," he said, holding up the windlass, "your goose would'a been cooked."

"I don' t... I don't ... understand," Tom muttered.

"What the heck did you do to piss this guy off, anyway?" Gav then asked, grinning in a way that Tom found highly unnerving.

"Honestly, Gav, I really don't know. He was going on about a lady. What lady?" Tom replied, looking down at the stricken man. "You hit him pretty hard. Do you think he'll be okay?"

Tom now noticed the gun, which had landed by his feet, and it suddenly occurred to him that Mickey could regain consciousness at any moment and make a grab for it, so he slid it away from him with his foot, afraid it still might go off. He knew nothing about guns and stared at it in horror. Why on earth would Mickey bring a gun to a stag do?

"Well," Gav replied, "the bastard got what he deserved.

Threatening to kill a man on his stag do over some lady just isn't on, Tommo, in my view."

"What are you blokes doing down there?" came a voice from above. It was Dave.

"Ugh!" Tom said, and bent down to pick the gun up, between finger and thumb, and gingerly put it into his coat pocket.

"Shit!" Dave said as he peered past Gav and saw Mickey's crumpled body. "What happened to him?"

"Merde," Gaston agreed, peering past Dave, their three heads an apparition in the doorway.

"I had to give him a good old whack with this," replied Gav, holding up the windlass once more.

"Why on earth would you do zis?" Gaston asked, slowly shaking his head.

"He was going to kill me," Tom muttered, his eyes back on Mickey, who still hadn't moved.

"Kill you! Why?" asked Dennis, the fourth head in the doorway.

"Honestly, I really don't know," Tom replied. "I came in the wrong end of the boat and mistook his backpack for mine. They're identical, you see. But as I realised my mistake, Mickey appeared and pointed a gun at me and started talking about ... about a lady ... but I had no idea what he meant, and then he said he'd give me three seconds to explain, and then Gav–"

"Where's this gun, mon?" asked Sherwin, as Gaston and Dennis made room for his head.

"We need to call the police, and I think we should probably tie his hands together in case he comes to. I really don't think Mickey is someone we ought to take chances with," Tom said.

The five men jostled and shuffled down the steps into the boat.

Dave bent to inspect the prostrate Mickey. "Not much point

in that," he said slowly. "Old Mickey here is dead."

"Dead?" Tom said, the word sending a tremor of cold panic through his body.

Gavin went a deathly colour and looked down at the lock key.

"Where's the gun?" Sherwin asked again.

"Who's dead?" Neville squeaked as he leaned into the boat.

"He's deffo dead, guys. I used to be a lifeguard back in Oz, and I've done enough first aid to know that this guy is a stone-cold goner."

"I don't understand why this is happening," Tom whispered.

"I'm not sure understanding is what we need to be doing," Dennis murmured. "We'll have to call the police."

"I'll make the call, Tom, if you want me to?" Dave said.

"Wait," Gav said. "Dave, can you check him again? He really can't be–"

"Yes, Dave, I think that would be a good idea," Neville said, his voice unsteady. "But would it be possible if ... if we all moved to the living area first?"

"I need coffee," Gaston said, and the men moved around Mickey in the narrow space.

"Check him, Dave, check him," Gav urged, a noticeable tremble in his voice, not following the others. Tom pulled his phone out of his pocket. "Please, Tommo, wait–"

"He's dead, Gav. He may have threatened us with a gun but, accidental or not, we have killed him," Tom said quietly, looking at Dave for confirmation.

Dave nodded.

"Shit, shit, shit." Gav collapsed onto the bunk. "But he was going to kill you, Tommo! It was defence, boyo!"

Dave took Tom's phone and flipped it open.

"I know it was defence, Gav, but we have no other choice. We need to make the call," Tom said.

There was a yell from the kitchen, sudden and terrified. They froze.

"End the call."

All three turned to see a huge man dressed in a black suit, black shirt and a long black leather overcoat, his head cocked to one side due to his vast height in the narrow doorway. For the second time, Tom had a gun, much larger, with an attached silencer, pointed at his chest.

"Wh ... wh ... what do you want?" he asked, his voice nowhere near as firm as he'd hoped it would sound.

"In here. Now."

Tom, Dave and Sherwin followed the enormous man into the dining area, where the others sat rigid with fear around the table.

"You know what it is I want. And would appear you have already killed to get it," the man said, pointing at Mickey's body. "And you have nerve to insult me with this stupid question?"

"Look, mon," Sherwin attempted, "please be cool, yeah. We mean no disrespect, but we're really strugglin' to understand what the hell this is–"

Doković jerked the gun and aimed it at Sherwin.

"If you really struggling to understand, then I will make easy for you." With lightning speed, he reached out and snatched Neville by his collar, pulled him up and wrapped his enormous arm around the panicked man's neck and pressed the gun's muzzle firmly against his right temple. "Tell me now where Lady is, or goodbye to your pal." The terrified Neville, who they barely knew, didn't utter a sound and looked like he might die of fear anyway.

"Again with this lady!" Dennis blurted out, instantly

regretting his comment as the man turned his horrible face towards him and tightened his grip on Neville.

"What you say?" The man's veins were bulging in his neck.

"The lady ... we ... what do you mean, mon? What lady?"

"Let him go," Tom said, fearing for Neville's life, raising Mickey's gun.

"No, mon!"

The man swung around to Tom. "I have had enough of this cra–"

For a seemingly eternal split-second, Tom was unsure what had made his body recoil so violently. His entire life entered a breathless void where time had no consequence, and he didn't know whether he had fired or been fired at.

Staggering backwards, he collapsed, the gun slipping free and onto the floor, his breath a gasp and his heart deafening in his ears. *My life is over*, he thought, his eyes closed tight. *On my stag do. Over. I'm so sorry, Jen. I'm so sorry. Oh shit. Am I dead? Dying? Or have I–*

"Wowzers, Tommo."

What was Gav on about?

"So that's where the gun went," Sherwin said, whistling through his teeth. "Tom, mon, you some kind of secret gangster?"

"Not helpful," Dave said.

"Took me by surprise, is all I'm saying."

"No shit," Dennis muttered, staring at the body of the man in black, who was lying on his back in a growing pool of his own blood. "Where the hell did Tom get that gun?"

"Mate ..." Tom heard Dave's voice. "Tom! Listen, mate, you need to get a grip."

Tom nodded, desperately trying to make himself get a grip,

but all he could manage was a mumbled, "My life is over."

"Your life isn't over, mate, but we do need to discuss this ... this situation."

"I'm dead. I'm a dead man."

"Not you who is dead. It's that man wot's a dead man, mon," Sherwin said.

"And this boat's a freaking horror movie," Dennis added.

"Where's Neville?" Dave asked.

"Here," Neville squeaked from where he had fallen beside the giant and sat up.

Tom opened his eyes and nearly vomited at the blood and brains splattered from wall to wall and embedded in coats and hair, and stuck to faces. He'd never liked horror movies. Gaston lit a cigarette and started muttering in French; Neville was staring into bloody space.

"Fou, fou, fou. C'est fou. Crazy English," Gaston continued, trying to pace in the small space, glaring at his once-immaculate brain-splattered white shirt.

"Put that out in here, mate," Dave said.

Gaston extinguished the cigarette with a curse.

"What the hell happened? How did this happen? How will we ever explain this? Oh help ... two dead bodies ... this is insane ... all over a lady ..." Tom rambled.

"If it was just that Mickey guy, then we might be able to explain things; that he attacked us and we had to act in self-defence. But we've got two guys dead, and one of them shot in the head. We need to think," Dave said calmly.

"I know ... I know. It's bad. Oh God, please help me ..."

"Tom, listen. I don't know who the hell this lady is, and why you're in so much trouble over her, but you saved my life, probably all of ours, as I'm pretty sure he'd have killed us all. But there's no guarantee the police are going to buy any story about a bunch of strangers on a stag do on a boat on the Norfolk Broads who end up with two bodies whether in self-defence or not, like." It was the most Neville had said since he'd arrived hours ago.

"Neville's right," Dennis said when they'd all recovered from the verbosity. "I did a two-year stint at her Majesty's pleasure, and I was innocent."

They all turned and looked at Dennis.

"I can see it in your eyes," Dennis continued. "You don't believe I was innocent either, do you? Trust me, the fuzz aren't going to believe any of us, what with two dead bodies and guns everywhere, and who'd blame them."

"You're not wrong, mon," Sherwin said. "The cops'll take one look at us lot and make their judgement call. We need a plan."

"We can't simply cover up the fact we've killed two men if that's what you're suggesting?" Tom said, keeping his eyes firmly away from the extraordinary amount of blood that still seemed to be seeping from the man in black. "And sooner or later, they'll be missed by ... people who miss people like this."

"These obviously weren't ordinary men, Tom," Dave said, nodding at the carnage. "They were hired killers, they had to be, they had guns, and it was them or us. Hell knows what they were doing here, but the way I see it is that if we get the police involved, then there's a chance we could all go down. Dennis is right. They're not going to believe us."

"What iz it you suggest?" Gaston said, folding his body into one of the benches around the dining table.

"We get rid of their bodies."

"We're not in the outback, Dave boyo," Gav said.

"Yeah, where we gonna put something that big, mon?"

Sherwin added, nodding his head at the floor.

Tom was still shaking – he'd killed a man; it was a natural reaction – but thinking. One thing he excelled at was thinking. It was something he did a lot of. He was also logical and practical, things he considered admirable traits as a computer programmer. Could he apply the same logic to being a killer?

"Someone may miss them," he said. "Well, perhaps not Mickey. I suspect he was a bit of a loner. But then there is the question of this 'lady'. She might be wondering where he is. But this other guy. Why would he just show up here? He was obviously looking for someone. He's a professional killer, I'd say. Probably on someone else's behalf, who I suspect will be waiting to hear from him, and most likely someone we would not want to run into. But ..." Tom had an uncomfortable thought. "Which one of us did he want?"

The silence that followed from seven live men and two dead was prolonged.

Gaston, who had been staring out of one of the circular windows at the night, turned and said, "I will level wiz you all ..." Not a word was spoken. "The only reezon why I am in zis country eez because I have big problems in France, and I do not want to be deported. If I do I will be in big trouble. But I do not know zis huge man. I have not done a crime to be killed for."

"I'm innocent. Always was, always will be," Dennis said. He looked at each man: they still didn't believe him.

"We can't stay here," Dave said. "And we need to do something about them. We all have lives. You're getting married, Tom. I've gotta girlfriend back home. Gav, Nev, Gaston ... whatever 'big problems' you've got going on France ... we need to sort this and then part ways."

"Dave is right. I think we should think about getting reed of those bodies and zen all go our separate ways. Why should we ruin our own lives for zeez orible people?"

"I agree," Sherwin said, and there were a couple of grunts of approval.

Tom slowly stood up. It was true. He was getting married. He couldn't go to jail. They had the venue booked. "Is there anyone here who still wants to call the police? Or shall we get rid of the ... well, move them to ... somewhere else ... and go back to our lives?" he asked.

There were various nods and further grunts.

"I think you have your decision, mate," Dave said.

"I guess I do. This is all insane. Insane. I wish to God ... anyway, it's too late for that. Like you chaps, I simply can't take the chance we won't be believed. We can't stay here tonight. We need to move a bit further upriver, away from the pub. If you guys could get the boat ready to go ..." He turned and walked away.

"Where the hell you going, mon?" Sherwin called after him.

"Back to the pub. I still haven't paid our bill."

Chapter Ten

SHADOW

Donnie Sykes was growing impatient. It had been three hours since he'd spoken to Doković. His deep criminal instincts were beginning to raise an alarm deep in his psyche. Had the Serbian retrieved the diamond only to keep it for himself? If there was one thing that Sykes knew well, it was never to fully trust his fellow criminals. He had spent an entire lifetime crushing (and eradicating) would-be usurpers to his crown and had he not beaten down, and sometimes disposed of, many similar men over the past decades, he knew unequivocally that they would have done the same to him.

But Doković had been loyal. A pain in his side for sure and certainly disrespectful at times, but this was a trade-off that Donnie had tolerated in return for the Serb's ruthless and impeccable talents – talents that had served him so well on his road to growing the largest criminal outfit south of Manchester.

Although Sykes knew that Doković worked alone, and this sometimes meant 'jobs' could take longer than sending in a team of clumsy mobsters, the impatience was growing, leaving less room for his tolerance of the Serb's radio silence. Sykes decided to leave it half an hour longer, and then he'd call the hitman to see if the job had been done.

* * *

They had not passed a single soul, either on the water or on the tracks that straddled the banks of the canal. Tom had taken charge, much to his surprise, and steered *May* in the darkness. Slowing as they passed a huge weeping willow draped over the waterway, he peered through the leaves.

"This looks like a good place," he whispered.

Sherwin squinted into the darkness and nodded. "True, mon. We can tie the boat to the trees."

"It'll do for tonight. We'll move on first light tomorrow."

Inside, the corpses had been rolled in rugs and tied with guide ropes that Neville had discovered in a utility storage area at the stern of the vessel. It was clear Mickey had been easier to wrap, neatly tucked in as he was, but the wrapping of the man in black had been a more complicated affair altogether, the top of his very bloody head and huge feet sticking out of each end of his rug.

"Sorry, Tommo," Gav said. "The boyo's just too long. Best we can do, I'm afraid."

"It's fine, Gav. It was never going to be easy," Tom replied.

"Tom," Dave said, "me and the guys have been talking. We need to find a secluded place and bury these guys. What other choice do we have?"

Tom knew Dave was right, but flashbacks of detective programmes on TV, with a foot sticking out of the soil and a kid pointing and dog digging, were not pleasant viewing.

"Where's the blood?" he then asked. "There was an awful lot. Especially from ... and quite a lot of other ... matter, shall we say."

"Gaston and me cleaned it up while Dennis and Dave wrapped," Neville said. "I doubt it would stand up to forensics, like, but then you'd never know if you weren't looking for it."

"It looks spotless to me, mon. Good job," Sherwin said as if congratulating the guy who just washed his car.

A phone rang, loud in the small space, and they all jumped.

"Whose bloody phone is that?" Tom asked.

"His," Dennis replied, pointing to the rug occupied by the body of the man in black. He pulled a Nokia out of his coat pocket. "It fell out of his jacket when we were rolling him."

"Bloody turn it down!" Tom hissed, grabbing it and trying to muffle the sound under a cushion."

The phone rang off and rang again.

"Merde!" Gaston said.

"Yes," Dave agreed.

"Don't touch it! Leave it!" Neville shrieked. "It could be a trap!"

The phone continued to ring.

"Give it to me." Sherwin held his hand out. "We need to know who it is."

"I don't want to know," Tom said.

"It'll be his boss, wanting to know where he is. We're going to have to make this up as we go along," Sherwin insisted. "Keep him quiet, off the scent."

"Sherw–"

Too late. Sherwin grabbed the phone and accepted the call, hitting the speaker button and laying the phone on the table. But he said nothing, waiting for the caller to speak.

A second later came a growl: "Doković? Where the hell are you? Is it done?"

All eyes were on Sherwin, but he remained silent.

"Doković?" Sykes said again, barely containing his anger. "Tell me you've got the Lady from that miserable little toerag, Mickey."

What was the deal with this goddamn lady? And Mickey? *Their* Mickey?

Finally, Sherwin spoke: "Your mon ain't 'ere right now."

There was a pause. Clearly, the man on the phone was unsure whether he should speak further or hang up. But then his curiosity obviously got the better of him, and he said, "And who the hell are you?"

"I'm da man what put your man in da ground."

"And Mickey?"

"He is not your concern."

"W H A T O N E A R T H A R E Y O U D O I N G ?" Tom mouthed, but Sherwin's face made it clear he was in no mood to back down. What happened to 'keep him quiet, off the scent'?

Donnie was silent once more, and after another long pause, Sherwin was beginning to wonder if the man-in-black's caller had hung up.

But Donnie, who had been pondering his best approach and had been contemplating the possible death of his best man, and the capture of Lawson, kept his voice low and steady. "So you're in charge now, are you? I guess we have underestimated you. So, are you going to tell me who I'm dealing with?"

Sherwin pushed out his chest and answered, "They call me the Shadow."

The rest of the crew simply stared on, dumbfounded. The Shadow?

"The Shadow?" Sykes repeated coldly. His mind was racing. He knew virtually all of the main players within the UK's criminal fraternity and was desperately trying to recall this name ever being uttered. He could not.

"That's right," Sherwin affirmed. "So if you wanna make a deal, then it's me dat you need to speak with."

"So, Mr Shadow," Donnie sneered. "Do you even know what you have?"

"Course I do, mon. The lady. So if you want a chance at ever getting your hands on her, den we need to make an accord. But I'm warning you, mon, you know what we're capable of, so if you mess with us den we put you in the ground too."

The crew looked on in greater astonishment. The repeated mention of this lady was escalating the absurdity of the situation beyond all comprehension.

Donnie dismissed the threat, but he knew now that the man on the other end of the line had the upper hand, for the time being at least. "Let's make this simple then. Why don't you name your price?"

"No," Sherwin said. "You tell me what you're willing to pay."

Again the line went quiet long enough for Sherwin to question if the caller was still at the other end.

"Two million," came the answer and through gritted teeth.

Sherwin's mouth fell open. For a moment he was completely speechless, but he forced himself to regain his composure. "Three."

"Do you have any idea how difficult it will be to sell this diamond?" Sykes growled.

They all looked at each other. Diamond?

"Unless you have the contacts I have, which I know for a fact you do not, you wouldn't spend more than two days as a free man before being picked up by the cops, and that's if you hadn't already been killed attempting to broker the deal in the first place. You will be dealing with some very ruthless people, and the black market is a very dangerous place. On the other hand, I have the valuable skills and essential contacts that will get the diamond verified, and a suitable buyer will be found within days. My offer stands at two million and, if you refuse, I will make it the rest of my life's work to hunt you down. Believe me when I say you will beg me to kill you swiftly after I have found you, which I most certainly will. But, if you agree with my proposal, I will overlook the fact that you have killed one of my own and that you have taken what is rightfully mine, and I will not seek vengeance once this transaction has been made. I hope this is clear, Mr Shadow."

"Two million. We 'ave a deal."

"Good. You have made the right choice." Donnie was relieved, but he would never allow this Shadow man to suspect this. "I need time to make preparations for the exchange. I will call you tomorrow at noon. But I warn you, if you are stupid enough to renege on this deal, I will find you, and I will kill you."

They listened, but it was clear the man was gone, so Sherwin ended the call and placed the phone back on the table.

"What the hell have you done, Sherwin?" Tom asked. "Or should I call you the Shadow?"

"So this lady person is a diamond?" Gav gasped.

"Two million quid?" Dennis said.

"Who the hell were these men?" Neville squeaked, looking at the rugs.

"I did what I had to, mon. Can't have these people coming at us, trying to kill us."

"But who was that man? And where the hell is this diamond?"

"Mickey's 'lady' is a diamond, that much is clear," Tom said, "and he would have killed me for it. Without the diamond, we're dead men. But we don't have a diamond. And now you've made a crazy deal with a crazed lunatic who thinks we do!"

"It has to be here somewhere," Dave said. "The man in black came here for it. He–"

"Wait! Mickey flipped when he found me looking through his backpack," Tom said, and hurriedly made his way over the rugs to the bow.

The others exchanged a few puzzled glances and followed, crowding into the small space between the bunks.

Tom tipped the contents of the backpack out again, rifling through a roll of cash, socks, underwear and a couple of T-shirts. He then put his hand inside, feeling around the pockets. Nothing. Hang on ... Remembering, he dropped to his knees and scrabbled around under the bunk. "Move away," he mumbled. "Give me some space. And light. I can't see a bloody thing."

"What are you doing, mate?" Dave asked.

"When I was emptying Mickey's bag, something fell out and rolled somewhere under here. But a split second later, he came in waving his gun at me, and I forgot all about it."

The others stood watching, each one holding their breath, as Tom moved his hand from side to side until he felt a piece of cloth with something hard inside.

"Got it," he said before reversing from under the bunk.

They crowded back in, circling Tom as he held the rolled-up piece of dirty black cloth in the palm of his hand.

"Well, open it, mon," Sherwin whispered.

Tom slowly unravelled the cloth to reveal the largest diamond any of them had ever seen outside of a movie. Each of them stood in silence, watching as the gem's beautifully cut facets caught the overhead lights and shone with such brilliance there appeared to be a pink fire in his hand. For almost a full minute, seven pairs of eyes were so entranced by the magnificent object they could barely breathe.

Sherwin whistled through his teeth. "I should have insisted on three million," he said.

"Just shy of three hundred grand each, like," Neville whispered, the first to complete the mental arithmetic.

"Crikey," Dave said. "My dreams of a condo on Bondi beach just might become a reality."

"It's a whole row of motorbikes for me," Dennis grinned.

"Have you all lost your minds?" Tom said, breaking the spell. "You don't seriously believe that the guy Sherwin spoke to, the same man responsible for sending that colossal giant who would have killed us, was the legitimate owner of this diamond, do you? It's clearly stolen! And if we take a cut when we give the diamond back to him, we're basically committing another crime on top of the other crimes – of, well, you know – we've already committed today."

"But we 'ave not committed any crime, Thomas," Gaston objected, motioning dramatically with his hands. "We are not murderers; we were defending ourselves against an intruder."

"Mickey wasn't an intruder. I effectively invited him here!" Tom said.

"But he would have killed you, boyo, if I hadn't have bashed his head in!" Gav protested.

"Yes, Gav, I agree, in principle. And that we acted against an intruder. But to keep this diamond and do a deal with whoever Sherwin was talking to, on top of burying their bodies rather than reporting this whole sorry mess, is a crime. I just wanted to have a stag do! And now I'm a murderer and a thie–" Tom bellowed, folding the cloth back around the diamond.

"Tom!" Dave interjected. "We've been through this already, mate. What difference does it make to add one more crime, which we're doing to keep us alive, just like we did when we had to kill those dudes in there?"

"What? What? Who the bloody hell are you?" Tom yelled. "This is not working for me!"

"Guys. Guys!" Dennis said, an odd look on his face.

"What?" Tom said.

"This stone isn't just called the Lady ... I think this is the Pink Lady."

"The what?" Dave asked.

"Pink? We can see she's pink," Sherwin said.

"Yes, pink," Dennis said. "It's all coming back to me. The Pink Lady was a diamond which was stolen at least ten years back. It's the largest and most expensive pink diamond ever found. If I remember, it was stolen while on loan to a gallery in London."

"On loan from where?" Neville asked.

"A Scandinavian royal family, I think. Anyway, that doesn't matter. What matters is that it was never returned. The reason I remember the heist is because, incredibly, it was done by only one man, at least as far as the fuzz were concerned. They caught him almost immediately, but somehow he'd managed to hide the diamond before they captured him. He's been in the nick ever since, but they still never found the Pink Lady."

"Oh my g–" Tom said.

"Zut alors!" Gaston agreed.

"Do you think that Mickey might have been the guy who stole it?" Dave asked.

"I can't remember much about the guy they caught, but I do remember he shot a police officer in the back during the getaway. Mickey had a gun and would have shot Tom here. It's possible he hid the diamond and the gun just before they caught him."

"So, you think this is the Pink Lady, then?" Sherwin asked.

"Mickey referred to it as the Lady," Tom said, unwrapping the shimmering diamond again.

"The intruder, the man in black, he also called it the Lady," Dave added.

"So we got the Lady, and the lady is pink," Gav surmised. "I think, boyos, that it's fair to say that young Tommo here is holding the Pink Lady."

"If that's true," Dennis said, "then this diamond is worth ten times what Sherwin agreed to."

"If that's true," Dave added, "then the guy on the phone won't be the only one interested in this stone. Half the criminal underworld would likely kill for it too."

"And if that's true," Tom finalised, "then we need to get the diamond to this maniac as soon as we can, well, after we've, you know ..."

On this, they all agreed.

After securing the famous Pink Lady in Tom's backpack, the guys gathered their stuff and went to the far end of the boat to get changed into clean clothes, and to try to sleep for a couple of hours as far away as possible from their deceased ... guests.

Chapter Eleven

AN ALLIANCE OF RELIANCE

Early the following morning, Donnie Sykes wasted no time in making his preparations. But these, he hoped, would be plans that would turn all of the cards in his favour. This Shadow man, whoever the hell he was, would not know what had hit him.

He selected a different mobile phone from the one he had used to communicate with his now-dead hitman, dialled a number and waited. Seconds later, the call was picked up.

"Yes?" a man said tersely.

"Hello, Superintendent Blakney ..." Donnie said.

The use of mobile phones was bad etiquette on the golf course, but a man of Blakney's standing was hardly going to be chastised by the other members that made up his four-ball partnership that morning.

"It's *chief* superintendent, actually, as you know, and I'm about to start a round of golf, so you'd better make it quick."

"Chief Superintendent, is this a secure line?"

There was a momentary silence, after which Donnie heard muffled excuses being made. Sykes did not like Blakney, and Blakney did not like Sykes, but the men had formed an uncomfortable alliance decades earlier and on many occasions over the years, had operated a quid pro quo understanding that had enabled both to prosper in their respective 'careers'. With a regular supply of information from Sykes as to the criminal deeds and whereabouts of a great number of the crime boss's rivals, the chief superintendent's career trajectory had been greatly enhanced. The cost, of course, and Blakney's role, was to divert unwanted police attention away from Sykes' growing criminal empire, allowing the thug to flourish unimpeded.

"It's secure. What do you want?"

"This is not just about what I want. I have information about Mickey Lawson and a certain Pink Lady."

There was another silence and more muffled excuses, and then, "Do you indeed?"

Sykes briefly described the past twenty-four hours as he knew it: the possible killing of Mickey; the killing of the hired Serbian; and the involvement of an unknown gang who were now in possession of the precious diamond.

"So, what is it you want from me? You understand that my aim was to recapture Lawson and the diamond in order to ensure my one hundred per cent success rate. Now that he's dead and the stone has fallen into unknown hands, this hardly seems like a possibility, does it?"

"Chief Superintendent, I am asking you to consider the possibility of overlooking a perfect career in favour of a very prosperous retirement. I already have interested parties who are prepared to pay handsomely for it, and I am suggesting that you and I retrieve the diamond and split this money between us. And you know full well the enormous sums we are talking about."

Blakney did.

"So you are in agreement with my proposal? You and I have been of mutual benefit to one another since the early days, and it seems fitting we now reap our reward for the hard work we have both done these past decades. I don't see you caring much for one single blemish on your near-perfect record when you take a private jet to Cannes to pick up your first yacht."

"I'm no sailor, Mr Sykes, but I do take your point. And if I were to enable you … us … to get to the diamond, how do you see this working?"

"It's actually very simple, and your part would be of minimal risk."

"That I doubt, but go on."

"I have a call at noon with the leader of the gang now in possession of the diamond. These idiots are chancers, and they are using the phone that belonged to my associate, who they killed. I need you to use police know-how to trace the phone number to their coordinates. Once you have those, you will send officers to arrest them and bring them – and their 'possessions' – back to your station, including the diamond, and therefore pass it to me ready for sale."

"Not quite as easy as you might think, but I should be able to make this happen."

"Then we have an agreement?"

"I think we do, Mr Sykes. But remember, if you were to double-cross me, then I have years of dirt that will put you away indefinitely."

"Chief Superintendent, that works both ways. But you know I am not a stupid man. We're not that dissimilar, you and me. And this time is really no different to all the other times we have helped each other. We want the same thing, and we have the power to make it happen."

"Send me the phone number, and I will get things moving."

"Good. I may even consider retirement myself once the deal is done."

"I doubt that very much."

Placing the phone safely back in the drawer, Donnie looked

over at the man who sat motionless in the corner of his office. "He's in," he said.

"He was never going to resist," the man replied. "His greed was the opening we needed."

"We're also going to need the best men on this, and immediately. They need to get in and out fast. The Serb said there were at least seven men in the gang, although he didn't feel they were in any way professional."

"And yet they were able to dispense with him easily enough, as well as whatever they've done with Mickey Lawson. We must not underestimate this gang, whoever they are. I have just the men. Ex-paras! They're primed and waiting for my call. We let Blakney do the dirty work. He'll lead us directly to them."

"What deal did you make with these mercenaries?"

"They will take ten per cent of the sale, which we will honour. They're not the type of men you cheat on. They're highly trained ex-soldiers, and they will wipe out this gang, bring the diamond to us, and then lay low while they wait for their cut."

"Very good. But we also need to eliminate Blakney. I will not allow him the opportunity to put two and two together and try to bring me down."

"Do what you want with the bastard. Once he's served his purpose, I'll be glad to see him gone. Make sure there are no loose ends."

"There won't be, that you can count on."

* * *

Donnie Sykes was not the only one eager to move things along with haste. Tom and his stag party were up, desperate to get the grim task of burying two dead men over and done with.

Dennis, who had been up on deck for a quick cigarette, stuck his head in through the hatch. "We have a potential problem," he said.

All six men inside froze.

"What is it?" Tom asked, definitely not ready for the answer.

"There's a cottage just set back from the bank. It looks pretty shabby, but we can't take the chance of being seen, you know, when we ..."

Tom and Sherwin quickly got up, stepped over the rugs, the contents of which were even more grisly as death set in, and went to look for themselves. The cottage did not appear inhabited, but both agreed the risk was too high.

"We need to go a bit further up the canal, find somewhere else," Tom said when they returned.

With barely a word, they got going, each absorbed in his own world of what had happened, what they'd done, and what they were about to do. A mile further up the canal, they found a wooded area off the port side of the vessel, still relatively dark as the dawn sun had yet to rise above the trees and thick with overgrowth and ferns. They agreed it was about as good as they could hope for.

"Okay then, boyos, how we gonna do this?" Gav asked as Tom and Sherwin moored up and tied *May* to the trees.

"Mickey'll be a cinch," Dave said. "But the other dude? That's going to take some muscle."

"I say we start with Mickey then," Neville suggested. "You know, so we can get a feel for it, like, if you get my meaning."

"A feel for it? I don't wanna get a *feel* for it!" Sherwin exclaimed. "This is irregular, mon! It's a bad thing!"

"C'est trés mauvais," Gaston muttered. "*Mauvais*. Bad."

"Yes. It is moyvay, Gaston mon," Sherwin agreed. "I've seen some stuff. But this is very moyvay."

Quickly they set about hoiking the dead men onto the bank. Gaston blanched, looked at the clean white shirt and pale grey trousers he'd put on, and was told to act as a lookout instead.

They found a ramp under a bunk and laid it across the gap between *May* and the bank.

"Steady, boyos," Gav murmured as he and Sherwin each took an end of Mickey's rug, with Dennis and Dave taking up their places to assist. "Take it nice and easy."

"Shut it, Gav mon. Nice 'n easy ... nice 'n easy, my arse," Sherwin muttered.

"Yeah, Gav, mate," Dave grunted. "And quit ya pommie whining, Shadow Man, and lift. There's worst to come."

"Pommie? Pommie! Mon!" Sherwin blasted (in a hiss).

"Cut it out," Tom said from the end of the ramp, watching and guiding the bickering men until Mickey was dumped in the ferns.

After gathering their breath and their tempers, they went back in for the man in black which as they'd anticipated, was the worst to come.

Two of them grabbed a protruding ankle and colossal foot while the others grappled with his vast, bloody head and shoulders.

"Bleedin' Nora."

"Couldn't we cover his head with a bag?"

"Come on, you big bastard."

"Muvva eff."

"Good grief, he's heavy."

"Argh, my back!"

Finally, the man in black was heaved and dragged and left sideways, leaning against Mickey, Mickey's head snuggled against the big man's chest.

Neville staggered back and landed backside down in the ferns a few feet away.

"What's with him?" Sherwin asked, noticing Neville's ashen face.

"He's having a bit of a panic attack," Dave whispered.

"Fair enough," Dennis said.

There was the unmistakable sound of a boat's engine.

"Zere iz a boat!" Gaston hissed.

"No shit," Sherwin said.

The men crowded into the helm, positioning themselves in such a way as to obscure the scene behind them.

Seconds later, a small white two-berth cruiser passed off their starboard side, and as it did so, an elderly man with an impressive Buster Merryfield beard turned from his mahogany steering wheel and called out in a jolly voice, "Mornin', fellas! Beautiful day for it!"

"Morning!"

"Alright there, alright."

"Waa gwaan."

"Good'day, mate."

"Bonjour!"

"Gaston, English would have worked here," Sherwin hissed.

"Je suis Français, imbécile," Gaston flounced. "And what is your waaah gwaaan, 'ey?"

"Shut up, the lot of you," Tom smiled, waving as the cruiser passed.

They turned back to the scene.

"Right. Let's dig," Tom said. The sun was getting higher. They needed to get on.

"Where, boyo?"

"Good point."

"Here," Dennis said. "We've already disturbed the ground a bit. If we go tramping about, we'll only make it more obvious we've been here."

"Innocent," Sherwin whispered.

"Innocent," Dave agreed.

The only shovel they could find was a half-size black thing used for coal and a couple of garden trowels, which they rotated until exhausted, they had a sizable hole in the ferns.

"Big man first," Dave said.

"Gently does it," Gav said as they pulled and dragged and heaved. "Have some respect."

"We're not burying the family dog, Gav," Sherwin replied.

The big man was shoved into the hole and landed face down, which was preferable, and Mickey was rolled in on top of him and nestled into his neck.

"Do you think we should say something?" Gav asked.

"Say something?" Dennis repeated.

"You Welsh are soft," Sherwin said.

"Nothing wrong with a bit of respect for the dead, boyo."

"For a pair of murderers?" Neville asked, still pale.

"Watch it," Gav said. "I'm technically a killer too."

"True, mon," Sherwin agreed.

"And him," Dave said, nodding at Tom.

"True," Tom said.

"So, you know, should we say something, like a prayer?" Gav asked.

"You are crazy people," Gaston said, from his watch point, cigarette held like a prop.

"No amount of prayer gonna do them no favour," Sherwin said. "So no, I ain't saying nothin good over them, but I ain't saying nothin bad neither, coz that's bad voodoo innit, mon."

"Okay, let's just say 'May God have mercy on their souls' and leave it at that," Tom suggested.

"And ours," Gav added.

"And ours," Tom agreed.

"May God have mercy on your souls," they said in unison, and filled the hole in.

Chapter Twelve

PATHOLOGICAL LOVE

"Do you ever wonder why we do this job?" Austin asked thoughtfully as he studied the array of surgical tools on the stainless steel instrument trolley.

"We're together, aren't we?" Shelly replied with a grin.

"Ha! Yeah, but it's a Saturday, and I have to share you with a new stiff!" to which Shelly giggled.

Detective Inspector Austin Williamson was certainly not a man known for grumbling, and in truth, he was only partially griping at the interruption to his and Shelly's weekend plans. Austin adored time alone with his beautiful fiancée, and being called into the station at all hours was simply part of the job – a job they both loved.

Since his move from sedate suburban surroundings to Central London, the young detective sergeant's studious commitment to the Metropolitan Police Service had won him much approval from those of loftier ranks and also within the press. After just four years, he had been promoted to detective inspector, and his sights were firmly set on yet higher ranks should things continue to go well. He was made for the job and could not imagine ever doing anything else.

Shelly, on the other hand, had almost stumbled into the role. After qualifying as a forensic pathologist, her intention had always been to go on to teach the profession at the Royal College of Pathologists. But her father, a career police officer, had convinced her to follow in his footsteps. At first, she was reluctant, but it didn't take long for her to realise that the sharp end of pathology – assisting police investigations and suspicious deaths – was the role she, too, was born to do. Within two years of arriving at the same station as Williamson, the pair had formed a romance that eventually led to Austin proposing. But as in love as they were, the two were also driven by the job. They were as comfortable chatting across one of the morgue's corpses as they were across a romantic dinner for two.

"So, let's talk shop," Shelly said as she pulled back the sheet. "Who are we looking at?"

"Colin Sturgeon," Williamson said after consulting the paperwork. "He was a probation officer, possibly killed by a prisoner recently released from Scrubs."

"I think I know what killed him," Shelly said, indicating the single gunshot wound straight into the heart.

"Ha. Funny girl."

"We need fibres, you know the drill, anything that could point at the killer."

"Including what the killer pointed at him."

"Again, funny."

"There's no exit wound from the bullet," Shelly said, "so it shouldn't be difficult to get detail on the weapon used. But the poor chap also took a real beating before he died, and there's very little to suggest he struggled with the killer."

"Too terrified, perhaps. Can I leave this with you? I have to pop upstairs to see the chief."

"Blakney's in too? So it's not just us monkeys who've had their day off interrupted; the organ grinder has too."

"Yep. He called me as I arrived. Needs to discuss some

highly classified case and, by the sound of it, it's got him all worked up."

"Oh, poor you."

"Call me when you know more about this." He handed her the clipboard with Sturgeon's paperwork.

"Will do, darling. Good luck with the boss."

They leaned across the corpse and kissed.

Williamson made his way up to the top floor. Thrown up in the early seventies, the building was a dreary six-storey block of decaying concrete. Still, recent refurbishments had improved the interior, including state-of-the-art equipment to rival any of the Met's other locations across the London boroughs. Blakney's office, in Williamson's humble opinion, must have soaked up a large part of the development funding. It seemed little expense had been spared to provide the man with every amenable comfort. From the wood-panelled walls to the eucalyptus globe drinks cabinet sitting beside his vast mahogany desk, it was clear to all deemed worthy of entry that the chief was a man with expensive taste.

The DI tapped on the ornate frosted glass window in the door.

"Come."

Williamson crossed the thick burgundy carpet to where the portly chief sat, studying the many documents spread out in front of him. The DI stood beside a chair in front of the desk, waiting for the invitation to sit that never came.

"Sir, you asked to see me?" he said after a few moments.

"That's right, Williams, this one's important."

Williamson resisted the urge to correct his superior's misnaming of his name. "Does this mean you're pulling me off the Mickey Lawson case, sir?"

"Far from it, man. I have new information pertinent to

the very same case. In fact, this information is of national importance and comes as a directive from the Home Office itself. The expedited capture of Lawson, and anything on his person or in the possessions he may be carrying, is now your primary objective."

"I don't understand, sir. His possessions? What could he possibly have in his possession that the Home Office would deem to be of national interest?"

The chief appeared slightly agitated at the question. "That does not concern us, Williams. And we have been expressly asked not to interfere with any of his possessions – under any circumstances, you hear. Once captured, his clothes, luggage, and anything he's carrying must be bagged securely and brought to me directly. Once I receive all items, I am to report to my contact at the Home Office and wait for one of their representatives to collect said possessions. Is this clear?"

"Crystal clear, sir. But what of the Sturgeon killing? Do we have any more intel regarding Mickey Lawson's possible connection with the murder?"

"That is yet to be determined, and, of course, finding this probation officer's murderer is still of importance. There are no new leads as yet, but I am expecting more intel later today as to his whereabouts. As soon as I have this, you will need to be ready to move quickly. And what of the autopsy?"

"Underway, sir. Shelly ... apologies ... Dr Baxter is about to perform the autopsy, and we should have forensic data soon enough. You're aware, sir, that the killer shot Mr Sturgeon?"

"I am. And you will need to take all precautions necessary when apprehending Lawson. If he is the killer, then he may well still be armed. As soon as we have coordinates as to his whereabouts, I suggest you take Sergeant Price along with you. Michaels is otherwise occupied until further notice. In the meantime, I will ensure that a team of armed responders are at hand should the need arise. But I will stress my earlier point: although bringing Sturgeon's killer to justice is very important, the retrieval of Lawson's possessions is our primary objective, and I wish to see no delay in ensuring the Home Office get what they're after before we seek the conclusion of the murder case. Understood?"

"Understood, sir."

"There is another thing ... There is a high probability that Lawson may now have accomplices, but it may even be the case that he's already dead."

"Dead, sir? Why would he be dead?"

"The man is a felon, isn't he?" snapped the chief superintendent, again revealing a certain agitation Williamson was not accustomed to seeing. "These people live by a different code, Williams, as well you know. Killers often associate with other killers, so whatever the Home Office are after, it may have been something worth killing for. If this is the case, then this possession may already have fallen into the hands of others. So, if Lawson is now in cahoots with other criminals, then they must also be apprehended and all of their possessions seized as well. Again, everything must be brought to the station immediately. I cannot stress enough the urgency and importance of what I am telling you. I want no slip-ups on this one."

"There won't be, sir. We'll do everything in our power to ensure complete success."

"Good man. So let's get cracking."

With his hand on the door, Williamson turned. "One last thing, sir. Do we have any idea where Lawson is?"

"We had some intel suggesting he was hiding out in Norfolk. Probably conjecture, but we'll know for sure soon enough."

After leaving Blakney's office, Williamson went to find Sergeant James Price. Price was a good man, and the two of them had been partners on many cases in the past two years. The younger man was intelligent, quick-witted, and, if truth be told, was the better officer of the two when it came to communicating with the general public. People just seemed to open up to Price because of his congenial disposition, and Williamson liked to have him as his wingman.

Williamson couldn't help replaying the conversation with Blakney in his mind on the way down to the second floor. The two men had a superficial relationship, and his superior was not a man for idle chit-chat. Still, something about the manner in which the chief had spoken seemed strange. There was an evident agitation and urgency about the way he had delivered his instructions. Was it possible that Blakney had not given his DI the whole truth? Or was it something he'd said that had not been true at all? Williamson couldn't be sure. But either way, the chief superintendent was his superior, and he was not about to question his motives. He had been given a task, and his job was to fulfil it to the best of his abilities. He shook the idea of deceit from his mind and greeted Price.

Chapter Thirteen

THE COUNTERBLUFF

Tom and his stag do crew travelled a further five miles along the canal. All fun was gone, and all they wanted was to put distance between themselves and the shallow grave where they'd dumped two strangers. Tom suggested only he stay up top, and the others remain below. The last thing they needed was to attract any unwanted attention. Still, with each slow mile that passed, the deep sense of foreboding continued to grow in Tom's gut. The fact they were even contemplating making a deal with the criminal caller seemed more and more foolhardy to him.

"We can't trust this guy," he muttered as he watched the bow of the narrowboat glide through the water seventy feet out in front. "We need to find a way of protecting ourselves." Leaning forward through the stern's doorway, he called, "Sherwin?" How the hell had his stupid stag do turned into this bloody nightmare? No doubt Jen was having a lovely, double-murder-free weekend in Prague ...

A few seconds later, Sherwin stuck his head out. "What's up, mon?"

"I've been thinking. I have a horrible feeling that dealing with this caller is a really bad idea. I know you, and the guys want to take his call, and I understand that the money he's offering is life-changing for all of us, but I think there's something really off. I think it's a pipe dream."

"A what now?"

"I mean, I don't think it's real. I don't think this guy, who tried to have us killed, has the slightest intention of giving us a penny. I think he's putting it out there as a carrot, trying to draw us to him. When he succeeds in getting the diamond, we'll immediately become witnesses to his crime and, ultimately, we'll be expendable. He's already proved he's capable of murder and probably has plenty more people who will do it for him."

Sherwin mulled this over. "So what're you suggesting, mon? Because I'm not gonna ignore all we've been through and not have something to show for our pains. It's payback time, mon. That dude may have bad intention but we have the diamond, so I think we have the upper hand."

"But that's my point: we do have the upper hand, for the moment, but only until he gets the diamond firmly in his own hand. This isn't the movies, mate. We have no idea how to make this exchange while protecting ourselves at the same time."

"So we need to think of a way to protect ourselves, yeah?"

"Yes. I do have an idea. It's not foolproof, but it may at least let us know if he really does plan to kill us."

"Okay, Tom mon, what's your idea?"

Sherwin listened intently, saying nothing but offering an occasional nod to confirm he understood. By the time Tom had finished, they were both in agreement that the plan was worth a shot.

"Right," Tom said, "it's 11.25. The guy said he'd ring at noon, so we'd better find a place to moor up and get ready."

Within fifteen minutes, they had found a suitable spot and nervously readied themselves for the imminent call. Although each man was expecting it, every one of them startled as the phone rang at 12.10pm.

The Shadow pressed the green button and growled, "You're late, mon."

"Hello to you too, Mr Shadow," Sykes replied, trying hard to suppress his utter contempt for whoever this usurper was.

"I said, you're late, mon."

What did this chancer want? An apology? No chance.

"The sale of an item as hot as the one you currently possess is not a simple task to organise," he eventually said, his voice controlled and his pace slow, "and takes time. I have been extremely busy setting up a potential buyer and organising the details of where and when we will make the exchange."

"So you have an interested party dat wish to buy the diamond. Who?"

"That does not concern you. What is of concern is that this purchase is time-sensitive and will need to take place in three days. At the latest, I will need you to deliver the diamond to me the day before. Where are you in the country?"

"Nice try, mon, but that does not concern you. All you need to know is it's no problem for us to make the exchange in two days' time."

"Very well. Do you know the club Peanuts, east of Soho?"

"Nope. Sounds like a batty boy club. Is it good?"

Sherwin's petulance was beginning to infuriate Sykes, but he needed to keep this irritant on the phone. "You can judge this for yourself when you arrive. I can assure you, Mr Shadow, that all of your needs will be met at my club. But I'm sure that in a couple of days' time, there will only be one thing you will be interested in, or should I say two million things?"

"About that."

"About what?"

"About your two million. Turns out we now know a lot more than you'd think about this Pink Lady, including the value. So the price has gone up. If you want to make a deal, then it's now seven million. If not, the deal's off. Your call."

The rest of the crew, with the exception of Tom, had not expected this move, and they glanced at each other in surprise, and fear, before turning back to Sherwin. Why was he pushing this? But Sherwin's eyes were firmly fixed on Tom's as they waited for Sykes' response.

"I see," Sykes responded through gritted teeth.

"I see what?"

Sykes had no choice but to appear to capitulate but took his time. "I can see you've done your homework, and it appears you have me over a barrel. So I agree with your terms. Seven million it is. Now get yourself a pen, and I will give you the address and instructions for the exchange."

After a lengthy description of the destination and how they must conduct themselves on arrival, the call ended.

Gav fell to his knees and punched the air. "Sherwin, you're a bloody legend, boyo! We're all gonna be MIL-LI-ON-AIRES!"

"No, we're not." Sherwin's face was a mixture of disappointment and annoyance. "Ask him." He nodded at Tom, removed the SIM card from the man-in-black's phone and bent it backwards and forwards until it broke into two pieces. He then dropped the phone on the floor and stamped on it with his boot, smashing it.

The men were justifiably confused, and all eyes turned to Tom.

"It's a trap," Tom said.

"A trap?" Neville squeaked.

"What do you mean?" Dave asked.

"Explain zis, please," Gaston said.

Tom looked at each man in turn. "Guys, I'm really sorry, but I've had this feeling something is very wrong ever since Sherwin's first call with this guy. Don't forget he sent that huge maniac to get the diamond from us, and he would have killed us unless I hadn't ... well ... you know. If the caller has already tried to kill us once, then why would he stop trying now? I don't believe he ever intended to give us anything for the diamond."

"Then why the hell would he give in to Sherwin's demands, like, and give us seven million quid?" Neville squealed.

"Because he's stalling. Sherwin and I agreed earlier that he would increase the asking fee in order to see what the guy's reaction would be. If he had argued with Sherwin and negotiated the price back down again, then I might just have believed the deal was real." Tom looked at Sherwin. "But he didn't."

"You heard. He agreed to seven million, just like that. I knew the moment he replied the man was lying through his teeth. He's trying to sucker us in, make us believe we're in control–"

"But I don't understand," Neville interjected. "How could you know he was stalling? And why would he do that?"

"The man made the call last far longer than he needed to," Sherwin said. "You know, the pauses, taking ages to give me the drop-off information. It was obvious, mon."

"But, like Neville asked," said Dave, "why would he do that?"

"Simple," Tom said. "He's tracking us, and he's using the man-in-black's mobile phone to do it. He kept Sherwin on the phone just long enough to pinpoint exactly where we are on the map. He's already sent one hired killer, and he's most likely mobilising a whole team now to hunt us down."

"So what do we do, like?" Neville blurted, his voice its customary squeak.

"Zis is some sort of crazy shit," Gaston said. "I should 'ave stayed in Leeds. Better still, France. Non, non, pas la France. *Problemes, problemes.*"

"We do the only thing we can do," Tom answered. "Get the hell out of here."

"Arghhhh!" Gav growled as though in great pain. "We had a chance of being millionaires, and now it's gone."

"Like I said, Gav," Tom sighed. "I really don't believe that was ever a possibility. It was always a mirage. And, anyway, I'm sure you'd rather live with empty pockets than die with them full."

"Whooah," said Sherwin, with a big grin on his face. "Empty pockets? Aren't you boys forgetting something? We still got the Pink Lady, remember?"

"Yeah," replied Gav shaking his head. "But your man on the phone said it would be impossible for people like us to sell it without getting picked up by the cops, or even get ourselves killed trying to sell the thing."

"Not true," a voice said quietly.

All eyes turned to Dennis, who was staring at the floor.

"Not true."

They waited. The man hadn't spoken at all, so what did he have on his mind?

Dennis looked up. "The likes of us might find it impossible to shift the diamond, but I know someone who has all the right connections."

"You?" Dave asked. "How would you know someone like that?"

"I told you guys that I did time, right?"

"*Oui,*" Gaston replied. "But you also told us zat you were innocent, non?"

"Well, I was. Sort of."

"And?" Dave said.

"A few years ago, my older brother and a bunch of his friends burgled a diamond store in Manchester. They got away with over a million quid's worth of precious stones. I wasn't involved. But my bro was like a father to me and brought me up after our mum ran off. I would have done anything for him back then. After the burglary, he and his mates had to lay low for a while, so he asked me to take the diamonds to an old Jewish guy at a jewellery shop in Hatton Garden, in London. This guy, he told me, would take the diamonds and sell them on the black market."

"So what happened, boyo?" Gav asked.

"I never made it. I got picked up when I arrived at Hatton Garden. Someone must have tipped the cops off, and because I was no longer a minor, I ended up with two years in the nick."

"This old Jewish guy, is he still active?" Dave asked.

"Last I heard, yeah. So unless anyone has a better idea, then I reckon he's our man. My brother told me he had used him to shift diamonds before. He said the guy was your old-school type of crook, in the game because of an obsession for precious stones, so I can't imagine he'd pass up the chance to be involved with such a famous diamond."

Sherwin gathered up the broken pieces of phone and the destroyed SIM card. "This problem is solved," he said. "Now we need to get outta here, get to London, and pronto."

* * *

After Sykes had hung up on Sherwin, he waited a frustrating fifteen minutes, fingers tapping on his desk and jiggling his legs, before calling Blakney. The chief superintendent would be gathering the results of tracking the location of the Shadow and his accomplices. He selected a phone and dialled.

"Mr Sykes," came Blakney's dispassionate voice.

"Chief Superintendent. Did you get what was needed? Do we know the gang's precise location?"

"We most certainly do. At least within a couple of hundred metres or so."

"And have you now dispatched your men to the site? They will need to move extremely fast."

"Mr Sykes, do not tell me how to do my job," the chief warned. Although he wanted the same outcome, he was not going to allow Sykes to press him. "I have two of my best officers leaving the station shortly."

"Will they have backup?"

"They will in due course. But I do not have the resources or enough motive to instantly send a sizeable team of armed officers to a site from which the perpetrators will possibly have now moved on. Don't forget that I must have perceived plausibility for my actions. If the commissioner were to get wind of the fact I have actioned a response team for no apparent reason, then I would immediately come under the spotlight. Remember, I am not meant to be aware that a man, your man, has been killed. I have given these officers the authority to secure the gang's position first and tail them if needed. As soon as they are sure of the gang's exact whereabouts, they will inform me immediately, and I will send in my armed team of officers."

"So, where is the gang?"

"Mr Sykes, with all due respect, I am not about to give you coordinates only for you and your associates to go in yourselves, all guns blazing. We are going to do this part my way. The diamond will come to me first. Then, and only then, will we set about trying to get this damn thing sold. I am as keen as you are to reap our reward, but I cannot risk the chance of any suspicion falling on me. I hope that's clear."

"As clear as day. But I only ask where they are as I'm interested in how quickly your armed officers will arrive at the scene once your men locate the gang."

"I see. Well, with blues and twos clearing their path, I'd say approximately ninety minutes."

"And your two officers ... they're on their way?"

"They are leaving now. Don't worry, Mr Sykes, as soon as they find these men and their leader, this Mr Shadow, we'll get what we've both been trying to get our hands on for almost a decade."

"We will, Chief Superintendent, we will. Before you go ..."

"Yes?"

"You ever heard of this Shadow character?"

"Can't say I have. Could be a new boy. It'll be of no interest to us soon enough."

"True."

Donnie ended the call and turned once again to the figure sitting in the dimly lit corner of his office smoking a cigar. "Your men need to move. There are two officers leaving the station now, and we'll need to tail them to this gang. Do you know who Blakney's men are?"

"I do, and so do my team. The moment the officers leave the station, my men will already be following."

"Okay. Once they find the gang and report to Blakney, we will only have around ninety minutes for your team to get in and get the job done."

"Ha!" scoffed the man in the corner. "As I told you before, these men were elite soldiers. I guarantee that after they make the call to Blakney, the two police officers and this gang of worthless shits will be eliminated within twenty minutes. Then the Pink Lady will finally be on its way back to us. Even if they have moved from the position we tracked them to, we'll find them, and it's just a matter of time before you and I become rich beyond our wildest dreams."

"I'll toast to that," Donnie added and pulled a bottle of Scotch from a drawer and placed it next to two crystal tumblers on the dark green leather desktop.

Chapter Fourteen

NOT LIKE LONDON, SIR

It was approaching mid-afternoon. After receiving coordinates from Chief Superintendent Blakney, Williamson and Price collected their designated unmarked Mondeo from the police parking lot, chucked their overnight bags in the boot and got on the road. A little over two hours later, they crossed the Norfolk border, and, according to Williamson's map, they were within three miles of their target.

"Take a right here," Williamson said.

"Here?" Price questioned, but dutifully readied himself to make the turn. "It just looks like a field."

"It does, but there's a small track that winds through farmland for a few miles. I can't see any other way that would get us close to these coordinates."

As Price turned the car onto the dirt track, it occurred to Austin that he couldn't recall passing a single car for at least ten minutes, and now they were leaving the narrow B road onto an even narrower track.

Within another ten minutes, the track had become distinctly more rugged. The churned mud surface had been baked by the summer sun, and the car was bouncing and jolting over the ruts. When the track came to an abrupt end, all that was left in front of them was a patch of wild meadow that led to an area of woodland.

"Well," Williamson said, surveying the area. "I think we should get out and see what's on the other side of those trees. If these coordinates are correct, then Lawson was tracked to a spot just beyond them."

"How accurate are the coordinates?" Price asked.

"Triangulated to within a few hundred metres, or so I've been told. But just look around; there really is nothing here. I'm not sure how these coordinates can be right."

"Not like London, sir, is it?"

"No, Price."

"But give me the fresh smell of manure over London pollution any day."

"Careful what you wish for, Sergeant, because if we don't get this job done in a hurry, then the chief may just demote us to the countryside. Anyway, they could still be lurking ... somewhere ... so caution required at all times."

"Yes, sir."

They made their way across the short stretch of meadow and cautiously into the trees. The woodland turned out to be a small grove which was only about fifty metres deep, and as they reached the opposite side, they were greeted with a vast vista of farmland that stretched out left and right as far as they could see. About ten metres in front of them was a bank that ran alongside an unkept canal or possibly a narrow river. The waterway appeared to follow the line of the woodland that ran north and south.

"So," Sergeant Price mused, "if Lawson was here, he doesn't seem to be here anymore."

"Evidently not. There really is nothing here at all, apart from this canal."

"Do you think Lawson was sailing through here when he

was tracked?"

"You don't sail on a canal, Price. But however unlikely it seems, I guess it's possible he was on a boat of some kind. Who knows? But that's what we need to find out."

The two men doubled back through the grove of trees, and once back at the car, Williamson spread his map across the vehicle's bonnet. After a few moments, he pointed to a particular spot.

"As I said, there is really nothing in any direction for miles from here, apart from this small group of buildings." Price leaned in to look. "They're by the side of this same stretch of canal but about three miles south of our current position."

"What do you suppose the buildings are?"

"No idea, but let's find out. If Lawson did pass through on the canal, then it's possible someone may have seen him. We have zero leads to go on right now, so it's worth a shot."

They made their way back along the bumpy track to the B road and headed south. Williamson spotted a sign – The Woolpack Inn, 500 metres – and instructed his sergeant to take a left turn.

"Looks like those buildings are a pub," he said.

"Hurrah! Perfect timing," Price replied.

"Ha! Nice try, Sergeant, but we're on duty."

Williamson took a moment to look around him, noting the pub garden and distance from the water. "If Lawson did pass by here, then let's hope he stopped for a drink. I can't see how anyone will have seen him on a passing boat when the pub is set this far back."

They made their way to the bar, and a short, cheerful woman in her late fifties asked them, in the local Norfolk drawl, what she could get them.

Williamson held up his Metropolitan Police ID. "We're

on duty, sadly. I'm Detective Inspector Williamson, and this is Sergeant Price. Would it be okay if we asked you a few questions?"

"Oh, well, now, this is exciting," the woman said, blushing a little. "I'll certainly try my best."

"Thank you, ma'am. May I ask if you work here regularly and, if so, approximately how much time have you spent here over the past few days?"

"My husband Phil and me we own this place," she said with a sweep of her short arm. "We live an' work here, day in, day out. We're always here. In fact, we haven't had a holiday in five years. You try having a holiday an' trustin' someone with yer pub!"

"I see. Yes. I can imagine that's quite tricky. Well, we're currently following a line of investigation and attempting to piece together the movements of a man who we believe may have passed by here in the past couple of days. It's possible he passed by on a boat and may have even stopped here for a drink or for food. Could you take a look at this and see if you recognise him?" Williamson placed a photograph of Mickey Lawson on the bar in front of the woman, who studied it for a few moments.

"Hmm. Well, now, he seems like he could be familiar, but I can't say for sure. I'm kind of drawn to fellas by their height, and this photo's not helping me much with that."

"I understand. He's approximately five foot eight, so not tall, with a lithe build. A bit of a loner, we're told. It is possible, however, that he may not have been alone. He may have been part of a group."

"A group, you say. Well, now, we had a group in here last night. Six, seven, eight of them. Can't quite remember. Seemed like a nice enough bunch of fellas. Lots of wedding talk, so I'm guessing they was out on a stag do, or something like that. They had a fair few to drink because they almost left without paying. One of 'em came bounding back in here all out of breath, full of apologies and the like. Funny lad, he was. Bit anxious to get going. But now I come to think of it, there was one of them that looked very much like your chap here, in the photo, I mean."

"Really?" Williamson was encouraged. "How sure of that are you?"

"Well, you can never be completely sure, can you? But, yes, I would say I'm pretty confident of it. He was about the right height, and he didn't half look sullen, just like in that photo of yours. Seemed not to fit with the rest of them, if I'm being honest. Like he wasn't having much fun."

"Are you able to give me descriptions of the other men?"

"Hmm, let me see. Well, the young chap that came back to pay was tall and thin with sandy coloured hair. Another one looked like a Hell's Angel, or some kind of biker at least. He was a big man, heavy set. One was French, possibly, or Italian, with black slicked-back hair. Another had a very strong Welsh accent. They was all white accept one chappie, who was black, and obviously the joker of the pack, as he got all the laughs. In terms of descriptions, I'm really sorry, but I really didn't take an awful lot of notice. It was a fairly busy evening for us on account of the fact it was a Friday night. That's the best I can do, I'm afraid."

"On the contrary, that's been very helpful. And when the group left, do you recall if it was by car or by boat?"

The woman let out a loud laugh. "By boat! I can tell you aren't familiar with this neck of the woods. It may have escaped your notice, but there's nobody around here for miles! Mostly I'd say all our trade is from folks stopping off on their boat trips. We've even got a few rooms upstairs for them who want a comfy bed for the night. I dunno how people sleep on those narrowboats. Too narrow, by half!"

"By boat, excellent, that's also very helpful."

"Wait! There's me telling you that most folks comes in here by boat, but now I remember something else about last night. There was this other fella, on his own, a giant he was. Had to duck when he comes in through that door." She pointed to the entrance. "He came in a bit later, when this man here in the photo and his group was in the garden. I don't think this other man had come from any of the boats moored up out front, and I didn't notice any car outside when I was putting bottles out, so presumed he had walked here from the station. We do get ramblers from time to time, not that he looked like a rambler. All dressed in black, he was. Looked more like an undertaker to me. Ordered a vodka in a funny accent and then just goes and sits by the window. I thought it was odd though because he looked as though he was watching this stag do group while they was out in the garden. I didn't notice when he left but must have been around the same time as your lot did."

"Okay, thank you, that's great," Sergeant Price said, looking up from his notepad. "Is there anything you can tell us about the type of boat the group were using? And might you recall whether they were headed north or south when they left?"

"No, not really, sorry. We get that many boats through here that I don't really take much notice of them anymore. Too busy pulling pints and cleaning tables. Plus, it was getting dark by the time those lads took off."

"And you don't have CCTV on the premises?" Price asked.

"Nope, sorry," the woman said with a chuckle. "It might be 2003 in London, but the twenty-first century ain't arrived in these parts yet."

"Okay," Williamson said, eager to conclude the conversation. "Thank you, ma'am, you've been very helpful and we appreciate your time."

"No problem, lads ... er, officers ... I hope you find the man you're looking for."

Williamson turned to go but then had a thought. "Actually, those rooms you mentioned, we may need to book two of them for a few nights while we continue our investigation. That's if they are available, of course?"

"They are," the woman nodded and pointed toward a shelving unit by the door. "Grab yourself one of our leaflets in that basket. If you call me later to confirm, then I'll make your rooms up for you."

"Great, thanks again."

When the two men were back outside, Price was the first to speak. "So, what do you think, sir? If she was right about this chap being Lawson, then it would suggest he's now regrouped and possibly with other criminals. And if that is the case then we will most certainly need backup in order to make arrests and confiscate all of their possessions."

"It would indeed," Williamson replied. "But that's only if she is right. We can't know for sure that this man is Lawson until we intercept the boat. At least if we found these guys, and Lawson was not among them, we could eliminate them from the investigation and find other avenues."

"What about this so-called giant of a guy who may have been watching the group? Do you think it may be relevant?"

"Impossible to say, but you've made a note of it, and if it is relevant, then we'll find out. Our focus needs to be on this group of men. We need to hope Lawson is one of them and that we're not off on a wild goose chase."

"So how do we find them? We're not sure which way they headed and no idea what type of boat they're on."

"Other boat people," Williamson said with sudden realisation. "And locks."

"Sir?"

"All canals have other boat people. People who live on boats and people who hire them. I imagine it's not a particularly common thing for so many men to be together on one boat, which means they wouldn't be hard to spot, which means they may have been seen, and certainly by the company they hired their boat from. They also have locks for navigating gradients. And I think most locks have lock-keepers who come out and chat and check all is going smoothly. I recall them as a child when my father once took us on a family holiday along the Thames ..."

"Which part, sir?"

"I don't remember which part, Price, more's the pity."

"You want me to start phoning around?" Price offered.

"Yes, call the station and get the contact details for all boat hire companies within a twenty-mile radius of here and phone each one. It's worth trying to contact the lock-keepers too. But don't get chatty. The guys in the boat may still be on the move, so we mustn't waste any time if we're to avoid losing them. In the meantime, I'm going to have a quick stroll along the canal path. I need to call the chief. Keep him up to date on proceedings."

Chapter Fifteen

HIT AND RUN AND HIDE

As Williamson and his sergeant were preparing for the next stage of their investigation, Tom and his crew had been implementing their getaway as fast as they could, at four miles per hour. While they could not be sure the call from Sykes had been deliberately tracked to their position, each of them feared it was a probability, as per Tom's suspicion, and they simply could not ignore that.

All men were up on the stern – except Gaston, who was down below preparing a meal for them all, and Neville, who was sitting quietly in the bow – and the discussions of how best to proceed were not going too well.

"We can't just ditch the boat, Gav!" Tom said. "It's been taken out in my name, and we have to get it back to Bill. In fact, in case you've all forgotten, your names are also on the paperwork."

"But Tom," said Gav, pressing his point, "we can't stay on this flippin' boat and get it all the way to London; it would take weeks at this ... this rate! We don't even know if this canal leads there! We could end up in the sea! And there's absolutely no way, boyo, we should turn around and go back the way we came, past the ... you know ... and past the bit where Sherwin spoke to this diamond guy. If he did actually track us, then that would be suicide, boyo!"

"He's right, Tom," Dave agreed. "We have to get off this tub and find another way to get to London. Several reasons. First, Mickey had this Pink Lady. Next, the man in black was prepared to kill us for it. Then we had the psycho on the phone. Who knows who else may be searching for the thing and what they'll do to get their hands on it?"

"And let's not forget that this Mickey guy might be working for someone," Neville added. "Someone, at some point, is surely going to report him missing, like. And then there'll most likely be police involved."

This thought sent fresh horror through Tom's already addled brain. This was carnage. Utter carnage. And all for the sake of a stupid bloody stag do he hadn't even wanted. He could throttle Jen with her good intentions. (What he wouldn't do to be safely at home with her.) He hadn't even thought to call her, and he'd probably missed a dozen messages while shooting one man and burying two.

"What about calling Old Bill and asking if he'd be willing to pick the boat up himself?" Dennis suggested. "Tell him we went through a lock and lost his windlass thingy. Like he told us, we only have one of them. We could tell him we got stranded on the other side."

Tom shook his head. "No, that won't work. We've travelled miles and haven't seen a single lock at all." He looked at the map. "And I can't see one coming up for miles either."

Sherwin turned to Tom, his hand still on the tiller, and shook his head. "This is bad, mon, bad. There's no choice but to keep going until we find somewhere quiet as possible, keep getting some distance between where we spoke to the dude, and then stop for the night. We can all eat–"

There was a shriek, which could only have come from Neville, and a loud shout. Sherwin's momentary lapse in concentration had allowed the bow to drift toward the centre of the canal, and they were heading directly for an oncoming craft. In desperation, he jammed the tiller hard to the right in a noble effort to avoid the collision, but it was too late. The two bows collided, and an unpleasant metallic clang rang out as the front of their hull scraped its way along the front starboard side of the passing boat, carving a deep scratch in the immaculate paintwork.

In an instant, the man who had been at the stern of the other boat started waving his arms around and shouting, and Gaston's head appeared through the hatch.

"What the hell are you doing, you absolute idiots?"

"Qu'est-ce que vous faites, espece d'idiots? It is like Titanic down there with the crashing! Everything is shaking!"

Sherwin had the intention of apologising profusely, but, as he did so, a bellicose Gav stuck out his fist and shouted back, "Oh piss off you old fart! It was an accident!"

Dennis immediately grabbed the lively Welshman by the scruff of his shirt and yanked him backwards. "What are you doing, you pillock?" he hissed. "You're making it worse."

Immediately after the impact, the man on the other boat had instinctively flicked his power off, but the inexperienced Sherwin had neglected to do the same. As a result, the seventy-foot *May* was still moving away.

"Stop, you morons!" the man yelled. "Come back and sort this out! You'll regret this! I'm going to report you! You're going to pay for this, you bastards!"

Sherwin reached out to kill the engine's power. As he did so, Tom grabbed hold of his arm. "No, Sherwin," he said quickly, not quite believing his own assertiveness. "We need to keep moving. You guys were right. Being on this boat is an absolute liability. We've got to hide it and find another way back to London. Perhaps I can swing things with Bill a bit later. I could offer to pay him for extra hire days until we've worked out what we're doing and then get his boat back to him. Does this thing actually move any *faster*?"

Gaston threw his hands in the air and went back below, muttering French insults in his customary way. Sherwin increased the power and kept poor *May* running at her full speed of eight miles per hour for at least another hour. Bill had told Tom the speed limit on canals was four miles per hour and slower when passing another boat, and the irony of such a laboured escape was not lost on him. His heart pounded as they cruised barely above walking pace, scanning the waterways for a place to hide *May*, desperately hoping they wouldn't encounter another boat. He made Dennis go up front to do the same, but it seemed he was also struggling to find anywhere, and then he turned and called, "Tom!" Followed by, "Sherwin, kill the engine!"

Tom made his way to the bow. "I just see masses of weeping willows, Dennis, with a wood behind. I don't understand."

"Look through the branches, mate. I almost missed it myself."

Sherwin joined them. "Look! It's another river, mon!"

"I think it's a weir of some type," Dennis said. "If we could push the boat through the overhanging willows, we could store it safely until we're able to return. What d'you think?"

"I think it's perfect," replied Tom. "Let's guide the boat into place, and quickly. If another boat passes us, our cover will be blown."

Between them, they managed to manoeuvre *May* into the narrow channel, parting the overhanging branches as they edged her hull into place and pulling them back over to obscure her.

"Careful not to slip off the bank," Dennis said as they struggled to secure her to low branches. "The weir is much deeper here than the canal, and it's very narrow."

"We only have another hour or so before it starts to get dark," Tom said, watching where he put his feet, "and this is the perfect spot to keep *May* safe until we're able to come back for her."

"So, what do we do now, mon?" Sherwin asked. He looked tired. They all looked tired.

"We must eet!" Gaston replied.

"Crikey, Gaston, that smells incredible! What have you made for us?" Tom said as they all went below.

"*Voila!* Boeuf bourguignon!"

"Wow. I didn't realise we had beef with us?"

"We didn't," Gaston said, throwing his hands in the air flamboyantly. "But all of ze other ingredients are in zere!"

All the men laughed out loud, something they had not done since the handful of hours before Mickey had been clobbered and the man in black shot.

Tom looked at each of them as they ate, unshaven, worn out and dishevelled, drinking beer and laughing. He couldn't have made it up if he'd tried, and he'd been good at creative writing.

Chapter Sixteen

ARSES FROM ELBOWS

"How's the chief, sir?" asked Price.

"Impatient at best. The Home Office is turning the screws apparently, and want a speedy result."

"Makes you wonder what Lawson might have in his possession that would warrant so much pressure from them."

"Not our concern, Sergeant," said Williamson dismissively. "It's above my pay grade and certainly above yours. We're here to do our jobs, not to second-guess our superiors. Any joy with the hire companies?"

"Well, sir, it would appear that your childhood holiday memories apply to the Thames canal system and almost all other canals in England, but on these local waters, there isn't a single lock-keeper I could find because these remote sections of the Norfolk Broads are completely free of locks. Although many people refer to the Broads as canals, the reality is they are mostly a bunch of rivers and lakes that interconnect. Because there is minimal rise and fall in the surrounding landscape, there is no need for locks or the keepers. Unfortunately, the inquiries of various hire companies didn't go well, either, sir. Most didn't answer the phone, or they had answer machines, and I didn't want to leave our sort of message on one of those, sir."

"Quite right, Price. Okay. Well, it was worth a go. But I can't see how we're going to find Lawson now. We don't even know if he, or his possible new associates, are still on these waterways."

"Oh yes we do, sir," Price continued. "After all the unfortunate lack of lock-keepers and too many answer machines, I got very lucky indeed."

"Really?"

"I thought I'd call the local station on the off chance they may have heard anything about these guys. You're not going to believe this. An hour or so ago, some chap had his narrowboat rammed by a bunch of men on another boat. I don't have confirmation of exactly how many men, but apparently, at least five or six were seen. This chap who got hit reported that they were aggressive, refused to stop, and simply continued their course northward, sir."

"Goodness, this certainly sounds like a solid lead. But they hardly appear to be the brightest bunch if they are trying to not attract attention to themselves. Did you get an exact location for the altercation between the two boats?"

"I did, sir. About thirty miles north from here. I was also informed that the local nick has a number of patrol boats on the Broads, and they are now sending one out to the location. But apparently, there are over a hundred and thirty miles of waterways around here, so it may take them a while."

"But they're not intending to intercept the boat, are they?" asked Williamson with a frown.

"No. I told them about the possible connection to the death of Lawson's probation officer and that there could be firearms involved. They put me through to their station chief, and I gave him full details of our investigation. He says they are more than happy to work with us on this one. In fact, he welcomes it. I get a feeling things are pretty slow around here, and when I mentioned guns, he was keen for us to take the lead. The moment they get a visual on the boat, they will get in touch with me to see how we want to proceed."

"Good. Good."

"There's another thing, sir."

"Another good lead?"

"I believe so, sir, yes. The name of the boat that we think Lawson may be on is called *May*. Turns out it's a rental boat and is currently out for hire to a bunch of guys allegedly on a stag do."

"Is that so? Well. If that is the case, then it's possible the company may have some sort of manifest with the names of the men aboard."

"That was my thought too, and I rang the hire company immediately. I say company, but it's basically one old man, a Bill Blakes, and *May* is his only boat. He swore blind he took all of their details, but the list is nowhere to be found. 'The scurviest bunch of sea dogs', he called them, sir. Said he doubted they'd get very far. Didn't know an arse from an elbow, he said, never mind a bow from a stern." Price chuckled. "To be fair, he sounded a little, well, geriatric to me, but I left him my number in case the list turns up."

"Indeed. Does he recall a Mickey being on the list?"

"Sadly not. He remembered only one name – a Tom Marshall – but cannot recall where he's from."

"Ugh, what a pain. But even if he does find the list, it seems unlikely that Lawson will have given a real name, and the same goes for these other men, for that matter. Even if the name he remembered is real, there must be a thousand Thomas Marshalls across the UK, so that doesn't help much at this stage either."

"That's true, but at least it's another piece of the puzzle that we didn't have an hour ago. I've passed on the name to the station, and they're going to compile a list of Tom Marshalls, with and without previous form. You never know; we may get lucky. Again."

Sergeant Price's mobile phone rang. When he finished the call a couple of minutes later, he snapped his phone shut and looked at Williamson. "Well, you're not going to believe this, sir."

"Try me."

"A local walker just reported that her dog found a shallow grave in woodland, just eight miles north of here, and it's on the edge of this same waterway. At this stage, they believe it to be the bodies of two men, but that's officially unconfirmed at present. The local station is sending out a forensics team now in order to cordon off the area and start to gather information."

"Good grief, things are escalating rapidly, Price. I suppose this shallow grave could be unrelated, but that would seem extremely unlikely given the current suspicions of Lawson's involvement in Sturgeon's murder."

"Exactly. Their chief is joining his team at the site and has asked if we are free to attend so we can work together in order to advance investigations."

"Absolutely. You have the coordinates for the site?"

"Yes, sir."

"Then let's get moving."

"It's getting late in the day now, sir. Should we confirm those two rooms at the pub?"

"Good point. I'll call the landlady from the mobile on the way."

It took the two men a little over twenty minutes to make their way to the site down another rutted and bumpy track. Ahead of them, parked up on a stretch of rough grass, they saw a couple of local police cars and also a white van with Forensic Investigation written in clear blue letters along its side. Price brought their car to a stop a few metres behind the other vehicles. As he did, so a junior officer jogged toward them with his hand held out in front of him as if to bar their way forward.

"It's okay, Officer," Williamson said as he exited the Mondeo and raised his identification badge. "I'm Detective Inspector Williamson, and this is Sergeant Price. We're here at your chief's invitation."

"Oh yes, I see, of course," the young officer said, relaxing his stance. "It was me that you spoke to on the phone earlier. Name's Perkins, sir. If you'd like to follow me, I'll take you over to the chief. I'll need you to both suit up first, though, if you wouldn't mind. Otherwise, Forensics will not be happy."

He opened the back doors of the van and picked up two pairs of white disposable crime scene suits, shoe coverings, face masks and blue latex gloves. Williamson and Price put the protective clothing on, and then followed Perkins around the parked vehicles and into the wooded area beyond. After a couple of minutes, the trees began to thin out, and they could see the crime scene ahead. A larger area of about forty square metres had been cordoned off with blue and white police tape tied to various trees. The light was beginning to fade, and a busy team had already erected generator-powered lighting that pointed downwards into the thick ferns. Three forensic officers on hands and knees were taking samples under the cover of a pop-up gazebo.

"Ah, Detective Inspector Williamson, I presume?" came a cheerful call from a stout man on the other side of the tape. He, too, was head to foot in protective gear, and after quickly lifting the tape, he strode over to them and shook both officers firmly by the hand. "I'm Chief Inspector Carlton. Pleased to meet you."

"Likewise, sir. And thank you for inviting us. Our investigation seemed a bit of a slow starter, but things appear to have escalated rather quickly this afternoon."

"Quite right, and most unusual for round these parts. I won't lie to you; this area's a far cry from the business you folks in London will be used to. And as this situation is most likely to be part of your own investigation, then it makes perfect sense to me for us to be cooperating. Our community is not used to such gruesome goings-on. So a quick result always helps to calm down the locals – and the bleedin' media for that matter."

"Well, sir, we're certainly happy to help in any way we can. But it remains to be seen whether these deceased men will have any connection to our own case."

"I agree. So let's go and take a look together. Follow me, and I'll see if we can pull Forensics away from their corpses momentarily so we can take a closer look."

All three men ducked under the tape, and Williamson and his sergeant waited while Carlton spoke to Forensics. The chief then beckoned the two officers over to join him. All three men looked down at a small area of excavated earth that had clearly been covered with ferns until very recently. Two rugs had been pulled from the shallow grave to reveal the corpses of two very different men.

"What do we know so far, sir?" asked Williamson.

"Well, we've not been here much longer than yourselves, Inspector, so it's currently early doors. But these guys are fresh as daisies, and we think they've been dead for no more than forty-eight hours. As you can see, this giant of a man has clearly taken a bullet to the forehead. Low calibre, so not a huge amount of damage, but fatal nonetheless." The chief then pointed to the smaller man. "This little chap, well, we think he's taken a bludgeoning to the back of the head."

"May I ask if anything else has been retrieved from the shallow grave? Any other possessions such as bags, coats, anything like that?"

"Not a thing. Just themselves wrapped in these rugs. A quick search through their pockets has given us nothing either. No possessions of any kind, and no identification either."

"Well, we can identify one of them, sir," said Sergeant Price, and he pulled a photograph from his jacket pocket.

"Lawson!" Williamson said with sudden realisation. He took the photo from his sergeant and kneeled to get closer to the face of the smaller corpse. The harsh lighting from above had made both of the deceased men appear ghastly white, almost blanched of features. Still, there was no mistaking that the smaller one was undoubtedly the body of Mickey Lawson.

"So, this is the man you chaps are after?" asked Carlton.

"Well, it was, sir. But the investigation has now widened significantly. We were originally tasked with bringing Mickey Lawson in for questioning, but it appears his association with this other man and the men on the boat has complicated things somewhat."

"So you're looking for a complete round-up?"

"Yes, sir, we are. And the reason I asked about other possessions they may have been buried with is also of paramount importance. We're under orders to bag up all possessions and get them over to the Home Office."

"The Home Office?"

"That's right, sir. I know it seems rather cloak and dagger, but those are my express orders from my chief superintendent."

"So you'll be wanting all clothing from the two deceased and, I imagine, from everything you find on the men on the boat when we finally catch them?"

"That's it exactly, sir. I fully understand you'll require the appropriate paperwork in order to release all items of clothing and possessions, so I will ensure these are faxed directly to your office first thing in the morning."

"Well, it's all very mysterious, but we can't go arguing with the Home Office now, can we? We'll certainly cooperate in any way that you see fit. To be perfectly honest, your chief will be doing me a favour, as I'd prefer it if this case didn't see the light of day, at least in these parts. This is the type of incident the local rag would love to get their hands on, and handing it fully over to you chaps will mean I get to dodge a tawdry and highly unpleasant press conference."

Price laughed, and Williamson allowed himself a chuckle. "Well, in that case, we're more than happy to be of service, sir. But the truth is, I'm very grateful for your help. I have no idea what it is the Home Office are so desperate to get their hands on, and I guess we'll likely never know, but they're applying a heap of pressure on our chief for results, and that same pressure is being diverted onto our shoulders."

"Well, gentlemen, that's the hierarchy of power, I guess. But what do you mean when you say you'll likely never know what it is that you're hoping to find?"

"That's the thing, sir. We've been explicitly requested not to tamper with any of the possessions we find. Simply bag it all up and get it back to London."

"I see. The plot thickens. Well, as I say, nothing has turned up here so far, so I imagine your focus will now be on intercepting the boat."

"That's partly correct, sir. Our initial task is certainly to find this boat as quickly as possible. But once we know their precise location, we will need to deploy Metropolitan armed officers immediately to the scene. There was already a murder attached to this investigation, and now there are two more. As there are clearly firearms involved, my sergeant and I will be required to momentarily stand down until these men are apprehended, and it's at that point we will confiscate clothing and possessions."

"I understand. Well, as you know, we have not located this boat so far. But based on what you've told me, I think I will ask for more patrol boats to start combing the wider area. It's getting dark now, so this will be at first light. Sound good?"

"That sounds perfect, sir. And again, thank you."

"Not at all. Where are you staying tonight? Somewhere local?"

"Very local. The Woolpack Inn. At first light, we'll head north and get as close as possible to the last place the boat was spotted, so at least we'll be closer to the scene."

"Very good," concluded the chief. "Forensics will continue to gather as much information as they can here, and I will ensure you'll be kept informed of everything they discover. But I can see your main focus is now on the boat, so let's hope we'll be able to track them down tomorrow. Nasty business all of this, far more the sort of thing you London boys are used to, and I would like to see a prompt conclusion as much as you would."

As Williamson and Price got back into their car, the DI turned to his sergeant. "The giant ..." he said.

"Yes. And all dressed in black. You're thinking he's the man the woman from the pub mentioned? The one watching the group that Mickey was with?"

"Precisely. I can't see who else it could have been. But who the hell was he? And who was he working for, if anyone? And why was he in the same shallow grave as Lawson? It appears this story is bigger than we realised, Price. A story I have a growing feeling we're only being allowed to understand in part. Let's get back to the pub. I need to call the chief to bring him up to speed. After that, I reckon we've earned an ale or two while we go over our notes."

"Amen to that, sir."

Chapter Seventeen

THE SMOKE SIGNAL

As he was accustomed, the man strolled elegantly across the office, sat down in a high-backed leather armchair in the dimly lit corner of the room, and reached into his blazer and pulled out a small box. After selecting and unwrapping a cigar, he lit it, took a few puffs, and then inhaled and exhaled.

Sykes placed his palms on his desktop and leaned forward. "Well?"

"Well?" repeated the man coolly as a spiral of blue-grey smoke gathered around him.

"Don't play games with me," Donnie responded. He kept his voice calm, not wishing to exude any sense of anger or frustration. The man in front of him was in a different league from himself. He was a man of substantive power, and mutual respect was essential in order to maintain their alliance.

"Donnie, it's all in hand. You need to relax."

"Do we know where this Shadow man and his gang are yet?"

"If you had pressed your Serbian harder as to where he originally tailed Mickey to, we would be on to the entire group by now. But no matter. We know where they are roughly. It won't be long now."

"And what area are they in? Roughly?"

"Somewhere on a canal boat in a remote part of Norfolk."

"A canal boat?" said Donnie with obvious surprise. "But that's ridiculous!"

"I agree. But perhaps it's so ridiculous that these halfwits figured nobody would think to look for them on a canal. But either way, that's of no consequence. What is of importance is we are very close to finding them."

"And how can you know that?"

"I know because it's my job to know. And knowing things is what I bring to this ... relationship. Is this not why you contacted me in the first place? I also know that by first light tomorrow morning, multiple police patrol boats will be scouring the canals in and around this area. It will not take long to track them down. Once the patrol boats find this group of men, they have been ordered not to intervene but to alert Blakney's officers, who, in turn, will go straight to the location and confirm that it is indeed the gang we're all after. And as soon as the call for armed backup is made to Blakney, my men will go in, do their job, and get out long before their response team are on site."

"And where are your mercenaries now?"

"Don't fret, Donnie. My men are in the area already and watching Blakney's men. The two officers are staying at a local pub and will be making their way to the boat's location at daybreak."

"Very good." Sykes allowed himself a quiet sigh of satisfaction. "Until tomorrow then?"

The man nodded just once. "Until tomorrow."

* * *

"Tom, wake up!"

Tom forced his eyes open and squinted at the sunlight coming in through the porthole by his bunk. Neville was leaning over him.

"Gaston's making some breakfast, like. The others have gone for a quick scout around to see if there are any roads nearby that'll take us in the right direction. It's what we planned if you remember. We drank a lot of wine."

"Yep. I remember," Tom said, wishing he hadn't remembered any of it. Whatever that French wine was, it was heavy-duty stuff. Should have stuck to beer. "Where's Gav? With the others?"

"Not sure. He was up before all of us. We put our stuff on the bank ready to go. You want me to bung your backpack with ours?"

"Yes. Actually, no. I'll do it."

Tom had a quick shower in the cramped bathroom, and then he and Neville went in search of the others, relieved when they saw them in the distance.

"About a mile behind us, we found a main road with a signpost that read A143," Dave said when they reached each other.

"I'm pretty sure that's the road I came in on," Tom said. "I'm fairly useless with road maps, but I do think I'm right about that."

"The rest of us came by train," Dave replied, "so I guess, without a map, we'll have to go with your memory on that one. Gaston arrived by taxi, but he's not going to know the road names." He pointed over Tom's shoulder. "The sun is rising over that way, on the other side of the canal, so we know that's east. As soon as we're ready, I say we get over to the road and make a left, and then we'll know that we're headed south, towards London."

"It's a long old walk to London. You know that, right?"

"Ha!" Sherwin laughed. "We ain't gonna be walking for long. Ma man Dennis here, he knows his stuff when it comes to hotwiring transportation. He'll find some old van, and then we'll be on our way properly."

Tom groaned. "How many more laws are we going to break before this nightmare is over?"

Sherwin laughed again. "This is the last one, mon! And anyway, we'll return the ve-hicle. After all, we're not criminals. We're–"

A deep, muted boom rang out behind them, and all five turned to where the sound had come from.

"That didn't sound good," Neville whimpered.

They then heard shouting and hastily made their way back towards *May*. What the hell had happened now?

Gav was standing on the bank beside the boat, which had smoke pouring from the centre, holding a large khaki jerry can in his right hand. Behind the Welshman was an incensed Gaston, cursing and shaking a large frying pan at him.

"Hey!" Tom shouted, and Gav spun around. He had a manic expression on his face.

"Boyos, you're back!"

Before he could say another word, Dennis grabbed him – by the front of his shirt this time – and holding tightly, he started to shake the gurning Welshman. "What the hell did you do, you complete lunatic!"

"I b-b-burnt the p-p-problem a-a-away!" Gav stuttered as he was shaken back and forth.

"Why?" Dennis yelled. "Why, Gav? Why would you burn the boat when we'd gone to all this effort to hide it? It was perfectly disguised behind all of these trees!"

"C-c-cops. They're h-h-here!"

"Cops?" Dennis stopped shaking Gav but did not loosen his grip on him. "What do you mean, cops? Cops don't hike around forests, you idiot."

"Woodland," Tom corrected.

"I went for a walk, really early, along the canal. When I was coming back, I saw them from the bank, boyo. I had to hide behind some trees so they wouldn't see me."

"Where?" asked Dave, worried the madman was telling the truth. "Where did you see them?"

"On the water. They were in a police boat. Ten minutes later, a different police boat came from the other direction, and I had to hide again. They're after us, boyos, and they know we're here, or at least they know we're somewhere here."

"Shit." Dennis released his grip on Gav, who staggered backwards. "Shit!"

"I think they must have found the bodies," Gav said. "Why else would they suddenly be going up and down the canal in police boats?"

"But burning the boat was a crazy thing to do," Dennis said. "Crazy!"

"Don't you get it, boyo?" Gav protested. "If they've found the bodies, then they are going to find the boat. And when they have both the bodies and the boat, there'll be enough evidence to link us all to those bastards' deaths. It won't matter whether we're innocent or not! None of you were here when I got back from my walk. So I made a split-second decision to torch the boat."

"But I was in the kitchen when you set ze boat on fire, you imbecile!" Gaston ranted.

"Why?" Gav asked.

"Cooking your breakfast, you idiot! I go to the bedroom

and boom! An explosion!"

"What with?" Tom asked.

"What with what?"

"What did you start the fire with?"

"We've gotta get outta here!" Neville squealed as flames appeared in the portholes and smoke poured from the ruptured roof.

"Gas."

"What gas?"

"The gas for the stove! I'm so sorry, Gaston boyo! I had no idea you were in there!"

"I was coooooking your breakfast!" Gaston hurled the frying pan into the boat.

"Oh shit!" Dennis said. Fierce flames were now shooting upwards, catching the low-hanging branches of the willows.

"Oh, good grief!" Tom yelled.

"Gav, you may have solved one problem," Dave hollered over the increasing roar, "but you've also managed to send up a huge bloody smoke signal telling the police exactly where we are! Guys, we need to grab our backpacks and go! Now!"

"Oh noooooooo! NO!" Tom wailed.

"What?" Dave said, grabbing his backpack.

"My backpack is still on the boat! The bloody diamond is in it!"

Without a thought, Tom dashed along the bank and threw himself inside the stern of the blistering boat. Thankfully he knew precisely where the backpack was, and blindly grabbed for it, his other hand over his mouth. He then turned and leapt from the boat, sprawling face down on the ground. He felt a number of hands grab him and yank him away, dragging him, spluttering and staggering towards the woodland as they all ran from the inferno. Frightened to look but drawn to the horror, they turned in time to see poor *May* consumed, hissing and spitting as she was sucked down into the weir, fire leaping and smoke pouring as she sank, middle first, then her bow and stern tilting and following.

The men stood hunched in the shadows of the trees in total silence, shaking and shocked by the destruction playing out in front of them as the flames from the trees shot high into the sky.

Sherwin was the first to break the silence. "Well, Tom," he said with a shake of his head. "You, I said right at de start, is one crazy fool. That was the craziest damn thing I ever saw. You iz damn lucky to be alive. Righteous!"

"Righteous? Righteous!" Dave said. "Look at what we've done! Look at what you've done, Gav!"

"Someone will have called the fire brigade," Neville squawked. "We gotta run, like!"

Tom's eyes were stinging ferociously, and his throat was raw. He knew he was lucky to be unhurt. He also knew he had been a damn fool. But he had the backpack. Which had the diamond. Which was their bargaining tool out of this mess. He looked down at the backpack. His present from Jen. And undid the clasp, just to check.

"Oh, God!"

"What?" Sherwin asked.

"This isn't mine. Oh God, this isn't mine!" he wailed, this time in utter disbelief. "It's not mine! It's Mickey's!"

"I wouldn't worry, mon," Sherwin said and patted Tom on the back. "It's not like there was anything precious in it."

Tom turned to Sherwin with a look of pure pain. "Not precious! Are you joking? I just said the diamond was in my backpack!"

"Yes, it was," Sherwin said quietly. "So it's a good job I lifted the Lady from your bag before you woke up." He pulled the black piece of cloth which held the Pink Lady from his jacket pocket.

"What the–"

Sherwin put a finger to his lips and whispered in his ear, "Nah mout. I took it because Neville was sniffing about your backpack, but I'll tell you about dat later."

"Sirens! Sirens!" Neville squealed and started running.

"Can I suggest you put it in Mickey's backpack, and then we can all get the hell out of here?" Dave said.

But my gift from Jen was in my backpack, Tom thought and was reminded again of the utter carnage his stag do had become.

They grabbed their stuff and ran.

Chapter Eighteen

ANIMALS, I TELL YOU

It was 6.50am when Detective Inspector Williamson's second call of the day came in. His first had been from Chief Inspector Carlton with an update.

"Ah, Miss Baxter, good morning. A little early for you, isn't it?"

"So it's Miss Baxter, is it? Not, hello Shelly, my darling, how was your lonely night sleeping alone?"

"Erm, I ..."

Shelly laughed. "I take it the handsome Sergeant Price is there with you?"

"Handso ... er ... yes, that's right. We're in the car and on our way to yet another crime scene."

"So the two dead bodies you mentioned in your goodnight call last night weren't quite enough for you?"

"We do seem to discuss corpses more than the average couple, I guess. And no, they were only a part of the investigation; we still need to track down the group of men who are somehow wrapped up in this whole mess."

"The men on the canal boat?"

"Exactly. Last night it looked as though we were about to corner them, but it appears they may have evaded us yet again.

I just took a call from the chief inspector of the local station, who asked if we'd join him at a new site where a badly burnt boat was discovered underwater earlier this morning. So we're now on the hunt for possible arsonists as well as killers. But it appears they've quite literally abandoned ship, which will make it all the harder to track them down."

"A possible bid to destroy forensic evidence, do you think?"

"It's certainly possible if this was the boat they were on. If it had been a domestic situation, the fire service would have been called, surely? But, anyway, you called me. What can I do for you?"

"Actually, it's what I can do for you. I called about the autopsy on Colin Sturgeon."

"Right, okay. What do you have?"

"Not a huge amount, but I can confirm that death was certainly caused by the single bullet to the chest. In terms of ballistics, we're looking at a 9mm at close range. There were no strands of any material on, or in, the wound other than fragments from Sturgeon's shirt."

"Why is that significant?"

"Well, the killing was committed during the day while a number of other staff were in and around the building. As you know, not one of them reported hearing a shot, or any commotion from Sturgeon's office, for that matter."

"It has a bustling street just outside, and the windows may have been open given the heat we're having."

"Even so. But the lack of other material strands suggests that a cushion or clothing had not been wrapped around the muzzle of the weapon in order to silence the shot. My guess is the killer used a silencer, or suppressor, as we now refer to them. This type of shooting is much rarer, as you know, and it does tend to suggest the murderer was perhaps a professional, for want of a better word."

"I see," said Williamson as he considered Shelly's analysis. "But what of the bruising? You mentioned that there appeared to be a great deal of rage involved. That doesn't seem to fit with a professional killer."

"You remember the bruising around his neck, which was obviously strangulation? I realised that the imprint of the bruising was from one single grip, not two, which is the usual case with strangling. The hand that strangled Sturgeon must have been enormous – and I mean enormous! The killer must have had the hands of a giant, and the grip was so tight that the killer's nails had dug in deeply, causing abrasions on the victim's throat. The back of his head had also been pounded into a hard surface, and he had bruising on his shoulders, indicating a wall or a desk. I'm almost certain the victim's DNA will still be under the killer's nails and of course, potassium nitrate particles on his hand from the discharge residue of the actual gunshot. So from what you've told me about Mickey Lawson, my opinion is his modus operandi doesn't seem to tally with anything I've learned from the autopsy. My money would be on a giant being the murderer ... but you're the detective."

"It appears that Jack may have already taken an axe to our giant's beanstalk."

"That's a bit cryptic. What do you mean?"

"Well, what I didn't tell you last night was that, while one of the dead men was almost certainly Lawson, the other was indeed a huge man – a giant."

"That can't be a coincidence?"

"It's doubtful, but just so you know, we'll soon have full details from the local forensics team in relation to the two dead men found yesterday. I'll ask them to forward this to you, and then you can cross-check Sturgeon's DNA against anything they found on this giant, as well as Mickey Lawson. With any luck, we may get a result and be able to conclude at least one part of this investigation. But one last thing before I go?"

"Sure. Shoot."

"We've been asked to prioritise the securing of the criminals' possessions ahead of solving Sturgeon's murder, so keep a hat on anything you find for the moment so we can deliver the Home Office's requests first and foremost."

"Understood. Speak soon, darling."

Williamson and Price ate a quick breakfast and then headed off to the site, keen to find out about the burned-out boat.

"Perkins?" Williamson called as he exited the car, and the junior officer looked up. "You're expecting us, I believe."

"Indeed we are, sir. The chief asked me to show you around."

"Good, good. Please, lead on."

"Ah, gentlemen …" Chief Inspector Carlton called. He was standing beside a narrow channel of water, his trousers tucked into wellingtons, with junior officers scuttling around him, scribbling notes or taking photos. A couple of men in wetsuits were sitting on a dry bit of bank. The rest had been turned to thick mud by the fire crew's hoses. The devastation of the area was evident, and the blackened and scorched skeletons of once-beautiful willows hung woefully over the scene. "Only a bunch of animals would do something like this," he said, shaking his head. "First double murder, and now wilful destruction of such a beautiful area. I tell you, officers, we are dealing with animals."

As the visiting officers slid their way over, the chief glanced down at their shoes. "Oh, yes, apologies about the mud. I probably should have warned you. Can't imagine you London chaps would even possess a good pair of wellies, though. But not to worry, we'll get you cleaned up once we're out of here."

"Please, don't apologise. We'll clean up well enough later."

He looked around him. "I can see it has been some task to put the blaze out," he added, seeing the devastation.

"Yes, but these boys did a swift and thorough job of putting out the flames. With the lack of rain we've had over the past two months this could have turned into a catastrophe had they not got on top of things so damn quickly."

"Indeed, sir. But where is the boat?"

"It's still in there," the chief responded and pointed into the water.

"And you think it's the same boat that carried the men we're trying to find?"

"I don't think it, Detective, I know it. The divers have just been down and confirmed that the boat is indeed *May* – the same name reported by the chap whose boat they hit yesterday. Because she sank so quickly, from the middle, it appears, her bow and stern survived the fire, and there was her name, loud and clear. Looks like they tried to hide the boat in among the willows before deciding to torch the damn thing, the bastards."

The acrid smell of smoke still lingered, and Williamson coughed. "And we're sure the boat is empty, sir? No more ... corpses, I mean?"

"Ha! No more corpses for the moment, at least not until I get hold of them. The divers checked throughout."

"So, where are they? The gang? Very few places to hide around here, sir."

"They must be on foot, but I'd bet my life on it they'll be looking to put greater distance between themselves and here, and quickly, so I imagine they'll be looking for transport of some sort."

"I would absolutely agree with that," Williamson said with a nod. "Are you considering ordering a stop and search operation in the surrounding area?"

"Already done, Detective. I've asked for an immediate stop and search for all major and minor roads within a thirty-mile radius. They can't have been gone more than two hours, three at the most, and on foot until they managed to 'obtain' a suitable vehicle – if they've managed to do such a thing around here."

"I sincerely hope that you're right, sir."

"Yes. Yes. By the way, Detective," Carlton said, "we'll have our forensic data for the two dead men ready a little later this morning. Would you like to see the results?"

"Yes, absolutely, thank you. There's a particular colleague of mine I'd also like the data to be sent to, down at our station. In fact, we have some intel of our own that potentially has some bearing on the case."

"You do?"

"Yes. It would appear that the victim of our original suspect, Mickey Lawson–"

"The smaller of the deceased men we found yesterday?"

"The very same, sir. We think the man in our lab, Mr Colin Sturgeon, is likely to have been killed by a much larger man. In fact, my colleague believes the man was practically a giant."

The chief's eyebrows raised. "A giant? So you think the real killer may actually be Lawson's sleeping partner, the colossus we dug up yesterday?"

"It seems too much of a coincidence to me, sir, and uncanny that the original suspect would be lying in the same shallow grave."

"Yes. All very mysterious. And now both men have been killed at the hands of the thugs who could have burnt this entire woodland down!"

"Well, sir, I cannot rule out the possibility that Lawson and the giant somehow killed each other, and the gang they were with then panicked. They may simply have been bystanders and buried them in order to hide their connection with the two men."

"Seems a bit far-fetched to me, Detective. But then we won't know for sure until we catch these reprobates."

"Precisely. We'll only be able to join the dots once we have them in custody. But if the gang did kill these men, then the question has to be, aside from panic, why?"

"Perhaps they got into some kind of altercation with one another. After all, they do appear to be acting like utter fools."

"Yes, perhaps. Or perhaps the deceased men had something the others were prepared to kill for?"

"I see where you're going with that line of thought. You're thinking about the Home Office instructions and the curious orders to confiscate all belongings from their persons. Then to hand the haul over to them, untampered, and possibly never know what this whole damn fiasco was actually about."

"Well, sir, yes. If that is the case, then we may never be able to find out why, or for what, these men were killed."

"Don't forget that the Home Office are our ministerial paymasters, and secrecy often safeguards their hallowed halls. I think that if this giant turns out to be your killer, then you will have to satisfy yourself with that. A result is a result."

"If only my chief thought the same, sir," Williamson ventured. "It's he who will need to be satisfied, and getting these men into custody quickly will be the only way to achieve that."

Carlton surprised Williamson with a firm slap on the back. "And that is exactly what we're going to do, Detective. Why don't you and your sergeant join me back at the station? We'll find it easier to coordinate our stop and search operation from there. Plus, I'll be able to offer you a damn good Norfolk brew and a ... a clean-up of your shoes."

"Thank you, sir. We accept."

Chapter Nineteen

THE FOX AND HOUNDS

"Police!" Gav said as they heard yet more sirens. "I knew this was going to happen."

"Why don't we duck down in the ferns and take a breather. It would be good to have some time to think, and I need some water and a snack. We haven't eaten yet, seeing as our breakfast went, erm, up in smoke," Tom replied.

His idea was met with a few grunts of approval. They'd been following the A143, but from under cover of the trees, and were tired. Gav opened his backpack and lifted out a twelve-pack of lager. He broke one out of the plastic loops. "Anyone?"

"You crazy fool, mon," Sherwin scoffed. "Have you seriously been carrying all dat weight this whole time?"

"Help yourselves, boyos," Gav chuckled. "Plenty more." He swivelled his backpack to reveal the shiny tops of twelve more cans, and they had to laugh despite still being furious with him for setting fire to the boat and sending up a colossal 'We Were Here'.

As they sat and drank, the conversation was quiet and awkward. They knew this was far from over and instinctively ducked when they heard yet more sirens.

"It's all getting a bit real now, isn't it?" Tom muttered, his face in the ferns.

"Sure is, mon," Sherwin agreed. "I think we just need to keep ourselves going and find some transportation. Come on, come."

Up ahead, they could see the woodland was coming to an end at a crossroads and didn't continue on the other side.

"Shit," Gav said. "Nowhere to hide."

"Look!" Dennis whispered.

Between the trees, they could clearly see a police car parked at the left side of the crossroads, and plastic police barriers had been placed across each of its junctions. As they watched, two uniformed officers approached a slowing car. They could barely breathe as the female driver was obviously questioned, but after a couple of minutes, the barrier was moved, and she was waved through.

"Well, that screws up our plans for driving out of here," Dave whispered.

"I don't think so," Dennis replied. "I think it's fair to say the cops found those dead guys and the boat, but I don't think they'd extend the search more than twenty or thirty miles each way. They don't have the resources."

"Meaning, mon?" Sherwin said.

"If we were to walk another fifteen miles or so, I reckon it'll be safe to find a van to, erm, borrow and get us back to London."

"But what if they have blockades set up around London, like?" Neville squeaked. "We'll never get there!"

"Don't be an idiot, Nev," Gav said. "How the hell would they know we're going to London? Dennis is right; once we get outside the search area, we're home free."

"But what can we do now?" Gaston asked. "How can we keep going in zees direction when *les gendarmes are just zere*?"

"I think we should follow the road east for a mile or so," Dave mused. "We can keep inside the edge of the woodland for safety until we see decent cover on the other side. Then we can cross over and continue heading south again."

"Good a plan as any," Dennis agreed.

"Yep, let's get going," Tom said.

From the safety of the woodland, they continued east until they spotted a country lane heading through some farmland on the other side of the main road.

"Think that's our road south," Dave said, and they edged out of the trees one at a time and crossed.

The mostly flat terrain now became hillier, and they walked solidly for at least three miles before stopping. From the top of the hill, they could see endless miles of farmland ahead of them, and, perhaps another three miles ahead and directly south, they spotted a large lake.

"We'll have to make sure we avoid that," said Dave. "Unless any of you fancy another boat trip?"

There were grunts and a firm "No!" from several, and Tom sighed. If they ever got out of this, he'd never set foot on another boat for as long as he lived. He thought of Jen again and pulled his phone out of his pocket. It was almost dead. Why hadn't he messaged her to say all was well when he'd had some battery left?

After another forty minutes of heading downhill, the lane sloped back uphill again. They were hot and tired and hungry by the time they got to the top. They also realised they had walked up the hill that edged one side of the vast lake, with nothing but surrounding farmland and woodland for miles.

"Shit," someone said.

"Yes," someone agreed.

There was little choice but to drop down to the lake.

They trudged down the hill, stumbling in the long grass and trying to avoid the thick brambles. When they got closer, they saw that the side of the lake they were on was for recreational use. To their left was a gravel car park, and to their right was a large grassy area used for storing boats. Some larger boats were up on rusting trailers and covered by tarpaulin, while other smaller vessels were stored upturned in the grass. It appeared the facilities had not been used in some time, and not a single person could be seen. On the other side of the boats, there was a rickety boathouse, and the ageing structure's far end jutted out over the lake to a wooden jetty about thirty metres long. Tied to the end of the jetty was a navy-blue speed boat of some kind.

Sherwin turned to Dennis and said, "You think what I think?"

Dennis frowned. "I've hotwired plenty of cars in my time, but I never tried a boat."

"But what if someone sees us?" Neville asked.

"Who is?" Sherwin said, spreading his arms wide. "The place is desert, mon. Would you walk all the way around?"

Neville said nothing but shook his head.

"I think Sherwin's right, Nev," said Tom. "I reckon it's a good mile to the other side. We were planning on hotwiring something today, anyway, so I guess a boat is fine."

"Besides, it's not like we're stealing it. We're re-parking it over on the other side of the lake," Dennis said.

"Good point," Sherwin said.

"Re-mooring," Tom said.

"Semantics," Dave said, and they all looked at him.

As they made their way over to the boathouse, it was clear the jetty could only be accessed through the front of the decaying structure, which looked more like a large and decrepit allotment shed. They were surprised to find the doors unlocked, and other than an old canoe mounted to the left-hand wall, the boathouse was empty. Quickly the men made their way along the worn and uneven planks of the jetty, stepping carefully and checking all around them, but there was no one about. It was sad, really, to see such a place so neglected but undeniably useful for their purposes.

"No keys, I'm afraid," Dennis sighed.

"Surely you weren't expecting it to be that easy, like?" Neville asked.

"I was joking," Dennis sighed.

Tom's phone pinged.

"Chaps, I've missed a call from Jenny. She's back from her hen weekend today. I need to call her back."

"Bonne chance," Gaston said. He looked untidy, for him, and thoroughly fed up. He'd barely spoken for the last two hours.

"He'll need it," Dave said.

"I'm not going to tell her anything!" Tom retorted.

"Sure," Dennis said.

"Seriously, what are you going to tell her?" Dave asked.

"I have no idea."

Gav opened another can of beer and sat down on the side of the jetty, and Tom walked back towards the boathouse. What was that sound? It sounded like a trumpet. Strange. Never mind. Things couldn't get any weirder. He pulled up Jen's number, praying his phone battery would at least last a short time.

"Hey!" it was Gav. "I'll keep you company."

Anxious to get a signal so he could speak to Jen, Tom didn't care and headed up the hill they'd come down just a while ago, checking his phone on the way. Gav drank his beer and chatted – where did the man get his energy? – until Tom asked for some quiet and some privacy.

"Sure, boyo, sure," Gav said. "Fill yer boots," and wandered off.

"Ah, Mr Marshall!" Jen said when she answered. "Too busy to pick up my call earlier, were you?"

"Ah, Mrs Marshall-to-be. Bad signal out here in the sticks, I'm afraid. You know I'd never ignore your call."

"I should hope not! I was calling to let you know I'm safely back from Prague. We had a lovely time!"

"Great. It's so good to hear your voice, Jen. I've missed you so much."

"Yeah, right, it's only been a few days! I'll bet you've been having a whale of a time up there in Suffolk."

"It's Norfolk, actually, at least, I think we're still in Norfolk."

"Think? What do you mean you think you're still in Norfolk? I'd have thought you'd be getting the boat back to the owner by now, given you're coming home tomorrow?"

"Erm, well, about that ... the thing is, we might be extending our little trip, just for a few extra days." He had absolutely no clue what he was going to tell Bill about his precious *May*, now a scorched, sodden wreck. But then, the police had most likely already contacted the poor old guy. Tom felt a horrible lurch of guilt. And fear.

"Really? Wow! That's so not like you, Tom. You must be having a good time with your new friends."

"Yes. Yes. It's been a ... we've had a ... good time, yes." He didn't even recognise his own voice anymore.

"Are you sure everything's okay? You do sound a little ... well, odd."

"Odd? No, no. I promise everything's absolutely fine. I'm just a little tired. I have got a lot to tell you, but it can wai–"

Tom was interrupted by a loud shriek – Neville. With his phone still pressed to his ear he spun around in shock.

"What the hell was that?" Jen asked.

About twenty metres away, he saw Gav with his arms outstretched in front of him, pointing at something crumpled on the ground. Neville was pointing at him. Where had Neville come from?

"Tom?" Jen said.

"Gav!" he called. What had the Welshman done now?

"Tom? What was that scream?" Jen asked, and Tom cupped his hand over the phone.

"Why have you got a gun, Gav!" Neville screeched.

Gav has a *gun*? Tom put the phone back to his ear. "Erm, I'm not entirely sure. But it's all fine. I'll call you back."

"T–"

Tom ran over to where Gav was standing over a dead fox, and Neville was jibbering. Gav had a gun in his right hand.

"Gav, where the hell did you get that, and why did you shoot a fox?" he yelled.

"Poor, poor animal," Neville said, flapping his hands and turning away.

"Neville, go back to the boat!" Tom said.

"It came at me, Tommo. Right at me. It ran over the top of the hill and came at me like it was possessed. I completely freaked and … shot it."

"Whose gun is that! The man in black's? The one he threatened to kill Neville with? I didn't know you had taken it. For goodness sake, Gav!"

"Yeah, it was his gun. You took Mickey's gun, so I thought it would be a good idea to take this one, just in case we ran into more people trying to kill us."

Dennis looked up from his hotwiring as shouting echoed

across the lake. "What the hell is going on now?"

"There it is again!" Sherwin said, looking up at the ridge. "That trumpet noise! The same one I heard earlier. It came from up there."

"Not that. But yes, that too."

Sherwin spotted Tom gesticulating at Gav. "What has that nutter done now?"

"Who knows."

"And the trumpet?"

"Who knows." Dennis stuck his head back under the boat's dash.

Gav looked up from the fox. "What was that?"

"I heard it too," Tom said, "but–"

A horse's head appeared over the ridge, followed by another, and another, and a whole row of red-jacketed horsemen stared down at them.

"Oh shit," Tom exclaimed. "It's only the bloody hunt! And you killed their bloody fox!"

"They look really pissed off," whispered Gav, sliding the gun into his pocket.

The stand-off continued, the horses looking as confused as their riders.

And then there was a loud roar, as over the opposite ridge appeared a large group of people with banners: 'Ban The Hunt!'; 'Fox Hunting Is Barbaric!'; 'Fox Off You Hunts!', and then a war cry went up: "Fox off you hunts! Fox off you hunts!" which fell silent when they surveyed the scene below them.

Another second later, one of the protestors yelled, "Murderer! He shot an innocent fox! Murderer!"

"Gav," Tom whispered.

"Yeah?"

"Run to the boat."

"Hey! That's our fox!" yelled one of the huntsman, and a hundred dogs howled in dismay.

"You killed our fox!" another shouted and gave the forward signal to charge. Horses and hounds launched themselves over the ridge as the protestors launched themselves over the other.

"Gav."

"Yeah."

"Run faster," Tom panted as they launched themselves towards the jetty.

"Dennis, get this thing started!" Sherwin hissed. "Speed! Speed!"

"I'm trying," Dennis hissed back as Neville shrieked; Gaston cursed in French, and Dave just swore.

Wisps of grey smoke curled from the wires as the boat fired, drowned out by hounds, horses, a trumpet, protestors and the shouts of "Wait! Wait!" from the two men racing down the jetty.

"One at a time! One at a time!" Dennis yelled as they all bent to hurl themselves and their backpacks into the boat.

Scrabbling and yelling as they tumbled one by one into the speed boat, Dennis opened the throttle and threw the boat right and out onto the lake.

"I can't take anymore," Tom whispered and slumped to his knees.

Chapter Twenty

PEANUTS AND CIGARETTES

After the morning visit to the site of the extinguished blaze, Williamson and Price spent the remainder of the day in the company of Chief Inspector Carlton. All were waiting for any news from the stop and search operation.

The local station was an altogether humbler affair than the Metropolitan officers were used to, but they were grateful for Carlton's solidarity and his, hopefully, invaluable assistance to their own case. The Norfolk brew they had been promised turned out to be something of a surprise, however. Rather than offering hot cups of tea, the chief had waited until his office door was shut before three chilled bottles of Woodforde's Wherry Amber Ale were removed from a small fridge in the corner of the room. Williamson, who had always been a stickler for observing abstinence of alcohol while on duty, had accepted all the same. They were guests at the station, and he would sooner flout the rules a little rather than disrespect the courtesy they were being offered. All the same, when the chief took a phone call, the detective inspector leaned toward his sergeant and whispered, "This will not become a habit."

Despite several calls to and from the stop and search teams, disappointingly, not a single sighting of the suspect group had been reported, and Williamson was beginning to lose hope that they would get the lead they needed.

Shortly before 4pm, the detective inspector's mobile phone rang and after excusing himself, he took the call.

"Shelly, hi. Did you receive the DNA samples from our two deceased men?"

"Yep, they arrived a few hours ago. The Norfolk colleagues were pretty efficient. And I've got results!"

"Really?"

"Yep. It turns out my hunch was correct. Skin particles taken from under our giant's fingernails do indeed match Colin Sturgeon's DNA. Also, fibres taken from the giant's jacket match those from Sturgeon's clothing, likely having rubbed off during the struggle. There was also discharge residue on his hands and his sleeve, meaning he would have fired at least one shot fairly recently. All in all, I think you have your killer."

"Hmm, shame he won't do time for it. All the same, good work. Thank you, Shelly."

"Just doing my job. That's not all, though. There are a couple more things to mention. There were traces of blood on the soles of our killer's boots, and it matched that of Mickey Lawson. This indicates that Mickey may have been the first to die, and also that Sturgeon's killer may also have killed Lawson."

"And the bullet used to kill our giant, did it match the type that killed Sturgeon?"

"Nope, 'fraid not. Ballistics confirm we're looking at a lower calibre weapon, which of course, means we're now talking about multiple firearms. And as neither weapon has yet been found – and you might not want me to nag – please be careful if you do find these men. It's quite possible you'll be dealing with potential killers."

"Our job is merely to find and identify these men first, and once we know we're not on a wild goose chase, we then call for the cavalry. But I'll be careful, darling, so please don't worry."

"It's not you I'm worried about; it's that handsome Sergeant Price."

"Ha! Very funny. You said there were a couple of things to mention; what was the other?"

"Turns out that our giant was a smoker. Norfolk pathology found a battered packet of Marlboro cigarettes hidden deep in the lining of his black leather coat like it had been crushed. The initial search missed that, but hey, we have them now. Finding a pack of cigarettes is not really of consequence, but what might be is the box of matches they also found. It was one of those strike-pad ones you can have your company logo printed on."

"You think it's significant? What was the logo?"

"As with the cigarette packet, the matches were pretty damaged, but the front is printed in black and silver and reads 'Peanuts, Soho'. It's a bar perhaps or a nightclub. Does it mean anything to you?"

"No, it's not a name I recognise. But it could certainly be connected, so we will follow it up."

"Leave that with me. I'll see what I can drag up."

"Great, thank you. And Mickey Lawson? Nothing more you can tell me about his death?"

"Not really. Straightforward blunt force trauma from a single blow to the back of the head. And it proved fatal. There were trace metal fragments that indicate he was hit with a steel object of some sort, about two inches wide. It would be conjecture to say what the object was, but my best guess would be some type of tool. Sorry, that's all I can offer."

"Okay, thanks again, Shelly."

"So no news on this group of men? Stop and search have not

provided any leads?"

"No, not a thing. It's as if they've vanished, for the time being, at least. Anyway, I really ought to get back to it, but I'll be in touch when I know more."

"Okay, take care. And I mean it, darling."

When Williamson went back into the office, the chief inspector was on the phone and grinning in a way that indicated he was receiving good news. A few moments passed before Carlton jubilantly slammed the phone down.

"I do believe we have the lead we wanted!" he declared.

"The men from the boat have been found?" Williamson asked hopefully.

"Not exactly, no." Carlton's jowls flapped as he shook his head. "But it seems certain they have been spotted. A group of men who appear to match their description have been reported to have caused an almighty ruckus down at Crossley Fields, which is about fifteen miles south of here. And the gang seem to have rekindled their penchant for boats."

"Sir?" Williamson asked.

"Crossley Fields?" Price added.

"That's right. This time they appear to have stolen an old speed boat in order to cross the boating lake situated at Crossley Fields – a dilapidated recreational area. It looks as though we may have underestimated them, as they've evidently been smart enough to steer clear of main roads and go cross-country."

"If it actually is them, sir. You mentioned a ruckus. Has anyone been hurt?"

"Mercifully, there were no human casualties, but they have shot and killed a fox."

"A fox, sir?"

"A fox, yes. As I said this morning, these men are complete

animals – worse than animals, in fact. There have been official complaints from two different sources. One from a group of anti-hunt protestors and the other from the actual fox-hunting party. I dislike either group at the best of times, especially fox-hunters, and hunting on a Sunday, of all things, that's just bad form. I can't imagine it will be much longer before they ban the abhorrent 'sport' completely. Apparently, the entire scene turned rather nasty, with both groups getting into a loud and sustained altercation while the gang made their escape across the lake."

"But why on earth would they shoot a fox and cause such a scene if they're trying their best to not attract attention to themselves?"

"That I cannot answer. Probably for the same reason they set fire to a narrowboat: they're animals. Animals, I tell you. But now that we have their approximate location, I am going to ask for the centre point of the stop and search perimeter to be moved to the lake immediately. It seems as though they are continuing south, and we won't take any chances. I want these men caught almost as much as you do, Inspector."

"I appreciate that, sir. I think my sergeant and I will get on the move if that's okay? We'll get ourselves down to the area south of this lake in the hope that new intel may come in. If it doesn't, then we'll head back to the pub we're staying at and reconvene in the morning."

"Very well. I'll continue to coordinate the operation from here and let you know if there are any new sightings. I'll also ask for calls to be made to all hostelries around that specific area. It's now late afternoon, and we might get lucky if the gang decide they don't want to camp out under the stars tonight."

"Good point. Thank you, sir."

"You're welcome. If you wish, I can ask for Perkins to drive ahead of you down to Crossley Fields. He knows the area well, and these Norfolk back roads can be a bit of a maze."

"If you're sure, then yes, that would be very helpful. Thank you again."

"Don't mention it. Right then, hopefully, we're getting closer to finally catching these animals. Do keep in touch, gentlemen."

"We certainly will, sir."

Chapter Twenty-One

LEFT OR RIGHT?

If they weren't hungry and tired before, they were now. And wet. Leaving the anti-hunters and hunters to their verbal brawling, the other side of the lake had been too steep and inaccessible to moor up. The men had had no choice but to carry their backpacks above their heads and wade the last few feet and then scrabble their way through reeds and undergrowth to a place to sit and assess this latest fiasco.

"I'm so hungry," Dennis said, tipping water from his boots and squeezing out his socks.

"Quit, would you," Dave groaned.

"Ya mon, cool it," Sherwin added.

"Hate to tell you this, but we've got to keep moving," Tom said. "We can't take the risk of staying here. One of those chaps is sure to report that we shot – you shot – a fox." He looked at Gav, who shrugged but didn't respond. "Come on, our clothes will dry as we walk."

"We still need transport, mon," Sherwin said.

"Ha, fat chance of that, like," Neville whined. "Look at where we are. No vans that I can see."

"Then let's walk." Tom forced himself to get up, his head spinning with hunger, exhaustion and leadership. When had he got so forthright? Ah yes, since the double murder, burial and arson.

All wearily agreed and began the steep slog up the hill on this side of the lake. There had to be a road of some description at the top? A road that led to vans that could be stolen?

Tom dropped back to walk with Sherwin, who was chatting to Dennis.

"Sherwin, erm, could I ask you something?"

"You want me to leave you to it?" Dennis asked.

"No. It's not private. At least, I don't think it is."

"What is it, mon?"

"You mentioned you, well, 'lifted' the diamond from my backpack because Nev had been sniffing around. You said you'd tell me about that later, so could you tell me about it."

"Sure, mon. The little man had been whining his mout about the money, and I get a feeling he might try for the backpack, take a little look for himself. Don't get me wrong, Nev's not a bad man, just a weak man, and could have create troubles if him lift the stone for himself, if you get me, so I lift it for you, to keep her safe."

"Good move," Dennis said, without thinking, but then turned to Tom. "It was the right thing to do, yeah?"

"Yes, it was the right thing to do. Nev's fine but jumpy. Who knows what he might have done with her. Thanks, Sherwin."

"Righteous."

After about three quarters of an hour, Neville, who had been walking fifty metres out in front as a lookout, turned to face them. "I've found a van!" he whispered.

"What did he say?" Dennis asked.

"I have no idea," Dave answered.

"I think I've found–"

"We cannot 'ear you!" Gaston said a little bit too loudly.

"Shush, Gaston mon!" Sherwin said.

"Who iz 'ere to 'ear me?" Gaston snapped, throwing his hands in the air.

It was true. Neville may have found a van, but there didn't appear to be anyone around who might own it.

They hurried to join Neville, who was pointing down a track. Sure enough, there was a scruffy white van parked by a power plant of some description, largely obscured by trees and not at all visible from the road, with a check-in booth next to the surrounding barbed wire fence but absolutely no one about.

"What do you think?" Tom asked Dennis. "It looks a bit wrecked."

"That's a good thing. The older they are, the easier they are to hotwire."

"Seems a bit risky," Gav said nervously, all out of gung-ho. "Maybe we should just keep moving."

"It'll be dark soon, and I don't fancy sleeping it rough, mon," Sherwin said. "And I don't fancy another step of walking tonight, either. I'm dead."

"Me too," Tom said.

"Neville, go and take a closer look. Check there's no man about, mon."

Neville looked over at Sherwin. "Why me?"

"Coz you saw it."

"I'll go," Dennis said. "I need to take a closer look anyway."

"I'll come with you," Dave said.

They set off down the track, glad of the dusk, and made their way around the side of the booth. They peered in the window.

"I wonder how long it's been since someone was last here?"

Dave asked, noting the piles of curling mail and old invoices.

"No way of knowing. Could just be bad at admin," he chuckled. "Let's check the van."

Dennis dropped to his knees on the passenger side of the van, out of sight of the road, and rummaged in his backpack.

"What you looking for?" Dave whispered.

"This." He pulled out a wire coat hanger. "You've seen the movies. I took it from the boat. I can use it to open the van door." He started straightening it out and creating a hook at one end.

Dave left him to it and went around to the driver's door. As with the booth, the van looked like it hadn't been used for a long time. He tried the handle.

"Dennis?"

"Just a sec."

"Hold the wire, mate."

"What?" Dennis stuck his head up.

"Tad-dah!"

"What! Who doesn't lock their van? That wouldn't happen in my town! If it ain't locked up or bolted down, it don't stick around. Guess I'd better get this rust bucket started."

A murmur of relief went up when Tom and the waiting guys heard the van splutter and choke into life, and they waited as Dennis turned it around and headed towards them.

"Which way, mate?" he asked when Tom joined him in the front, and Sherwin, Gav, Neville, and Gaston climbed into the back.

"I've been trying to calculate how many miles we've walked today. I think the average walking speed is about three or four miles per hour, but I'm not entirely sure we've managed to average that pace simply because of the nasty terrain we've had.

Plus, we've had the odd break and … erm … the situation at the lake. All the same, we did set off super early this morning, and it's nearly ten o'clock at night now. So we must have come a fair old way."

"Which way, mate?" Dennis asked.

"I'm not sure whether we should be considering that the centre of the stop and search would have been where the narrowboat sank or whether it's now moved to where the fox was shot, and the lake is the new centre, which means we're still potentially in the search area."

The van sounded rough like it might stall.

"Tom," Dennis said.

"Yes?"

"Which way?"

"Left. I think."

"Anyone else?"

"Well, we turned left down the track where I found the van, like, so right would be back the way we came, so left, yes," Neville said.

"Tourner à gauche, tourner à droite, tourner à gauche," Gaston snapped. *"Tourner à gauche!"*

"Anyone else?" Dennis rammed the van into gear and let the clutch out.

"Left!" Tom said. "Definitely left."

The left turn took them down yet another narrow country lane, but lights up ahead indicated a main road and hopefully a road sign. The van had half a tank of fuel, with any luck, that would be enough to get them at least close to London. And then they saw the blue lights of the roadblock ahead.

"No, no, no, no, no," Dennis breathed and slowed the van to a crawl.

"There!" Tom said, pointing to a side road just ahead on the right. "Turn in there."

Pulling the van into a gateway and turning the lights off, Dennis turned to Tom in the dark. "This is it for tonight. This is it. Nothing for it." He disconnected the wires, and the van went dead.

He was right. Unrolling their sleeping bags and making room among the boxes and rubble in the back of the van, they were too tired and hungry to argue and fell asleep almost instantly.

Chapter Twenty-Two

THE NUCLEAR DISASTER

The following morning, Tom was the first to wake, and the first thing that struck him was the stale smell of breath and sweat from the six unwashed men around him. A quick check of his armpits confirmed he was the seventh. He carefully unzipped his sleeping bag and climbed over the men nearest him to get out into the fresh air.

He was surprised to see thick fog, and yawning, he decided to do a quick recce before the other men awoke.

"An odd place to camp," he muttered when he ventured further down the lane and saw the vague shapes of tents in an adjoining field. He then smiled. That 'odd place to camp' had served them well enough, hadn't it? Surprised to see yet more tents, he walked on and spotted a white sheet draped over a hedge. Curious, he lifted the edge and peeled it back. Daubed in rough letters, the sheet had 'New Age Festival' painted on it. "Weird," he said and put it back down.

The fog was clearing, and he saw dozens more tents as he walked and the outline of people wandering about. It occurred to him that they really ought to get on the move and he turned around and headed back the way he had come. It really wouldn't be a good idea to be seen, despite them not looking dissimilar to the ragged-looking folk wandering around in the fields. In fact, they'd probably fit in quite nicely! Even so ...

As he walked, he heard shouting and stopped to listen. It sounded like a fair few people. He quickened his pace. *I thought New Age people were supposed to be peaceful*? he mused. *Time to put some distance between whatever has made them angry and get back on the road to London.* But as he neared the van, he realised the shouting was getting louder, not quieter, or was the fog distorting the sound? His question was answered when he saw a large group of people up ahead. Just where the van was parked. Oh good grief, what was happening now? He was alarmed to see dozens of people surrounding the van, shouting and banging on its sides. Some had long, multicoloured hair and equally as bright clothing; some wore combats and black boots and green army coats; they all looked furious. What on earth had happened in the short time he'd been walking? They then started rocking the van from side to side. Evidently, New Agers were not averse to a bit of a violent protest, but what about? And what could he do to stop them from tipping the van over? They needed that stolen van to get back to London with the diamond and hopefully get the deal done!

CRACK!

The sound of Mickey Lawson's pistol discharging into the sky was deafening, and the New Age mob instinctively ducked and fell silent. The swaying van wobbled to a standstill.

A man near the van's rear turned and tentatively took one step in Tom's direction. He was dressed in a full-length khaki trench coat, and his shaved, tattooed scalp gave him a severe look. "Who the hell are you people?" he asked softly. "This is a peaceful festival to promote clean energy, man. Why would you mock us by driving this filth onto our field and then fire a gun to frighten us?"

Tom had no idea how to respond but lowered the gun. "Well, I, well ... I'm sorry I startled you, but ... but what are you doing? And what filth?"

The crowd stood in silence for a few seconds more before the man in the trench coat turned back to the mob and gave a nod. They parted like a colourful Red Sea, and that was when Tom saw the lettering on the van they had missed in the dark the night before: Hawk's Nuclear Power. Ah ...

"We're all about the peace, man, and the clean. You know what filth nuclear energy creates, man?"

"No, I ... I admit I do not. Well, a little, but not a lot."

"Put the gun away, man. And educate yourself, right?"

"Yes. Yes, of course. My sincere apologies."

"Peace, man."

"Yes, erm, peace. Thank you."

With another nod from the man, the crowd wandered away, offering lots of "Peace, man, peace," as they did.

"Yes, sure. Peace. Yes," Tom agreed.

"Good timing, Tommo!" Gav shouted through the driver's window. "What took you so long, boyo? We thought we were gonna get torn to shreds by those nutcases!" A couple of nutcases turned around. "Peace, boyos, peace ..." Gav called, waving.

"Why would they do that to us?" Neville squeaked through the back window.

"It's not us they took offence to, Nev, not personally." He pointed at the van.

They all piled out, and Sherwin gave a long whistle. "Whoa, mon. We managed to pick ourselves a pretty conspicuous ride!"

"We really did," Tom said.

"And now we're a bunch of gun-toting guys in a nuclear van on top of everything else. Yeah, I'd report that," Dave said, flicking his head at the disappearing crowd. One of them was on a mobile phone. Of course they didn't know they were being reported for sure, but it was time to go. Again.

"Shit," Gav said. "I bet those people do a mean bacon sarnie, too."

"Vegetarians, mate," Dave said.

"Oh yeah. Bloody New Age unwashed bloody vegetarians."

"Watch it," Gaston said. "You are unwashed yourself, *non*, and I'm a vegetarian."

"Sure you are ..." Gav said.

"I am. I made you vegetarian boeuf bourguignon, did I not?"

"You had no choice, Gaston. We had no beef," Tom said.

"Zis is true."

"Don't talk about food," Gav groaned.

"Ya, mon," Sherwin agreed. "Let's get outta here. Find some grub."

"And some paint," Tom said.

"Paint, mon?"

"So we don't work for Hawk's Nuclear Power anymore."

"Good point, mon."

Chapter Twenty-Three

JOINING DOTS

Chief Superintendent Blakney jumped at the loud buzzing of his mobile phone. It was 9.15am.

"Mr Sykes. Good morning," he said.

"Chief Superintendent," came Donnie's reply. He noted the unusual sheepishness in Blakney's voice, a clear sign that the chief had no new information for his criminal accomplice. "It's now Monday morning, and I'm keen to know if there have been any further developments. Have your men located the gang yet?"

The chief cleared his throat. "No, they have not. But I'm expecting an update this morning from my chief investigating officer. I assure you, Mr Sykes, I am doing all I can to apprehend these men. During the course of yesterday, I received certain intel as to their whereabouts on two separate occasions, but when my officers arrived at these sites, the group had already moved on. It seems as though they are smarter than we may have given them credit for."

"I don't need to remind you what is at stake here, Chief Superintendent. If we let these bastards continue to slip through our hands, we may never get another chance of retrieving the Lady."

Blakney stiffened in his chair, irritated by Donnie's tone.

"I've given you my assurances already, and I do not like to repeat myself. My men are following the trail. As soon as they have confirmed visuals on the suspects, they will immediately call this in so we can mobilise an armed response team to apprehend these men, and with deadly force if necessary. All of my men have been briefed not to tamper with any baggage they might be carrying but will retrieve all possessions and return them directly to me. Let me remind you that this remains a police investigation, and I need to tread very carefully so as not to arouse suspicions. My officers are closing in, and they will find these men, but for the moment, we simply must exercise patience. We both want the same outcome, Mr Sykes. For differing reasons, perhaps, but our ultimate goal remains the same. As I say, I will know more very soon, and, when I do, you will too."

"Thank you, Chief Superintendent," Donnie breathed through gritted teeth. "Then I look forward to your update very soon.

* * *

The previous evening had failed to produce any further leads for DI Williamson and Sergeant Price. Chief Inspector Carlton had released Perkins from station duties in order to escort the Met officers to Crossley Fields, the scene of the lakeside altercation between the gang, the fox hunters and the anti-fox hunters. On their arrival at the recreational side of the lake, there had been no visual clues as to which route the gang might have taken. In the fading light, Perkins had dutifully driven the officers up and down various lanes in the hope of spotting the gang, but it had quickly become obvious the group must have either retreated into one of the nearby woodlands for the night or found some form of transport that would allow them to create even greater distance between themselves and the area of their last sighting. Either way, it soon became evident that nothing more could be done at such a late hour, and Williamson and Price had reluctantly returned to the Woolpack Inn for a second night.

It was now just after 9am the following morning. Although Sergeant Price had heartedly finished his full English breakfast, Williamson's plate had remained untouched. The DI was frustrated with the case, and he simply had no appetite for anything other than strong black coffee. As he gazed out of the window, lost in thought, his phone rang.

The DI nodded to Price and took a stroll while he talked.

"Good morning, my darling. How are you?" Shelly asked.

"Ugh. We're okay, but a conclusion to this investigation appears to be evading us."

"Still nothing on the gang?"

"Nothing concrete as yet, but I'm expecting a call from the local chief shortly, so we can plan our next move. Any news at your end?"

"Yes, that's why I'm calling. I have some very interesting news."

"Go on."

"You recall the strike-pad of matches we found in the jacket belonging to our giant and the logo on its cover?"

"Peanuts?"

"That's it. Well, Peanuts is a club. But not your average club. It has a rather shady reputation if you get my meaning."

"My darling, most clubs in London have something of a shady reputation, always have done and probably always will," Williamson offered, partly in jest. "But I do get your meaning, and it's not much of a surprise that this lowlife would frequent such an establishment. But just because he had these matches on his person, it does not necessarily mean there are any connections between him and the club."

"True, but our giant had absolutely no other item of identification on him. Anonymity was obviously so important to this man that even the labels in his clothes had been removed, so it's interesting that he would carry such an incriminating item. Perhaps he never imagined for a minute he might be shot or even caught. Anyway, there's something else I've discovered."

"Which is?"

"Peanuts is owned by none other than Donnie Sykes."

Williamson paused momentarily, calling up the memory. "Sykes? The London gangster?"

"The very same. But not just in London. The man is notorious and has criminal connections all over the country."

"Allegedly. My understanding is he has evaded all prosecution, despite being implicated in dozens of historical crimes, some heinous ones too."

"But you and I, and the entire police force, know that he's not only a criminal; he's also a powerful underworld player too."

"Yep, I know. He's a dangerous character, for sure. But to have never been caught means he's a pretty slippery customer, which also makes him dangerous and smart. But I still don't see there's a clear link between him and our killer."

"I haven't finished yet. We have two men dead, remember? And it seems as though I may have found another connection, but with the second man."

"Lawson?"

"Yes, Mickey Lawson. How much do you recall about the

case details of his theft of the Pink Lady, the famous pink diamond?"

"Not a great deal. I was a junior officer at the time, working out in the suburbs. But obviously, it caught everyone's imagination purely because of the audacity of the robbery. I mean, the fact that Mickey almost pulled it off all on his own was pretty incredible."

"If he was working alone."

"I don't follow ..."

"I've done some digging and discovered something very interesting. During the robbery, the police conducted a desperate search for Lawson, who was on foot, and finally found him hiding out on some building site. But what I didn't know is that the initial stage of his attempted getaway had been made by car. After Mickey was apprehended, his car was eventually found. But guess where?"

"Where?"

"Parked outside the premises of a certain London strip club."

The penny dropped. "Peanuts!"

"The very same."

"So was Donnie Sykes ever implicated as being an accomplice?"

"He was certainly implicated and thoroughly investigated, but the lack of any concrete evidence eventually led to him being exonerated of any involvement. It seems Mickey was a loner in crime, and Sykes claimed Mickey left the car outside Peanuts in order to falsely and deliberately implicate the club's owner. But nothing ever stuck, and the case was closed."

"Until now, perhaps?"

"Perhaps. But it does seem we now have some sort of a connection between the two dead men and Donnie Sykes, or at least his club."

"It does," Williamson agreed. "I'm not sure we have enough dots to join all of the connections yet. But the thing that appears to link them together could well be the missing diamond. It was never found, is that right?"

"That's correct. The police never retrieved the diamond and, what's more, the theft and the failure to find the jewel all happened ..." She lowered her voice. "On Chief Superintendent Blakney's watch. I've spoken to a few of our longer-serving colleagues here at the station, and it's fairly well known, although never mentioned, that this was the only blemish on his record. Some here still remember how his name had been dragged through the mud and that he's been an absolute sod to work under ever since."

Williamson took a sudden intake of breath. "Good grief."

"What is it?"

"I may have just joined a couple of those dots together. You recall there are two parts to my investigation. The first is to apprehend all of the men now involved with this case, but the second is to bring all of their possessions and clothing back to the station ... untampered with."

"The possession of 'great importance' to the Home Office. You think it could be the–"

"Shelly, wait. We need to keep this quiet for the moment. We simply can't go second-guessing Blakney's motives, innocent or otherwise. But something has been bugging me during this investigation, something that has left me feeling slightly uncomfortable. For the time being, though, we just need to keep this ..." His voice trailed off as he realised Price was trying to get his attention. "Darling, I've got to go. You have been brilliant; thank you so much. But as I say, we need to tread very carefully for the moment. I love you, and we'll speak again later." He turned to his sergeant. "What is it? Do we have a new lead?"

"We sure do, sir. You're not going to believe this one." Price grinned. "I've just been speaking to Chief Inspector Carlton. He tried to call you first, but obviously, you were on the phone, so he called me instead. First thing this, morning the chief's station took a call from a nuclear power facility about fifteen miles south of the lake we were at last night. The facility reported a stolen van, which appears to have been taken during the night."

"So they now have transport, if, of course, it is the gang who have stolen the vehicle."

Price could barely control his enthusiasm and continued with the grin still in place. "Oh, I think we can presume it's the gang, alright."

"Go on ..."

"The station also took a bunch of calls from the attendees of some sort of New Age festival which was set up in fields not far from the nuclear power facility. Apparently, they were deeply offended by the presence of a van parked in a lay-by where they were camped. A van with Hawk's Nuclear Power written on it. Not only that, when these hippies got a bit vocal, one of the group fired at them with a handgun."

"At them?"

"So they say, sir."

Williamson went quiet, thinking of Shelly's warning and still connecting dots. "I've just been speaking with Shelly, and based on some of the information she has discovered, I do believe this gang are headed for London."

"Certainly seems that way, sir, and Carlton agrees. He's been in touch with Suffolk and Essex forces, and their traffic officers are to be immediately briefed on the gang's possible route. The chief also assured me he has their full agreement that, if caught, as well as detaining the men until our own team arrives, any of their possessions will be confiscated and remain untampered with. The A12 corridor to London will be monitored, but it seems unlikely these men will try to journey too far in such a conspicuous van. They can't be that stupid, surely?"

"That remains to be seen. But the reality is, there's no longer any point in us staying here. We need to head back to London. If any new sightings are reported along the way, then we can divert, but things are escalating quickly now, and I have a hunch that the next time this gang rear their ugly heads, it will be back on our own turf. After speaking with Shelly, I feel we have a few possible leads. We must ensure the trail doesn't go cold."

"I agree. Erm, sir?"

"Yes?"

Despite the fact the two men were alone in the bar, Price lowered his voice and leaned in towards the DI. "Apologies, but I overheard the end of your conversation with Shelly ..."

"Yes ..."

"Well, sir ... well, do you have suspicions and apologies for asking, sir, of wrongdoing by the chief? You know, the moment we walk back into the station, he will want to be fully debriefed. Do we need to discuss making sure our stories align, just to ensure you have time to investigate any potential compromises? I've sensed you've been uncomfortable about something during the past couple of days, and I can't say I am fully sure about the validity of our instructions, either. Something doesn't seem right; that's all I'm saying."

Williamson was a little taken aback by his sergeant's questions. But he trusted Price implicitly and knew the younger man's intentions were honest.

"I should have been a little more guarded, but what Shelly told me came as a shock, and it has potentially strengthened the suspicions I've had during this entire investigation. What we must not do is jump to conclusions, however, as it's entirely possible there is a perfectly valid explanation for the chief's curious instructions. All the same, let's discuss this on the way. As I said to Shelly, we must tread carefully and only make assertions once we're fully in the picture. The chief will want a debrief on our arrival, you're right about that, but I think it would be prudent, at least for the moment, that we only convey what we are supposed to know and not any ungrounded suspicions."

Price nodded to confirm his agreement.

"Okay, Price, you go and grab our stuff. I'll get us all paid up with the landlady, and then we'll get on the road."

Chapter Twenty-Four

A BIT OF BOTHER

Dennis, Tom and Sherwin were on high alert as Dennis drove east along the busy A14. The upside, as Dennis put it, was that the road was far too busy for the police to deploy a stop and search; but the downside was there were bound to be more traffic cops – and they may well be on the lookout for a van with such distinctive branding on its side. But each man took some comfort in the belief the police had no clue where they were headed. There was little comfort in the fact, however, that the fuel light had just come on.

"How many miles?" Tom asked.

"Tops about thirty," Dennis said. "But there's no telling with a beat-up van like this."

"We should have painted over the bloody logo," Dave said.

"With paint we don't have, boyo," Gav replied.

The next few miles were tense, and all in the back were relieved when they heard Dennis mutter "Thank God" when he saw the bright green BP garage sign in the distance, along with signs for Starbucks, Marks & Spencer and Burger King. "I say we fill up and then park around the back somewhere," he added. "We all need to get something to eat and use the bathroom, but let's be discrete, yeah?"

"It's a sound idea," Tom said. "But Dennis is right. We do this as discretely as possible. No dramas. No shooting anything." He looked back at Gav, who rolled his eyes.

"It was the one fox, and you shot a whole man, Tommo."

"Fair point." But Tom's stomach lurched with the memory and with hunger.

As they pulled into the service station, they were relieved to see there were no queues for diesel, and Dennis filled the tank while Tom went in to pay, using cash from his stag do fund. *What a ridiculous thing to have to do*, he thought. *I bet no other groom-to-be has had to fill a stolen nuclear power plant van with diesel on his stag do.* Dennis then parked the van in a space between a large truck and a coach around the back of the service area, thus obscuring them from view. They then used the facilities and bought coffee and food, collapsing around a table in Burger King to eat. For a while, they barely spoke, too hungry to think about anything else other than the food in front of them.

"So when we make it to London, Dennis," Tom finally asked quietly, "do you know where in Hatton Garden this jewellery dealer actually is?"

"Absolutely," Dennis said, wiping burger grease from his fingers with a paper napkin. "I was arrested right outside his shop. But as I said before, I never actually got to meet him. The cops nabbed me before I could pass my brother's stolen goods over to him."

"But this was some time ago. What if his shop isn't there anymore?"

"Well, that's possible, but I doubt it. From what my brother said, he's been there for decades and is very well established, so I can't see why he'd move on. Another thing I remember is that the guy was so old that he refused to have a phone; he didn't believe in them. Thinking about it, he might even have died. But let's hope he's still alive and still in business."

"What's the name of the shop?" Sherwin asked.

"Do you know the man's name?" Neville added.

Dennis thought for a moment. "Solomon's Place. No, Solomon's Ice. Pretty sure that's the name. And he's called Hershel Cone. I remember because I'd never heard a name like that before. My brother told me he was a gem cutter by trade but was a buyer and seller of precious stones too. As I said, my brother had dealings with him on plenty of occasions. He's particularly obsessed with diamonds. An old-school crook, really."

"But as you 'ave never met zis man," Gaston asked, "do you think he will want to deal with us?"

"After I left prison, I decided never to get involved with any of my brother's shady business dealings ever again. I got myself into mechanics, landed a good job and never looked back. But my brother has never given up his thieving, so I imagine he will still be in contact with Cone. Even if he isn't, I'm sure the old guy will remember my brother, so I'll be surprised if he won't at least talk to us. And if he seems reluctant, just the mention of the Pink Lady may change his mind."

"The thing is, though," Tom ventured, "if I was him, I'd take one look at us and tell us all to shove off. I mean, just look at the state of us."

Each of the men looked around, and it dawned on them just what a dishevelled bunch they had become. They were all on their last set of clothes, having only expected to be away for a few days, and were unwashed and unshaven. Tom still had soot in his ears and hair, and on his face and clothes, along with the mud and general filth they all had from hiding in woodland and sleeping rough in a grubby old van. Being on the run was a dirty business.

"If we want to stand even half a chance of pulling this diamond deal off, we need to smarten up. As soon as we get into London, we must buy clothes and try and clean up before we go walking into his shop. As we are now, he may take one look at us and use the panic button if he has one – or something more serious."

"Fair dinkum," Dave said. "I think we can all agree on that. Okay, Dennis, if you're feeling revived, I reckon we should scoot."

They gathered up their backpacks and unfinished coffees and made their way across the sprawling car park.

"Shit!" Dennis suddenly whispered, ducking behind a huge truck. "Shit. Shit. Shit."

None of the men needed to ask what the problem was. The coach they had parked behind was now gone and in its place, parked diagonally across the front of the nuclear power station van, was a police SUV, its blue lights flashing. Two police officers were pacing around the vehicle, one of them talking into his radio. They knew without a doubt they had been compromised, and the van was being called in as suspicious.

"We're screwed, boyos," Gav said, leaning heavily against the truck.

"Zis is game over," Gaston agreed.

"Quick!" hissed Neville. "This way!"

They turned to see Neville clambering over a fence and into a long stretch of conifers at the back of the truck. They followed, ducking through the dense branches as they went. On the other side was a huge area reserved for trucks, rows and rows of them backed into lines.

"Now, what do we do?" Neville asked, in his returning squeak, hoping for at least a glimmer of an idea from the men around him. But they looked just as panicked as he did.

"This place will be crawling with police in no time," Dennis whispered. "I doubt we even have time to find another suitable van."

"So, what do we do?" Neville repeated.

"We hitch a ride."

All eyes turned to Tom and then followed his gaze to a high-sided old truck with wooden panelling. Ducking in and out of the trucks, they made their way over and peered inside. Inside were stacks of dusty crates piled up and tied down with old canvas strapping. Each crate had a wire mesh window. Through the windows, they could see chickens. About fifteen or twenty to each container. Equalling hundreds and hundreds of chickens. The smell was wretched.

"You can't be serious, Tommo?" whispered Gavin.

"You don't expect us to get all the way to London in that, do you?" Neville squawked.

Tom was watching an elderly man in dirty blue overalls smoking a cigarette next to the open driver's door. He looked every bit the owner of a decrepit old truck loaded to the hilt with stinking fowl.

"Who says he's going to London?" Tom replied. "At this point, it doesn't matter which direction we go, as long as we get as far away from here as possible."

The man flicked his cigarette butt to the ground and dragged the sole of his tattered black boot over it. He then raised his hand to grab the inside handle of the door.

"Wait here!" Tom hissed, shocked by his decisive command. "Excuse me?" Tom called up to the old man, who was now behind the wheel. "Excuse me, sir?"

"Yes, laddie, what can I do for you?" His hand was on the key in the ignition.

"I was wondering if I could, erm, hitch a lift?"

"Hitch a lift?" the old man repeated. "Gracious, it's many a year since I was asked that. Nobody trusts nobody nowadays. But luckily for you, I'll always help a fella out who's in a bit of bother. Where're you headed?"

"Oh, I'm not in any bother, at least not of the serious kind, as bother goes, and, erm, nowhere really. I mean, anywhere is fine. Well, London ideally, but not to worry if not."

The man wheezed with laughter. "Not in any bother. Not in any serious kind of bother. Nowhere, anywhere, or London. Now that is a curious situation and destination for a hitch-hiker. Ah well, you likely have your reasons and, as I say, I'm happy to help. I'm actually heading toward London but can't get you all the way. Romford is my stop. That any good to you?"

"It certainly is, and thank you so much."

"No problem. Let yourself in the passenger side." The old man then closed the door but stuck his head through the open window. "One thing, though ..."

"Yes?"

"There's only room for you up front," he said. "So tell your fellas not to upset my chickens when they ride in the back. It's a couple of hours to Romford, and I want to get these birds there without any stress."

Tom suddenly felt ashamed of his dishonesty. His plan had been to secretly usher his friends into the back of the truck on his way around the vehicle. But there were no flies on this wily old coot.

"Sir, I'm so sorry. This is so kind of you. I would never normally have tried something like this on, but ..."

"You're in a bit of bother." The man finished Tom's sentence with a chuckle. "Go on, laddie, pack your stowaways and let's get going. Just slide the bolt fully back when you close the doors."

"Get in," Tom said, going to the back of the truck and reaching up for the long bolt holding the doors closed. "We can get as far as–"

"Zere iz no way I will travel wiv zees stinking poulet! Zis iz–" Gaston gesticulated, but the sound of sirens silenced him, and he climbed up behind the others.

"Just keep out of sight!" Tom said. "And don't upset the chickens."

He slid the bolt back, dashed around to the passenger side and hauled himself in.

* * *

Sergeant Price was driving southward on the A12.

"Sir? What's the news?" he asked as his DI placed his phone back into his jacket pocket.

"The van has been found in a car park at a service station on the A14, somewhere near Bury St Edmunds. But as you likely heard, once again, the gang have disappeared. A dozen officers are combing the area, and interviews have already started. A waitress has reported that a group of six or seven men ate in Burger King, but it doesn't necessarily mean this is the group we're looking for. Frustratingly, there was no CCTV in operation in the car park, only in the restaurant, and this will be sent to us shortly. The issue is, of course, that we still have no real idea of what these individuals look like. The waitress's statement mentioned that one of the group was a black male, and this tallies with the reports from the pub, the collision on the canal and the lake. But this still does not mean these are our guys."

"So we're not turning back?" Price asked. They had passed the service station at least half an hour earlier and were approaching Chelmsford, less than an hour from Central London.

"No. There really is little point. The gang have stolen one vehicle already and clearly has the ability to do the same again. If that's the case, hopefully, the vehicle will be reported missing very soon so we can get a registration plate and model. But we have to assume they are again on the road, and if they're not in London already, then most likely they will be very soon."

"If they really are headed for London. This is still an assumption on our part."

"It is. But we have to start somewhere. The more I think about the connections between Lawson, the giant and possibly Donnie Sykes, the more I'm convinced London is where the gang's next move will be made. We just need them to slip up so we get the chance to finally track them down and bring them in. Either way, I believe that doubling back to where the van was found is futile. We need to get back to the station, report in with the chief, and then start digging at these new leads."

Chapter Twenty-Five

RESERVATIONS, SIR

The absurdity of the cat and mouse antics was not lost on DI Williamson as they overtook a rattling old chicken truck trundling down the A12. But Tom didn't notice the two officers in the unmarked Mondeo, engrossed as he was in conversation with the driver of the decrepit vehicle.

"Well, laddie, I'll be making my turn soon. Sorry, I couldn't take you boys all the way, but I reckon you'll be fine from here."

"We certainly will. And thank you again for your kindness. You've helped us out of a spot of bother, as I said, and you've not even asked me why, which is extremely generous of you."

"Nonsense," the old man replied merrily. "Truth is, it's been nice to have someone to talk to, to drown out the constant chatter of those bleedin' birds back there. As to your bit of bother, that's none of my business. But I wish you all the best and hope you manage to square things away. I'm guessing those sirens back there were calling for you and your friends, but I knows a wrong'un when I sees one, and Tom, laddie, you ain't one of them, so best of luck to you."

"I do hope you're right. My life has been pretty straightforward, boring even, well, until the last few days, when things sort of got quite complicated quite quickly, and your help has probably saved the day, as it were. I won't forget your kindness, and once I've sorted things out, hopefully, maybe I'll come and find you and tell you all about it. I owe you a full explanation."

"You owe me nowt, laddie. But if you do ever seek me out, I'll take a nice, tasty ale in return. Right, there's a bus stop up ahead. Shall I drop you there?"

"That'll be perfect. Thank you so much."

With feathers and the smear of chicken mess now added to their filthy clothes, six very disgruntled men held their noses through the stench and dropped down to the pavement.

"The next bus to Central London is in about five mins, and it'll take about an hour," Tom said, looking at the bus timetable rather than at the six angry men. "First stop, an H&M or somewhere, to get an inexpensive change of clothes."

"I totally agree with the need for new clothes, Tom, but there's no point heading to Hatton Garden today. It's half three now. By the time we've sorted out new clothes, Hershel will have shut up shop for the day," Dennis said. There was no response from the others.

"You're right," Tom said. "We'll have to head to Hatton Garden first thing in the morning. But what do we do until then? We can't sleep under the stars in Central London. I know people here and can't risk anyone seeing me. What do you guys suggest?"

"I got a mate in Lambeth," Sherwin sighed, trying to pick feathers out of his hair. "I could see if he'll put us up for the night."

"It's a nice idea, but maybe a bit late notice, even for the best of mates?" Tom responded. "And besides, there's seven of us. That would be too much of an imposition, well, in my opinion, do you not think?"

"He cool, but yeah, maybe a big ask," Sherwin agreed.

"Then ze only real option eez to stay in *un hôtel, non*?" Gaston said.

"Or some kind of cheaper place," Dave offered.

"Either sounds fine to me," Dennis said. "Right, lads, look lively. Here comes the bus."

Tom pulled his mobile phone out. Perhaps Jen had messaged about when he might be home? He hoped there might be just enough battery left to message her back, but it was dead. He'd need to find a phone box and call her at some point, or at least get somewhere he could charge his phone. She'd be worried sick. The others hadn't seemed that bothered about checking in with home. Neville wittered on about his wife occasionally but didn't seem inclined to call her. Plus, he didn't have a mobile phone. Dennis spoke mainly about his kids but didn't speak about any kind of relationship. Gaston didn't speak much at all and mainly cursed and smoked. Dave's girlfriend was back in Sydney and was no doubt used to long periods of radio silence. Sherwin seemed very much the free spirit. He'd spoken about various mates but not about any particular girl in his life. Gav mainly burnt things, shot things, at least in their company, and talked about Swansea, but again never really mentioned a partner or girlfriend. And they'd learnt nothing about Mickey, and then Gav had bludgeoned him to death on that first night, so that had been the end of that – apart from Dennis' sudden recollection about Mickey and the diamond. The diamond. The million-year-old lump of compressed carbon that had been the reason for this whole damn bother. He climbed onto the bus with the others and slumped into a seat by the dirty window. Dennis sat next to him. He stank. They all stank.

* * *

For the past half an hour, Sergeant Price had been waiting patiently outside Chief Superintendent Blakney's office. He had not been invited to attend the debriefing, and given the amount of desk pounding and shouting coming from their superior, he almost felt grateful for the snub.

Eventually, Williamson emerged, and the young officer knew his DI well enough to see he was fuming at the barrage of abuse he'd endured. Despite his anger, Williamson was a man in complete control of his emotions and calmly closed the door behind him.

"He's not happy, then?" Price asked.

Williamson raised his eyebrows and shook his head as he ushered his sergeant away from the office and along the corridor. "Just imagine what he'd have been like had I raised my concerns over some of the odd instructions we've been receiving! The chief's obvious desperation to get his hands on the gang's belongings is only increasing my concerns. Strangely, though, he didn't mention pressure from the Home Office this time, so it seems more and more like this is based on some personal objective, perhaps even a grudge. But I cannot be sure about anything until we have more details. We simply have to find this gang and then see where it goes from there."

"Easier said than done, sir."

"Agreed. But Shelly's intel was good, and this Peanuts club is definitely a lead we need to follow up. Let's get down to her office and see if she has anything new for us. At the very least, the CCTV footage from the service station's restaurant ought to be in by now and could give us more of an idea of what the suspects actually look like."

When the two officers made their way down the several flights of steps to Shelly's office, a figure was waiting for them at the bottom, barring their way.

Police Commissioner Douglas Hawke-Staines was

impeccably dressed, as he always was. But the high-ranking officer was rarely seen in the station, let alone in uniform, preferring expensive suits from Italian makers such as Brioni and Boglioli. His slicked-back hair completed the look of a man who demanded attention purely through his meticulous air of authority and respectability. He looked up at Williamson. "I'm glad I've managed to intercept you," he said, his voice as impeccable as his uniform.

"Me, sir?" Williamson had only ever spoken with Blakney's superior on two, perhaps three occasions, and their exchanges had been fleeting at best.

"Yes, Williamson. I was actually on my way up to see you. I wondered, would it be possible to have a word ... in private?" he asked, with a sideways glance at Sergeant Price, the question purely rhetorical.

"Yes, of course, sir. Sergeant, would you mind heading to Shelly's ... er ... I mean Dr Baxter's office, please? I'll join you as soon as I can."

"Of course, sir."

Once Price had left, the commissioner led Williamson into a vacant side room and quietly closed the door behind him.

"Thank you, Williamson. And I do apologise for delaying you, but I have something rather delicate to discuss."

"But of course, sir, I'll help in any way I can."

"Good man, good man." Despite being alone in the small room, Hawke-Staines stood strangely close to the DI and kept his voice low. Williamson detected the sickly sweet odour of whisky and cigars, despite the mask of expensive cologne. "As I said, this is a delicate matter, so I trust I can count on your complete discretion."

"Naturally, sir. Please, go on."

"It's about your latest case and this baloney with those

bloody pen-pushers at the Home Office."

Williamson was surprised by the commissioner's candid opening but did not show it.

"The truth is, Williamson ... we may suspect some form of ... corruption. I'm not saying this is necessarily a reality, but I've been asked to get a handle on this investigation, but surreptitiously, you understand."

"Yes, sir, I think I do. But corruption? Are you able to be more specific? Who exactly is under–"

"Chief Superintendent Blakney," the commissioner cut in and left the name along with a long pause in the air while he studied the DI's face. "You don't seem surprised, Williamson. Which leads me to think you may have your own suspicions."

"Not suspicions as such, sir." Williamson felt the commissioner's eyes bore into his own. "Perhaps *reservations* would be more appropriate."

"Reservations? In what respect, exactly?"

"Assuming you are fully up to speed on the proceedings of this case ..."

"I believe I am, but please continue."

"Well, sir, our initial objective, as you'll know, was to apprehend Mickey Lawson in connection with the possible killing of his probation officer, Colin Sturgeon. But once his body was found and has now been identified beyond doubt, we also retrieved a second body buried in the same makeshift grave. This man has yet to be identified, but we now suspect, based on forensics gathered by Dr Baxter, that it was this second man who is likely responsible for Sturgeon's death, not Lawson. Although, given the fact these men were found together, and not to mention previous convictions, Mickey is likely to have been involved in some capacity. Further intel we have gathered, and strongly suspect to be correct, is a direct link to a group of men who may also have been involved with Mickey and this other man. The capture of these men has now become the sole focus of our investigation, although, despite numerous sightings, we have been unable to apprehend the gang so far."

"How can you be sure that each of these sightings have been the same men each time?"

"The fact, sir, that witness statements match in terms of the group's appearance, but also that they have repeatedly used a firearm."

"But what of your reservations?" Again, the commissioner's eyes bored into his.

"Well, given this was a murder investigation, and now multiple suspected murders, it seems odd to me that the capture of the perpetrators, in order to bring justice for these murders, no longer seems to be the main objective." Williamson waited, wondering how the commissioner would respond.

"You are referring to your instructions to obtain all of the items and personal effects carried by this gang? But why should this be odd?"

"It's not that which is odd, sir. This would be normal procedure in the capture of any suspect during part of a murder investigation. It's the fact that ..." Williamson paused. This was the awkward part, as any potential accusation from him, as a subordinate officer, could potentially prove his undoing. "It's the fact that the items this gang may, or may not be carrying, seems to be of far greater importance than the apprehension of the murder suspects."

"But you said yourself, the second dead man was likely responsible for the murder of Sturgeon. Why should the focus of operations not alter now that he himself is dead?"

"We suspect it was him, but only that, because following Sturgeon's death, we now have two further bodies. Criminals or not, we have to treat their deaths as crimes too, and we simply cannot allow this gang to slip away. We do not know what they are capable of. Given that they are armed, surely public safety must come first? What could the Home Office possibly want that supersedes this?"

"And you feel that Chief Superintendent Blakney has placed more importance on the retrieval of these items, whatever they may be, rather than the capture of the murder suspects?"

Williamson hesitated again and then said, "I do, sir. I appreciate he may well be under huge pressure from the Home Office, but there seems to be ..."

"Seems to be what?"

There was nothing for it. He needed to be honest. "There seems to be something personal about his instructions. Sir, I have just spent the last half an hour debriefing the chief, and yet at no point did he acknowledge the potential hazard to the public from this gang, only that we retrieve their belongings at all costs. The anger toward me for not yet locating this gang is something I can take, and I will, of course, continue to do all I can to bring them in. But of the orders to obtain their belongings 'at all costs' ... this is where my reservation lays."

The commissioner thought about that. "Okay, Williamson. I understand your concerns. Is there anything else you want to tell me?"

Reservations of orders were one thing; suspicions of corruption were quite another. The DI had already resisted the urge to speak of the revelations that Shelly had uncovered regarding Blakney's previous dealings with the diamond theft case and the possible idea that the item that was so desperately being hunted was, in fact, the Pink Lady. Revealing this to the commissioner at this stage seemed a step too far for Williamson. If he was to share more, he must first attempt to gather hard facts, facts that may or may not exist.

"No, sir, nothing more at this stage. I was on my way to speak with Dr Baxter and to hopefully come up with a few more leads before Sergeant Price and I continue the investigation."

"Very well. But before you do, I want you to listen to me very carefully."

"Of course, sir."

"As I said at the outset, this is an extremely delicate situation, so this is exactly what I want you to do ..."

* * *

The last stop from Romford was the southeast corner of Trafalgar Square, and Tom led the way north to Covent Garden.

"Here," Tom said turning left and then right down some narrow streets off St Martin's Lane. He eventually pointed to the H&M on the opposite side of the road. "This isn't a fashion show, chaps, so we just grab something simple, pay, and get out of here as quickly as possible. Change into your new clothes, and shove your old ones in your backpacks, and I'll meet you at the checkout in fifteen minutes."

One by one, they returned in blue or black jeans and dark sweaters or sweatshirts. Despite the budget price tags, Gaston still looked slick and French.

"Where's Neville?" Tom asked.

"Haven't seen him," Dennis said, pulling the tag from his dark grey sweatshirt.

"Oh no, boyos," Gav said, and they turned to look.

Neville was on his way. In orange cargo-style jeans and an orange sweatshirt.

"What the ... I told you to get something simple!" Tom scolded.

"You look like some kinda prison dude, mon!" Sherwin hissed. "Subtle, no!"

"What? I like it!" Neville squeaked. "My wife always says I should be more bold, like!"

"Coz this is a good time to listen to the missus, mate," Dave said. "Go and change!"

"I like it!"

"We don't have time for this," Tom snapped. "Anyway, I work in this city and, I see more interesting outfits than Neville's every day of the week. Trust me, nobody will bat an eyelid. Right, give me all your tags, and I'll pay." He handed all the tags to a checkout girl with blue hair and green-painted nails. "Hope it's okay, but we needed to get changed into the new clothes," he said. "We got a bit ... erm, muddy, and anyway, I'll be paying for it all, so don't worry about separating the tags out." He dug out his credit card and again pondered the ridiculousness of his purchase. First diesel for a van he didn't own, and then a whole pile of clothes, in multiple sizes, for men he'd only known seventy-two hours. His credit card company would wonder what on earth had possessed him. He wondered what on earth had possessed him.

The checkout girl didn't look up. "Cash or card?" she asked in a monotone.

"Card, please."

"Do you require a bag?" She started scanning the tags.

"No, thank you. As I said, we need to wear the clothes because–"

"Do you want to open an account? Fifteen per cent off all purchases today, and no need to pay for a month. APR 29.5 per cent, and–"

"No, thank you."

The girl finished scanning. "Three hundred and forty-two pounds," she droned. "Cash or card?" Still no eye contact.

Tom sighed. "Card, please."

She held her hand out and took Tom's new chip and PIN credit card, which he was quite proud of. He typed in the PIN.

"I'm afraid your card has been declined, sir."

"Really? That's odd. There's plenty of credit–"

"Would you like to try again, sir?"

"Absolutely. There's plenty of credit on that card, and I know I put the right number in, but then again, so let me–"

"Declined again, I'm afraid. Do you have another card?"

He did, but a horrible mix of realisation and fear began to stir in Tom's mind as he studied the face of the blue-haired girl who was now reading something on her computer screen. And then she looked at him, her vacant face showing a flicker of something. "If you don't mind waiting, sir, I'm just going to ask my manager to come over and deal with this."

Tom just nodded. Without saying a word, the girl shuffled away, his card in her hand.

"Dennis!" he hissed.

"Yeah? What's up? What's the delay?"

"I think my credit card has been frozen. They must have my name from when I paid for the boat, dammit! The police must know who I am! They've frozen my accounts so I can be tracked!"

"Why didn't you use cash?"

"I didn't have enough left."

"We would have chipped in, mate."

"Too late now."

"Where's she gone?"

"To get her manager."

"Shit. We need to go. Now."

Tom spotted a dumpy man in a cheap grey suit waddling across the store floor towards them. "Now!"

Instinctively, the others followed the moment they saw Tom and Dennis move. What the hell had happened at the checkout? Tom made it to the doors first and charged out into the street. For almost five minutes, they kept up the pace, twisting and turning through one lane after another until Tom dived into the entrance to Holborn Tube station and doubled over, hands on his knees, trying to get his breath back.

"Keep moving!" he gasped. "And keep up!" He merged in with the crowd.

Eventually, he stopped in one of the endless passageways and leaned against the wall. He burst out laughing.

"What's so funny, boyo?" Gav asked.

"Proper fugitives we are now!" Tom laughed.

"Reminds me of my younger days, 'shopping' in Swansea!" Gav said.

"Mate, we gotta keep moving," Dave said.

"And we need to find somewhere to stay," Dennis added.

"This. Is. Such. A. Mess. Such a. Bloody awful. Bloody mess." Tom was still laughing and feeling a little bit unhinged, if he was honest, but the guys were right. They couldn't risk staying still. Too many CCTV cameras. But where on earth were they going to stay for the night? And how would they pay?

Chapter Twenty-Six

A SWITCH OF MASTERS

DI Williamson went directly to Shelly's laboratory after his peculiar encounter with the commissioner and received a welcome hug from his fiancée. Price turned away momentarily to give his superior a few seconds of privacy.

"So, my darling," Shelly said with a grimace, "James tells me you got a bit of a grilling from the chief."

"That's one way of putting it. Thankfully Sergeant Price here was spared the experience. The chief is not a happy man. To be honest, I'm pretty frustrated myself. Have you turned up anything new since we last spoke?"

Shelly shook her head. "Nope, 'fraid not. Peanuts is still the only real lead we have. But the more I think about the pressure you're receiving to seize this gang's possessions, the more it makes perfect sense to me that the Pink ..." She paused momentarily, glancing in Price's direction.

"It's okay, Shelly," Williamson assured her. "Sergeant Price is fully up to speed on our suspicion that the gang may be carrying the diamond. The three of us need to work together on this one and share all thoughts openly if we're going to get closure on this case. And I agree with you; I think the likelihood these men have the stolen jewel has gone from suspicion to genuine probability. And speaking of sharing, there's something else I need to discuss with you both. Something that absolutely must remain between us."

"Is this to do with your conversation with the commissioner?" Price asked tentatively.

Shelly looked from Price back to Williamson. "The commissioner? Hawke-Staines is in the building?"

"He is indeed. He waylaid me on my way over to you."

"Blimey. What did he want?"

"To tell me that something smells bad."

"You mean ..." Shelly paused as she processed her thoughts. "You mean he, like us, has suspicions over this case?"

"He does." He knew he needed to share the instructions Hawke-Staines had given him before they'd parted and took a deep breath. "Not only that, but he's asked me to bypass the chief with any important new leads or evidence that may arise during further investigations. I'm to deliver only mundane advances to the chief, but anything substantial, including any new orders from the chief himself, must be reported directly to the commissioner and not shared with anyone else. I know it may appear a little against normal procedure, but I have my orders."

"But you've decided to share this with us, sir?" Price said quietly.

"I have, Sergeant. And the reason for that is I cannot do this on my own. We simply have to work together. I trust you both implicitly – in fact, you're my most-trusted colleagues – and I know we'll be able to keep this between the three of us."

"Of course, sir, that goes without saying."

"So, just to be clear," Shelly said. "Hawke-Staines suspects the chief of ... corruption?"

"I think it's more that he believes something is not quite right. But possible corruption, yes, is certainly on his mind.

Why else would he ask me to hold out on Blakney?"

"But why would the commissioner have eyes on this particular case? I don't recall him ever bothering himself with the day-to-day running of this station in the past."

Williamson considered that point. "Maybe it has to do with the Home Office," he then said. "Perhaps they've had eyes on Lawson for years, waiting for him to be released, expecting him to return to the place of his hidden treasure. It would certainly be a feather in their cap were they to retrieve the stolen jewel and repatriate it. Imagine the fanfare. Her Majesty's police force would be hailed for its dogged pursuit of justice, and the British government praised for its generosity and cooperative goodwill."

Shelly frowned. "But this doesn't explain why the chief might be under suspicion of corruption."

"If, as we suspect, the Pink Lady is indeed at the centre of this investigation then the commissioner will certainly be aware of the chief's involvement during the original investigation, and his failure to retrieve the diamond. Hawke-Staines may be asking me to report directly to him because he feels that, although he may well be innocent, the chief's judgement might not be helpful to the new investigation due to his desperation to retain his unblemished career."

"Or perhaps," Price mused, "he suspects the chief of corrupt intent, meaning he may intend to retrieve the diamond for himself. After all, he had asked for none of the gang's clothes or baggage to be tampered with and to be returned only to him. For his eyes only, so to speak. He told us the possessions would go straight to the Home Office, and this would mean he would have the opportunity to intercept the diamond before these items were passed on."

The three stood silently for several moments, each one considering the possibilities.

Eventually, Shelly looked up at her fiancé. "Austin, knowing how the hierarchy works, we have to be aware the commissioner is likely to have only passed on to you the very minimum he needed to. There are bound to be aspects of this case that are only known by those higher up. We've already connected the dots between Lawson and the diamond and between the giant and the probation officer he killed. We've also connected the dots between this killer and the club Peanuts, which we know is owned by Donnie Sykes. Another connection to consider might be one between this thug and the chief himself."

"You mean a partnership of some kind?"

"Seems unlikely, for sure. But given the shadow of corruption that appears to have fallen on the chief, perhaps the commissioner is aware of a previously suspected link between Sykes and Blakney. We know that the getaway car was found adjacent to the club's premises, and we know that Sykes was exonerated of any involvement. The chief himself would have had to sign off on that exoneration. And given we know Sykes has a criminal empire, one that has grown strong seemingly by evading the long arm of the law, then is it possible there has been, or still is, a 'special' relationship between Sykes and the chief?"

Sergeant Price shook his head, letting out a long whistle as he did so. "Wow. Connecting some of these dots could get us into a whole heap of trouble if we're wrong."

"Agreed," Williamson said. "But Shelly is right to consider all possible connections. We need to tread very cautiously, remain objective, but continue to test every door that may lead to the truth. At the moment, everything appears to lead us back to the club. So one door we will be knocking on is Donnie Sykes'. I want to question him about our dead giant and see what his reaction is. We can request all footage from the club's CCTV and see if we can find anything that connects him to the killer, or to Mickey Lawson, or to the gang, or even to the chief himself. We'll also need to bring a team of officers with us in order to conduct a thorough search of the property. It may turn up nothing, but it's all we have for the moment."

"I doubt Sykes will agree to any of that without a warrant, sir."

"I dare say he won't, Price. But I will speak with the commissioner again and see if a warrant can be obtained by the morning. If the commissioner is as keen as I think he is to get to the truth, then I can't see him objecting to us ruffling a few of Sykes' feathers."

They were interrupted by a muffled ringing, and DI Williamson retrieved his mobile phone from his jacket pocket. After a brief exchange, he ended the call and looked at his junior officer with a smile. "We were right, Price. The gang are here in London. Seven men were reported an hour ago for stealing clothes from the H&M near Covent Garden."

"Blimey, we needed a slip-up, but that's some slip-up! But how can we know for sure this is the same gang?"

"Because the gang's leader tried paying for the clothes with a credit card which was declined. That's why they scarpered. Would you like to hazard a guess at the name on the card?"

Price's eyes lit up. "Tom Marshall? From the boat hire place?"

"Precisely. Not only do we now have a name, we also have CCTV footage of all gang members. We know what they look like, we know what they're wearing, and we know they must be in London for a reason. Perhaps to connect with Donnie Sykes? Well, that remains to be seen. Sergeant, I want you to get a hold of the footage immediately and get images out to all stations within the M25. Also, get a request out for surveillance on all London-based CCTV. We need to track these thugs down urgently–"

"Sir, that's–"

"It's a huge undertaking, I know, but you must stress that we have explicit orders from the Home Office that these men are suspects in a murder investigation and that they are armed. If you have any resistance, then let me know, and I'll get the commissioner's weight behind the order. He expressly asked that I appraise him immediately with any developments, so I must call him now to let him know about the gang's sighting and also request an armed response team to be assembled and ready for when we locate the gang. I'll also ask him to sanction a warrant so we can get things rolling first thing in the morning. Things are hotting up, and we now have two leads, but we must move fast. All other information discussed in this room stays between the three of us, yes?"

"Of course."

"Sir."

Chapter Twenty-Seven

I'VE HAD A BALL!

In fear of using their debit or credit cards, the guys decided it would be safer to pool resources and use whatever cash they had left to pay for some accommodation; but the combined sum did not amount to a great deal, and as a result, they were forced to dismiss one hotel after another as they wandered through the backstreets of London, not daring to use the main roads. Tom's knowledge of the streets was impressive, having worked in the city for so long, but he'd rarely stayed there. He was relieved when they eventually discovered a drab-looking building not far from Tottenham Court Road with a red and white sign that read YMCA.

"Actually, the standard of these hostels is pretty good," Dave said. "I've stayed in plenty of them when travelling. They're clean and tidy, and cheap too."

By that point, the group couldn't have cared less where they stayed. They were exhausted and on edge after leaving the clothing store and just wanted to eat and sleep.

* * *

During bacon sandwiches and coffee in Russell Square Gardens the next morning, Tom suggested they use the final bit of cash to pay for a cab to Hatton Garden so they could sell the diamond and then get on with their lives.

"Sorry, Tom, but that's ridiculous," Dennis said. "Even if Hershel is there and is interested in the Pink Lady, it makes no difference to our immediate situation. The diamond is worth millions, and he's not going to have that kind of dough hanging around. Surely you guys realised we were never going to get paid today? This is simply the first part of the process, and he'll need time to set up a buyer. This gem is one seriously hot potato, and Hershel's role will be to find someone rich enough and crazy enough, to want to make the purchase. I couldn't even guess at how long that might take."

"So what are we supposed to do till then?" Neville squeaked. "We're still robbers! We–"

"Not to mention we're – what did you call us? Fugitives, zat was it," Gaston said.

"Gaston's right. The police are on to us now, no doubt. We've left a trail of bad behind us on this crazy stag do, mon – sorry, Tom – and we're now out of cash and places to go," Sherwin said. "We can't just go home."

"So we'll be on the run with no money until then?" Neville said. "If he agrees to sell it for us, surely he'd be able to give some kind of deposit, just enough to get by for a few days? I do need to go home. The missus'll be, you know. I'll be in the doghouse, like."

Dennis shrugged his shoulders. "I have no idea. Like I told you guys before, I was young when I was mixed up in my brother's criminal dealings, so I only know the basics of how this all works. I guess we'll just have to find out."

"And after that?" Neville piped. "We're wanted for double murder, arson, shooting a fox, stealing a boat, stealing a van, stealing a dia–"

"Yeah, alright, boyo," Gav said. "Enough of the doomsday stuff."

"Neville's right, Gav. We're in all kinds of trouble. Even if we sell the diamond, we face arrest, questioning, court, prison, unless by some miracle none of this actually bloody happened, and I'm at my desk at work daydreaming, not dressed from head to toe in H&M talking to you lot about selling a diamond. No one's going to believe this. Who would ever believe this?" Tom said, again overwhelmed by all that had happened. "And I feel so bad about Old Bill's boat."

"Me too," Neville said. "Never been on a boat before except a dingy with my old man off Blackpool beach."

They fell silent and Tom, not for the first time, realised he knew so little about these men, consumed as they had been by basic survival since the death of two men on the narrowboat. As he watched the normality of his surroundings, the passing city-dwellers and the commuters and the tourists, all concerned with their own affairs, not one of them stopped to look at the group, but then why would they? They were just seven friends eating breakfast in a park. On the run with a priceless diamond.

"What a mess I've got us all into," he said. "I'm so sorry, guys. I wish I'd never auctioned those bloody tickets. What can I say? I'm sorry."

"Don't be daft, Tommo," Gav said. "I think it was a cracking idea. I've had a ball!"

"A ball?" Dennis asked, incredulous.

"None of us has done anything wrong, boyos. None of us could have known that someone like Mickey would have turned up and pointed a gun at Tommo so I'd have to clobber him, or Tom would have to shoot that huge dude for pointing a gun at us, or there would be a bloody great diamond or any of this. This whole thing has been thrown on us, but we've stuck together. Amazing, really. We've all been part of the story, you know."

"Still wouldn't call it a ball, mate," Dennis sighed.

"Don't beat yourself up, Tom," Dave said. "Gav's right. We all thought we were going to have a pretty dull weekend on a narrowboat with a man with no actual mates. But we've had an adventure so crazy you could write a book about it."

"We'll have plenty of time to write that book if we all get thrown in prison," Neville said.

"You've got the garb for it, mon," Sherwin chuckled.

"Shut yer fa–"

"Cool it, Nev," Dennis said quietly.

"I hope your British jails 'ave better food than zis *merde* we are currently eating!" Gaston grumbled, pulling a piece of bacon gristle out of his mouth.

"Apparently, the food is great in Scrubs," Gav said.

"Mickey would know," Neville replied and then shuddered.

Dennis rolled his eyes, stood up and brushed the crumbs off his sweatshirt. "I know what it's like to be in Her Majesty's, and I'm certainly not going back," he said. "I reckon it's time to go, boys. Find out if Hershel is in business or not."

"Find out how much we're actually gonna get for the gem," Gav said. "Make ourselves a nice little nest egg. Change my life that will, boyos."

"Yep," Tom said, sounding more positive than he felt. "Dennis is right." And yet he was conflicted on multiple fronts. As well as the fear of not knowing what the future held, never mind the rest of the day, he also felt a huge sense of guilt, but surprisingly not for the deaths of the giant and Mickey Lawson. His guilt was for the lies he'd been telling the woman he loved more than anyone else he'd ever known. As far as Jenny was aware, he had simply extended the hire of the narrowboat to spend a bit more time with his new friends. He had never lied to Jenny, not once, but this morning – now that his phone was charged – he had sent her another message to say he was fine, enjoying the Broads and would be home in a couple of days. Back in Venice, he had convinced himself he was choosing to become a risk-taker to get the most out of the rest of his life. But it now felt that choice had been stolen from him. Fate had made a mockery of his choice. What blow would she deal next? Or would they end up with some life-changing money? He imagined telling Jenny about the house they could buy, the holidays they could have ... either that, or he'd be calling her from a police cell.

Tom and Dennis led the way back to the park's gate but stopped dead when they saw a police car parked on the street just the other side of the railings. It could have been a coincidence they were parked there, but it also might not be, and it wasn't worth the risk.

"Other gate," Tom whispered. "Try and walk normally. Don't run."

The others nodded in agreement, and in a bid to obscure Neville's prison attire, they surrounded him as they strolled as nonchalantly as possible towards the other gate.

"Do you think they spotted us?" Tom asked.

"I kind of feel like we're being watched wherever we go, especially with this one's subtle attire," Sherwin sniped.

"There's nothing wrong with my outfit, you arse," Neville hissed.

"Don't call me an–"

"Okay, okay, once again, *drop it*," Dennis said. "Getting lairy with each other isn't going to help."

"Over there, across the road," Tom said, and they saw a couple of Hackney cabs parked up along the kerb. "Let's split into two groups and meet at Hatton Garden. Dennis and Neville come with me. Sherwin, you take Gav, Dave and Gaston." He split the last of the cash and gave it to Sherwin.

The cabs slowly pulled away from Russell Square Gardens. Sherwin's suspicion was correct: they were being watched.

Chapter Twenty-Eight

AN UNHOLY UNION

"Croissant?" Donnie asked as he slid the plate across his desk.

The response was a puff of smoke from a newly lit cigar and a dismissive wave of a hand. "Thank you, but no. I do not eat before midday."

"So ... what brings you here so early?" Donnie asked, helping himself to a second pastry.

"I bring good news, and I bring good news. Which would you like first?"

"Don't play games," Donnie sneered. "Give me both."

"Last evening, I spoke with the detective inspector tasked with bringing in the late Mickey Lawson, and who is now attempting to track down the gang in possession of the diamond – not that he knows about the Pink Lady. I had to agree to allow him to interview you and also to the release of a warrant to search your premises."

"What?" Donnie spat, puff pastry spraying across his desk. "How the hell is that good news?"

Commissioner Hawke-Staines waved his manicured hand for the second time in a bid to encourage Sykes to remain calm.

"It is good news because I am letting you know well in advance. At the present time, the DI has nothing on you, only some tenuous link to your club. It transpires that your Serb was stupid enough to carry one of the club's packs of matches on his person. As stated, tenuous at best, and we need to play his game in order not to arouse further suspicion. All you need to do is comply, say as little as possible and, for all our sakes, keep a lid on your temper. The warrant will not be in his possession for at least a few more hours, allowing you time to remove anything that might ... shall we say ... incriminate you in anything unlawful. Don't forget, Donnie, that my role is not to help you run your business. Our relationship is one where I inform you, in advance, of what is coming. A relationship that makes things more convenient for you."

Donnie's reddening face was evidence of his displeasure. "This is not sodding convenient! This late notice allows me very little time to make sure there's nothing here that could compromise my operations!"

Hawke-Staines bristled and replied, "Good god, man, what have you got laying around? Dead bodies? You do what you need to do, and I will do what I need to do. And while you're at it, I would make any CCTV footage you have disappear, as the DI will almost certainly request you hand it over."

For fear of his temper boiling over, Sykes didn't respond but simply nodded his head to indicate he understood. The commissioner had dealt with Donnie Sykes many times over the years, and the crooked men had benefitted handsomely as a result. But once in a while, Hawke-Staines felt the need to ensure Donnie was kept in his place, to issue a firm reminder that their special relationship had clear boundaries. The men's unholy union meant they had a hold on each other for different reasons. Understanding these boundaries was crucial to ensure the alliance did not break down, a result that would be disastrous for both as they individually sought to increase their illicitly gained wealth and power.

Content that Donnie was now back in his place, the commissioner continued. "Listen, Donnie, I cannot be seen to obstruct my officers, but I can certainly slow things down when I need to. If you need more time, then it is in my power to ensure this happens. I will make sure the warrant takes a little longer to land on my DI's desk."

"Understood," Donnie allowed begrudgingly. "So, what is the other good news?"

Hawke-Staines, who had leaned forward to deliver his reprimand, now eased back into his chair, and a rare grin spread across his clean-shaven face. "We've had a sighting of the group here in Central London."

"Here?" Donnie asked, almost in a gasp. "Where exactly?"

"They were spotted yesterday on high-definition cameras near Covent Garden. We now know exactly what they look like and what they are wearing."

"I asked where exactly?" Donnie repeated.

Hawke-Staines ignored the question a second time. "We have the entire police force on high alert, and images of these men have been provided to all officers. We can only be hours from finding them now."

Donnie was infuriated by the fact the gang were still evading them, despite being so close by. But he knew the commissioner was as eager as he was to bring things to a conclusion. They had waited so long, and Hawke-Staines's confidence was as palpable as it was contagious. Surely they would soon bring the Pink Lady into their possession? But then he had a dark thought. "But what if they've gone to ground again?" he asked.

The wave of the hand again. "Not a chance. They've made a desperate journey into London, and they are here for a reason. It must be in order to set up a deal for selling the diamond. They will know that the longer they leave this, the greater the chance of them being discovered. They will show themselves very soon. After all, they most likely believe we still think they're up on the Broads, unaware that the entire London police force is either watching them or watching out for them."

"And our team of mercenaries? Are they ready to intercept the moment–"

"The very moment," Hawke-Staines interjected. "I spoke with them on the way here. They are holed up in Central London, locked and loaded. They're on standby for my call and will be on the scene before the police armed response team has even left the station."

"So you're sure your detective inspector won't release the response team the second the gang is located?"

"Absolutely not. He has not been delegated to do this. I have instructed the DI to call me the moment eyes are on the target and that I alone will make the call to the officer in charge of the armed response team." Donnie caught the treacherous glint in the commissioner's eye. "But he will not get my call until I've allowed our mercenaries the time they need to get the jump on these officers. Our men will be in, out, and away with the diamond well before they arrive."

The two sat quietly, each one allowing themselves a smile of satisfaction. This was the reason for their partnership; this was the reason their unholy union had functioned so well for so many years: greed for ill-gotten gains. The commissioner's role in this illicit operation would soon be complete. With the diamond finally in their possession, the baton would be passed to Sykes. Donnie would then gather the most secretive of his underworld contacts, offering them a once-in-a-lifetime opportunity to purchase one of the world's most valuable treasures. The Pink Lady would soon make them rich beyond even what they could have envisaged.

As Donnie was escorting his accomplice to the door, the commissioner lifted a finger to his lips and took a call on his mobile phone.

"Williamson?"

"Sir, good morning. I'm not calling to chase the warrant, sir. I have other more pressing news."

"Go on."

"It's the gang, sir. We firmly believe we've located them. Sergeant Price just took a call from Traffic. Apparently, two officers spotted a group they suspect to be the men we are looking to bring into custody. Descriptions and clothing are a precise match to the images provided. They are convinced these are our men."

"That is very good news. Where are the gang now?"

"The group of seven men got into two cabs at Russell Square. The officers trailed them to Hatton Garden, where they exited the vehicles just over a couple of minutes ago."

"Hatton Garden, hey?" the commissioner repeated, glancing at Donnie. Sykes was all ears.

"Yes, sir. We've instructed the officers not to approach but simply to keep eyes on them from a safe distance and inform us of their movements."

"Which way did they head?"

"They haven't, sir, at least not yet. Intel is live and ongoing, but it seems the men are currently lingering on the corner of Hatton Garden Road and Greville Street. Perhaps they are waiting for someone. But surely we mustn't wait for their next move? We ought to mobilise the armed response team immediately. Is this your thought too, sir?"

"Detective Inspector, I too am a man under authority, and this investigation involves powers even above my station."

"Yes, sir, I understand."

"I must first call the Home Office," the commissioner lied. "I appreciate this will mean a slight delay, but it will only be a short one. In the meantime, please ask the response team to ready themselves. How long will that take, Williamson?"

The DI was slightly taken aback by the question, as he felt sure the commissioner would know procedures just as well as his subordinate.

"As you'll be aware, sir, the team have been in readiness for the past few days, so realistically they could be deployed within ten to twelve minutes and be in Hatton Garden very shortly after that."

"Okay, get them ready to go. I will call them with the direct order just as soon as I can. Keep me apprised of any movements and, if the gang do move, make sure the trailing officers maintain constant visual. We cannot afford to lose these men again. Clear?"

"Crystal clear, sir."

Hawke-Staines pulled a number from his quick dial. "Mr Sykes, the game is afoot," he said, and then, "We're on," as the call was answered. "Get your men over to Hatton Garden now. The men on the image I sent you are currently on the corner of Hatton Garden Road and Greville Street. Keep this line free, and if their exact location changes, I'll call you immediately."

"Understood. ETA is approximately nine to eleven minutes."

Chapter Twenty-Nine

DANGLING THE CARAT

It had been some years since his first and only visit to this area of London. What should have been a simple drop-off for his thieving older brother had turned into a period of his life he would never forget and did not wish to repeat. For some young men, a stretch in prison often had the adverse effect of leading them to a deeper life of crime rather than dissuading them from a criminal path; but for Dennis, the latter had thankfully been true. It was somewhat profound and disturbing, therefore, to find himself outside Hershel's once again, and once again, by proxy, in possession of a stolen jewel.

The shop was shut.

"Bugger," Dennis said, peering through the bars covering the discoloured glass.

"*Oui*."

"Yep."

Old blue paint was peeling around the door, revealing layers of equally peeling paint in the various blues of the passing decades.

"We can't hang around here. Let's walk. We'll come back in half an hour," Dennis said, nervous now.

They crossed the road and started walking uneasily,

bumping into each other.

"Cool it," Dennis warned. "Just cool it."

"Wait," Tom said. "Look."

All eyes turned to a stooped man who had just turned onto Hatton Garden Road, shuffling along the pavement in a black fedora and a dark raincoat, a black umbrella in his right hand used as a sturdy walking stick.

"It's our man, like. Has to be," Neville whispered.

The man reached the shop and dug into his coat pocket, and hauled out a large jumble of keys. Starting from the top, he unlocked a series of lever mortice deadlocks that ran down the right-hand side of the shop's front door.

"Tom," Dennis said. "Follow me. The rest of you stay here. Let's not overwhelm the old guy."

The others nodded and sat on a bench, trying to be cool but not quite succeeding.

"Excuse me," Dennis said softly. The man hadn't heard and pushed firmly at the heavy door, blue flakes of paint gathering with the rest at his feet. "Excuse me, Mr Cone?"

This time the man looked up, pushed his wire-framed spectacles onto the bridge of his nose and squinted up at the large man with the gentle voice. "Yes?"

"Mr Hershel Cone?"

"That's right. Who are you?"

"Sir, you won't remember me, but my name is Dennis Slaughter." Hershel placed a small liver-spotted hand on the doorframe to support himself. For a moment, he studied Dennis but said nothing. "You knew my older brother Alex."

Dennis was concerned that the man, who must be in his eighties, was perhaps too old to remember much of anything.

"My brother Alex used to be ... well ... acquainted with you," he continued. "And I wondered if–"

The elderly man raised his left hand. "Oh, I remember Alex alright."

"I'm his–"

"His younger brother, yes. I heard you the first time. You must be twice Alex's size. And you don't look anything like him." When Dennis opened his mouth to answer, Hershel grabbed him by the wrist with surprising force. "You!" he hissed. "You're the idiot brother!"

"I'm sorry, I'm–"

"You're the idiot who brought the Old Bill knocking at my door. You're the boy who got nicked. Am I right?"

"You're right about the second part, sir," Dennis admitted. He waited as the man's sharp eyes raised a question about the first part. "But I'm not an idiot."

The man shuffled through the door but kept his hand on the frame. "Why are you here?"

"I'd like to talk to you, sir, if you have time. I–"

"I'm not interested. I don't make time for idiots. Get away from my door and don't come back here."

Tom and Dennis stared at the closed door. Through the barred window, they watched as Hershel locked the exterior door from the inside, unlocked a second interior door and disappeared into the unlit gloom of the shop.

"There are other dealers, I'm sure ..." Tom said, not remotely sure.

"I'm not giving up on him. He's our man."

Dennis knelt down and lifted the letterbox. "Mr Hershel, sir?"

"Did you not hear me, idiot boy? Get away from here." A single overhead light came on, and Hershel started moving things about from one corner of an untidy counter to the other.

"Nothing for it," Dennis said. "Mr Cone, I've come to talk to you about ..." He lowered his voice. "The Pink Lady."

Hershel went still.

"Mr Cone, sir, have you heard of her?"

Hershel still did not move, but he was listening.

"Mr Cone," Tom said, crouching down beside Dennis, who made room at the letterbox. "I think you know exactly what the Pink Lady is and as incredible as it may sound, I have her right here in my backpack. The reason we are here, sir, is that Dennis believes you might be able to help us?"

Still, the man stood perfectly motionless.

"Sir, we'll leave if you are not interested," Dennis said. "But if you'd take a look at her, I think you will want to speak to us."

Slowly, Hershel made his way to the door and looked down at them through the glass. "How do I know you're alone and not part of some police trickery?"

"We don't have anything to do with the police, but we're not alone," Tom said. "We're with a group of men who helped rescue the diamond from falling into the wrong hands. If you would be kind enough to let us all in, we could let you take a look at her."

The old man looked at the group of men on a bench on the other side of the street, one of them in some kind of prison garb. "No more than two in my shop at a time. That's always been my rule."

"Mr Cone, the jewel was discovered by all of us, so we're in this together, so to speak. If you wish to see the Pink Lady then I'm afraid you will have to meet with us all."

Hershel took a step back, and for a few moments, Tom was worried he may have pushed the jeweller too far.

"Okay. Call your friends. But quickly now, I don't want the

world to know my business."

Tom waved to the group and they crossed over to the shop, and Cone stood back to let them in. He locked the door behind them.

"Come, come," Hershel said. "Not here. We'll go out to the backroom."

Cone switched another overhead light on, as ancient and dusty as the first, as he guided them through a maze of cabinets overloaded with gold and silver chains, old goblets and medals to another locked door. They were now in a very different room altogether. All around them were pieces of worktop-mounted machinery, cutters, lathes and buffers, and shelves stacked with hundreds of tools. This was clearly the old jeweller's workspace.

At the far end of the room, at an angle to a heavy steel bolted rear door, stood a large desk with one chair behind and two in front. Hershel sat himself down behind the desk. He held his hands out towards the other two chairs. He looked at Dennis and Tom. "You. And you. Sit." He motioned for the others to stand against the far wall, away from the desk and then switched on a powerful desk lamp. "Your name?"

"Dennis Slaughter."

"Not you. You."

"Tom Marshall."

The man smiled for the first time. "Well, Tom, let's see if the Pink Lady is indeed in our midst, shall we?"

* * *

Commissioner Hawke-Staines took a call from Detective Inspector Williamson. He listened for a moment and then asked, "And you're quite sure?"

"Yes, sir, one hundred per cent. All seven suspects have entered the building. We believe the men have moved to a room at the back of the building as we cannot see them from the front."

"And the name of the shop?"

"A small jewellery shop called Solomon's Ice. Sir, have you spoken with the Home Office? Armed response is ready to go on your say-so."

"I have, Williamson. Take this as the green light. It's time to take these scoundrels down."

"Thank you, sir. May I have your permission for Sergeant Price and I to attend the scene? Tracking down this group has been our mission since this case began, and I'd like to be a part of bringing them to justice."

Hawke-Staines paused momentarily. Denying this request would seem odd, and he knew the DI had been intelligent enough to have made connections that led to raised suspicions of Blakney's erratic behaviour. He must ensure Williamson would have no reason whatsoever to level any suspicions in his own direction. The commissioner knew that once his mercenaries had made their raid, the diamond would no longer be in the gang's hands. When the armed response team arrived, there would be nothing for them to find. Agreeing to the DI's request would only be beneficial in protecting his own agenda. He simply must agree. But then he had another idea, one that would ensure the DI's unequivocal trust in his superior.

"You have my permission to attend the scene. But there is something else I would like to entrust you with."

"Yes, sir."

"Your original order, from the chief superintendent, was not to tamper with the gang's effects. However, I can now share with you that we believe this gang may have in their possession a highly significant jewel, a priceless diamond, in fact, and one of utmost importance. Once the armed response team have disabled this gang, I would like you to conduct a full search of these men, their possessions, and the immediate vicinity of their capture. Conducting this search in situ should ensure this priceless object is not 'lost' on its way back to the station if you understand me. In short, Williamson, I am trusting you and your sergeant to finish what you started, and this time without one hand tied behind your backs. Is this understood?"

Williamson was both surprised and flattered by the commissioner's request. A *priceless diamond* ... So they had been right; the Pink Lady was what this whole show had been about. "Fully understood, sir. And ... thank you. I assure you that Sergeant Price and I will not let you down. If the diamond is there, we will find it."

"Good man. But, Williamson, I don't need to tell you to exercise caution when you arrive. These men are armed, so let armed response do their job first, then you can do yours."

"Sir."

Hawke-Staines ended the call and immediately made another.

"Jewellery shop called Solomon's Ice. Do you see it?"

"Yes."

"Enter via the rear of the building. Two officers are currently watching the front."

"We've already clocked them, useless morons."

"Move now. My next call will be to armed response. You'll have no more than twelve minutes to get in and out."

There was a chuckle. "We'll be out in three."

"Once you have the diamond, bring it directly to the club. We'll be waiting."

Chapter Thirty

ROZE DAME

Tom placed Mickey's backpack on the desk, right in front of Hershel Cone. Hershel nodded. His hands trembling, Tom unbuckled the strap and reached inside. There was a deep silence in the room.

"Sir, the Pink Lady," he said holding the wrapped diamond out in front of him.

Hershel did not speak. So was this really she? The famous Pink Lady? He reached out and took her in his hand, feeling the weight of her. He felt a strange lack of urgency, happy to just hold her – if this really was her. But there was business to be done.

"If this is indeed what you believe it to be," he finally said, laying the wrapped diamond on a black velvet cloth in front of him, "then how on earth has it come into your possession? You must have done some bad things to get your hands on this."

"Sir, that's a very long story and, to be honest, I'm not sure you'd believe me if I told you. The truth is, we did not set out to find her."

"Tom is right," Dennis added quietly. "The Pink Lady found its way to us, not the other way around."

Hershel gave Dennis a sharp look over his spectacles and then pushed them back up his nose. "I will decide if this is the

Pink Lady. Very few people know more about this object than I do. Do you even know who it belonged to?"

"I believe it was the Scandinavian royal family," Tom said.

"The Nords? Pah!" The old man waved a disparaging hand. "No. They wouldn't know a diamond if Odin himself was to cast it into their laps. The Pink Lady belonged to the *Dutch* royal family. A most priceless legacy of the Boers and their aggressive exploitation of Afrikaner mines. A blood diamond, washed clean by centuries of so-called respectability."

Neville, who had been standing behind Tom and Dennis, stepped into the light in his garish outfit. "But if it is priceless, does that mean it can't be sold, like?" he asked.

Hershel looked directly at Neville with no little disdain. "Young man, priceless means its value cannot be determined, not that it cannot be sold. This is very true in this case because the Pink Lady simply cannot be replaced. Yes, it can be sold, and I know of many who may wish to own it. But if it were to be replaced, then this would affect its value. Quite significantly, in fact."

"I don't follow. What do you mean when you say replaced?" Dave asked.

"Soon after the Pink Lady or the *Roze Dame* to give it its Dutch name, was stolen, the Royal Palace of Amsterdam desperately sought ways to see it returned. So desperate were they, in fact, that they sent out messages to underworld contacts with offers of a reward for its return. The reward was offered without recrimination or reprisal, and discretion was guaranteed. In other words: we will pay to have it returned without any questions needing to be answered."

"How much was the reward?" Sherwin asked.

"I seem to remember it was in the region of ten million pounds. This is a fraction of what you could make were you selling it on the black market, but it would certainly be the safer option, not to mention you'd be doing the 'noble thing' by returning it to its rightful owners." Hershel placed his hands on the desk, one either side of the precious object in front of him. "However, none of this matters for the moment. The first thing we need to establish is whether what we have here is the *Roze Dame* or not." He looked at Tom. "With your permission?"

"Yes, of course," Tom replied quickly. "It's why we're here."

Hershel nodded and gently began to tease the edges of the black cotton cloth, unravelling her slowly, a moment at a time, until there she was. Each member of the group breathed in involuntarily, transfixed by her beauty. It was as though they were seeing her for the first time all over again. They looked at Hershel. He was mesmerised. Hardly breathing.

Silently he reached into a drawer and brought out a small leather satchel. After unclasping the opening, he removed and then fanned certain items out across the desk before selecting a black eyeglass. He then lifted the diamond and began his meticulous inspection, turning her this way and that in the light of the lamp. Each of the men found themselves leaning in, willing Hershel to speak, to tell them what they wanted to hear. To tell them what they needed to hear.

Gavin raised a hand to ask the question the others had dared not ask. But before he could utter a single word, he was blown backwards by the steel door exploding from its hinges. The shock of the deafening explosion sent the group to the floor, cowering and scrabbling as ten men dressed in black combat fatigues and ski masks burst through the gap, weapons raised.

"Make one fuckin' move, and I will shoot every single one of you. I'll ask you once, and once only. Where is the diamond?"

But no one needed to answer, as shining through the dust where she had fallen from Hershel's fingers, the Pink Lady lay on the black velvet cloth on his desk. Instantly, the man strode to the table and picked up the shimmering stone. He studied it momentarily before rapidly zipping it into the sleeve pocket of his jacket. He then raised a hand and made a swivelling motion with his index finger. The masked men acknowledged the signal and turned to leave. In and out. Two minutes.

"Give that back!"

They spun around and saw a Welshman with a pistol pointed at the man who had just relieved them of their treasure. But Gavin's protest was short-lived. With great speed, the closest intruder slammed his automatic rifle's butt into Gav's shoulder and caught the falling pistol as he fell in a single fluid movement. "Anyone else carrying a weapon?" he roared as Gav fell, whacking his head on the counter behind him.

"Er, sorry, just me."

The same man turned and jammed the barrel of his rifle into Tom's chest. "Where?"

Tom was thrown backwards and clutching his chest gasped, "In my backpack, there on the table."

The man nodded to a team member, who quickly retrieved the handgun.

The leader then took a step forward and growled, "We're leaving now. If any of you try to follow us, you will be shot."

In and out. Four minutes. Damn.

"What the hell were you thinking, Gav? Those maniacs could have shot us all!" Sherwin yelled. "You are out of control! You and that stupid gun, mon! First a fox and then a masked bloody maniac with a machine gun? You're insane. Crazy in the head!"

"I wish they had killed us all," Neville wailed. "The diamond's gone, and we don't have anything to show for all the shit we've been through."

"You're alive, Nev," Dave said. "That has to count for something, so stop bloody whining."

Tom writhed on the floor. "Someone check on Gav, for goodness' sake. And Hershel!"

"Gav, mon," Sherwin said, crawling through the carnage to where Gav was groaning. "You okay? I'm sorry, mon. It's just you're such a foolboy."

"No, mate. N-not okay," Gav muttered.

"Who were zoze guys? And how did zey know we were 'ere?" Gaston asked, his head in his hands. "I am going home to France. I am never ever coming to ze UK everrr again."

Dennis was bent over, hand on his knees and shaking his head. "I don't know, and I don't care. What does it matter now? Nev's right, all this shit for nothing."

Dave inspected the back of Gav's head. "Just like Mickey, you've taken a proper whack. I'd call that karma," he said. "But you'll need some ice, that's all."

Tom pulled himself to his feet. He hadn't heard a word from Hershel. "Mr Cone?" he asked, noticing that Hershel had his head buried in his hands and was gently rocking back and forth. "I really am so sorry these men burst into your shop. You must believe us that we had no idea ..."

Tom stopped. This was awful. This was all just awful. But then he had another dreadful thought. The police would be on their way. Again. They had to get out of here! But all eyes were now on the old man as he rocked.

"We really are sorry," Dave said. "We'll help you tidy up. We're so very sorry about your shop." He brushed some debris from the desk as a strange sound filtered through the old man's hands.

All men were up now, moving the rubble with their feet and brushing off the tools and dust.

"Priceless," the old man gasped. "Priceless."

"I know, we're ... so sorry," Tom said. "If there's something we can do? Or would you just prefer us to go?"

"A waste of time," the old man said. "A waste of time."

"We should go." Dennis was agitated. He did not want to do time. That much he did know.

Hershel raised his head, and they all looked at him.

"Are you okay?" Tom asked.

"We need to go," Dennis said.

"Not only have you had a wasted journey coming all this way to find me," Hershel whispered, scanning the men, "you've just lost yourselves a valueless stone."

"You mean priceless, like?" Neville said.

The old jeweller threw a look of scorn at Neville. "No. I mean valueless."

No one spoke as the word sank in. Valueless. No value.

"I don't understand," Tom said. "Or I might. Do you mean?"

"She's a fake, Tom," Hershel said and started chuckling.

Fake. Not real. Again, no one spoke.

"But Mickey would have killed you for it?" Dennis eventually said to Tom.

"And the giant would have killed all of us for it," Tom responded. "Surely they can't both have been wrong?"

Hershel did not care much for this Mickey or a giant, but he cared about diamonds, and the fake diamonds had had men fooled since time began. "The stone was a brilliant fake and would have fooled most, but it was a fake nonetheless," he said.

"A ... *fake*?" Tom asked, barely breathing.

"A fake," Hershel confirmed. Then he had a thought. "This Mickey, did he have another diamond?"

"I don't understand," Tom said for a second time. "Why would he have two?"

The old man leaned forward in his chair. "He could actually have had three."

"*Three*?"

"Many of the world's rarest gems have copies, especially those loaned to public exhibitions. It's a safety thing. The Pink Lady had not one but two replicas cut, both so perfectly fashioned you would need to be an old expert like me to notice a single difference from the real thing."

"This was the only stone Mickey had," Tom said. "At least that we know of. I have his backpack. There isn't another diamond in there. If he did have another diamond, then it can be found in a burnt-out narrowboat at the bottom of a canal in Norfolk. And in police hands now, if it existed at all."

"What have you men been doing?" Hershel asked.

"It was my stag do," Tom said. "But it got a bit, you know ..."

"And where are Mickey and this giant now?" Hershel asked.

"Erm ... well, they're dead, sir."

"And you and your friends killed them?"

"They're not my friends; actually, they–"

"Thanks a bunch, mate!" Dave said.

"Yeah, boyo!"

"I didn't mean it like that. I really didn't. I'm sorry. You're not going to leave are–"

"It's okay. We're still here for you, mate," Dennis said. "We're not out of the woods yet, though–"

"Oh, no more woods, mon," Sherwin groaned.

"Or vans," Gav added.

"Or–"

"Armed police! Armed police! Get down on your knees and place your hands behind your heads!"

All men dropped to their knees, but Hershel put his hands

behind his head and leaned back in his chair. "I'm afraid you're too late," he said. "The Lady has gone."

Well, who would have thought it, the old man mused as one by one, his new acquaintances were cuffed and searched. *The infamous Mickey Lawson dead for a fake diamond. I wonder if they know who they've been fraternising with?* He raised his hands for the cuffs. I must speak to Tom alone.

Chapter Thirty-One

THE PINNACLE

"It's a job half done, Price," Williamson sighed as he watched the armed response officers leading the handcuffed gang away to police vans parked in the back street.

"No Pink Lady," Price confirmed.

A thorough search of their possessions, as per Hawke-Staines's directive, had revealed just that: this motley gang did not have the diamond, and their belongings were returned to them, along with their backpacks, and they would now be transferred to the station for full questioning. During the searches, however, preliminary questions had been asked, and the answers had only compounded the DI's frustration.

"Do you believe them, sir?" Sergeant Price asked as the last man, a slim Frenchman, had been escorted into a van.

"They certainly seem convincing," the DI responded. "One thing is for sure: they didn't blow that back door in. It's also very doubtful they would have smashed Lawson's head in. They just don't seem the type, if I may be so bold. But even on a basic level, each of their accounts matches."

"So what now?"

"First, we cordon off this entire building. During our brief search, we haven't found the diamond, and this shop is a maze. I want a team in here today to conduct a meticulous search of the entire premises."

"But you're convinced it's not here?"

Williamson turned to his discerning sergeant. "Do you think it's here?"

"No, sir, not for a minute. What's more," he added, with a nod towards the dishevelled men, "this gang are nothing like I expected them to be. They just don't fit the profile of a gang involved with killing and diamond theft. They have been respectful, they have been compliant, and they appear, on the face of it, to be telling the truth. So much so that I don't think they are a gang at all, and I'm inclined to believe their story of being a stag party that simply had the misfortune of coming into contact with an extremely dangerous character such as Mickey Lawson. Sir, we've been in this job long enough to smell bullshit – pardon the language, sir – when it presents itself. But all I smell at the moment is truth. They had no weapons in their possession, no stolen items on their persons, and I even suspect that the proprietor of this establishment is telling the truth: the diamond was a copy."

"You may be right, Sergeant. But we need to wait until they've been processed and questioned. But there is now a more pressing concern."

"You're referring to the battalion of armed men who beat us to it?"

"Precisely. Fake or not, we have been tasked with bringing it in, and this is now our sole objective for the time being. And, once again, I believe there is only one person we know of who would have had the audacity to have organised the raid on this jewellery shop. Certainly, only one person who has previous – although tenuous – connections to this case."

"Donnie Sykes."

"Precisely. Let's cordon off this area now, and we'll call for a search team while we're on the way to Sykes' place."

"We're going to the club?"

"That's right, while the game is still in play."

"But, sir, we have no warrant yet."

"Sod the warrant, Price. I want to see the man face to face. I want to witness his reaction when I ask him about the Pink Lady and the meticulously orchestrated 'smash and grab' that just occurred. Let's get moving."

* * *

"They've gone," Hawke-Staines said.

"About time," Donnie muttered. "And we can trust them to keep their mouths shut?"

"Mr Sykes, as I've said before, these men are of the highest order. They have been in my service for many years and have never let me down. I can assure you they know how to 'disappear', shall we say."

"And exactly how long will they be prepared to disappear for?"

The commissioner tapped his jacket pocket where the jewel was secreted. "As long as it takes for them to receive their cut. My role is complete, so I ought to turn this question to you. How long will it take to set up one of your buyers and have the monies in our accounts?"

"I already have two interested parties, and perhaps three more will come to the table within the next forty-eight hours. It's in our interest to create as wide a bidding game as we can to ensure the largest payout possible."

Hawke-Staines allowed himself a satisfied smile. "Very good. I like the sound of that."

Donnie shuffled impatiently in his chair and leaned forward. "Right, show it to me. I want to see it for myself."

"Patience, patience, Donnie. I believe celebratory drinks are in order first, and then we can have a look at our prize together." He pointed towards the drinks cabinet. "May I?"

Donnie nodded his approval. "I'll have a Scotch."

"The Macallan?"

"Yes, the Macallan."

While the commissioner poured a large glass for them both, Sykes rose and turned to the wall behind his desk. At head height hung a large gilt-framed portrait of himself mounted on a white horse. Hawke-Staines had always detested the painting and shuddered when he had first laid eyes on it. He considered it to be the grotesque indulgence of a man who clearly had no observable taste, let alone panache. Donnie lifted the painting down to reveal a safe built into the wall and typed a long combination into its digital keypad. He retrieved an eyeglass, much like the one Hershel had used earlier that day. After reseating himself behind his desk, he waited for Hawke-Staines.

"You know, Donnie," the commissioner said, as he placed Donnie's Scotch down on the desk, "what we've achieved here today is most likely the pinnacle of what we could ever have hoped to do in a single lifetime. In fact, the money made from the sale of this diamond will be more than we could have hoped to accumulate over a dozen lifetimes. The outcome is, I believe, a toast to this victory as our last adventure together. I make no secret of the fact that I intend to retire in the sun and make the most of the rest of the time I have on this godforsaken planet. How about you?" He raised his glass.

Donnie raised his glass in a return salute and took a large gulp. "I'm not so sure I'm willing to give up my operations just yet, Commissioner. But first things first, let's check the diamond."

Donnie held out a hand. Hawke-Staines smiled again, almost revelling in his accomplice's growing desperation to see their spoil. He slowly placed his glass on the desk, reached into his pocket and removed the diamond. Donnie was almost childlike, fidgeting at the thought of his birthday present, and the commissioner laid the gem in his upturned palm.

Donnie, like all before him, breathed in sharply as he marvelled at the shimmering pink diamond. She was as beautiful as he had imagined her, all this time, and he watched the light flicker and dance over her multiple facets. He put down his Scotch and picked up the eyeglass and, just as Hershel had done, rotated the gem under his lamp, studying her closely. Hawke-Staines watched, a self-satisfied smile on his handsome face. But the smile evaporated when Donnie suddenly froze.

"Donnie. What is it?"

Donnie's face was now a fiery red. And then the fury exploded.

Hawke-Staines had to jump clear as the man's six-foot-four frame launched upwards, causing the desk to crash forwards, its contents propelled across the floor.

"What the hell is the matter with you, Sykes?"

But Donnie had lost control and hurled the stone across the room, sending it smashing through the pane of his office door. Launching into a tirade of profanities, he started to kick at his desk with his heavy boot, smashing the drawers, the lamp, and the whisky glasses.

"Good god, man, what is wrong with you?" Hawke-Staines cried as he backed away toward the office door, his immaculate shoes crunching over the smashed glass. He knew Sykes was prone to rage, but this was in a league of its own, and he stayed back, hoping the man would tire. What had made him so angry?

Eventually, Donnie did begin to tire and soaked in sweat, he dropped back into his chair.

"Are you going to tell me what that was all about?" Hawke-Staines ventured.

Donnie's chest was heaving, and he did not respond. Instead, he stood up, still in a mighty rage but silent, and stamped over to the safe. Reaching inside, he pulled something out, but the commissioner did not see what it was as it was hidden in a clenched fist. Turning toward Hawke-Staines, Sykes slowly moved forward. Completely unnerved, the commissioner's heart beat fast with fear. He was unsure what Donnie would do next. Sykes stopped three feet in front of him. He was breathing hard, and he held out the clenched fist.

"Donnie, what–"

Donnie unclenched his fist. In his hand was another pink gem. Identical in every way. It shone with the same brilliance, and light danced and sparkled across all of its intricate facets.

"But … what? … how? I don't understand?"

"It's fake," Donnie growled. "This one is a fake."

"So … what is–"

"Also a fake. *They're both fakes.*"

The commissioner stared wildly at the gem. "Fake? But how can it be fake? Why on earth would there be two fakes?"

"There have always been *two fakes*," Donnie roared.

"But why? Why are there two bloody fakes?"

"They are replicas. The Pink Lady has always had two identical replicas."

The commissioner's growing incredulity could be heard in his voice. "But why do you have the other one? I'm confused, Donnie. What have we been trying to find all this time? I don't–"

"This is the one that that thieving streak of piss, Mickey Lawson, gave to me ten years ago. We had a partnership, too, much as you and I have had. But he double-crossed me, and I have been waiting for the bastard to be released ever since so I can get my hands on the real thing. And now someone else is double-crossing me ... *for a second time*!"

"What's that supposed to mean?" the commissioner asked, frightened by the seething rage in Donnie's face. "How the hell would I know there were two replicas?"

"You expect me to believe you've had a desperate need to get your hands on the Pink Lady all this time, but you had no idea there were *replicas*?" Donnie sneered.

"Now, you listen to me, Sykes! I had absolutely no idea! What we need to do is discuss this and work out a way to find the real diamond." The suave, pristine commissioner was feeling an unaccustomed fury of his own now.

To the commissioner's relief, Donnie said nothing but turned away and trudged back to his shattered desk, moving a few broken items around with his foot. But then he felt the return of his fury: his fabulously rich future had hung on the retrieval of this diamond too!

"So you're giving up? Is that it? Hey, we had a deal, in case you'd forgotten!" he snapped, taking a couple of steps towards Donnie. "Come on, Donnie!"

Donnie walked over to the safe.

"Talk to me, for goodness' sake!"

"Either your so-called team of mercenaries have double-crossed you, or it is *you* who has double-crossed me," Donnie said, his back to Hawke-Staines. "You see, Commissioner, it really doesn't matter to me which way round it is. They were *your* responsibility, not mine. So either way, I hold *you* responsible."

Donnie turned around to face the commissioner, and Hawke-Staines's face turned pale with horror.

"Now, just wait!"

But Donnie didn't wait. Calmly he fired six times, emptying an entire cylinder of bullets from a shiny revolver into Hawke-Staines's chest. The commissioner died instantly and toppled gracefully to the floor.

Chapter Thirty-Two

YOU HAVE MY WORD

Hershel had made sure he was paired with Tom for the short journey to the station, and the two men sat alone in the rear of the van while the officers rode up front, a metal mesh screen dividing them.

"How on earth am I going to explain all this to Jenny?" Tom sighed, his head in his hands.

The older man leaned towards the younger. "Who's Jenny?"

"My fiancée."

"Ah, bride-to-be, hey?"

"Or not-to-be, maybe. She may change her mind after all this. As I said before, the whole story is so utterly ridiculous I wouldn't blame her if she didn't believe a word of it. I can hardly believe a word of it. And to think all I did was promise myself I'd take more risks, you know, in life, after I'd proposed in Venice. It was the reason I booked the stag do. To prove I could be a braver man, less the old safe me and more what I wanted to be. I blame Tillich."

"Tillich?"

"Tillich, the philosopher who talked about risk and courage and freedom."

"Does she love you?"

"Love me? Yes, she loves me."

"Then she'll believe you. It may take a while for her to take it all in, but, if she loves you, then she'll believe you. Simple as that."

"I hope you're right. But look at the state of me. All of the belongings I arrived with are gone. I'm wearing a set of stolen clothes that don't even fit me properly. I've got a dead man's backpack instead of my own, which was the one thing Jenny bought for me to take on my stag do."

"Who cares about the backpack, lad? It's you she'll want back!"

"I care because, and it seems so silly, but Jenny had hidden a present in a secret compartment in my backpack and told me to open it only once I was alone. But then Mickey, the guy who had the diamond, had the same backpack, and I opened his instead of mine, and he saw me, assumed I was looking for the diamond, held a gun up to me, and it all got chaotic, and I ended up with his backpack instead of my own."

"So what happened to yours?"

"When our boat caught fire, I mistakenly rescued his bag instead of my own."

The old man laughed out loud, and one of the officers turned around and gave him a sharp look through the mesh. "Your Pink Lady isn't the only replica in this whole sorry tale," he whispered.

"I had no idea about that until you said so."

"And your Mickey is Mickey Lawson, the renowned criminal, you know that?"

Tom looked at Hershel and registered the intense look in his eyes. "Yes. Dennis made the connection."

"And the replica was in Mickey's bag?"

"Yes."

"Where in the bag?"

"I don't know. After the mix-up with the bags and Mickey getting so angry, I only remembered something had rolled out of his bag later on, on that first night. I found it under a bunk on the narrowboat."

The old man thought for a long moment. "So if your backpack was identical to Mickey's, have you looked in the secret compartment in his bag?"

Tom looked at Hershel. "I haven't, no."

"Don't you think you should take a look? He may have shoved some cash in there, for all you know. No good to him now. Or even ... go on, take a look."

Tom opened the backpack and started to fiddle around inside, his heart pounding. He probed his way around the entire lining – nothing. Maybe it was a slightly different design, after all. But then his fingers brushed against a flap in the thick padding at the back. There was a small zip under the flap. Checking the officers were still facing the front, he pulled back the zip and reached inside. There was a roll of cash, no doubt, but then he almost stopped breathing.

"Hershel."

The old man looked at him. "Is it her?"

Tom carefully slid the object out of the concealed compartment and allowed Hershel to look inside the bag. He reached in and touched her.

"Tom, it's her," he whispered.

"You're sure?"

"She's warm. Diamonds are good conductors of heat, not like glass or synthetic gems." He looked again. "I would almost bet my life on it. This is no fake, Tom. This is her, I'm telling you." His cheeks flushed scarlet, and his eyes shone brightly, like the joy of a man who holds his newborn for the first time.

"Put her back and zip her up."

Tom did as the old man instructed and replaced the flap firmly back over the zip.

"Now you listen to me, Tom, and you listen good. I'm not as squeaky clean as you might imagine. In my younger days ... well ... let's just say I know my way around the police system. When we get to the station, we'll all be questioned individually. If, as you say, you boys have done very little wrong, then it's best you all stick to the truth. Yes, you might get a slap on the hand and have to do a little time inside, but it won't be for long. You'll have your clothes taken from you when you arrive and any belongings, including the backpack. You'll sign all of your items – and Mickey's – over to the station for safekeeping, and, of course, everything will be checked inside and out. But as you've discovered, the secret pocket is almost impossible to find. The officers didn't find it back at the shop, and we only found it because you knew it was there. When you're released from the cells or prison, you'll get the bag back. I don't see what they can keep me in for, so they'll let me go quite quickly, especially at my age. But I'll wait for you, Tom. You come to me with this diamond, and I'll make sure we get it sold to the highest bidder. Agreed?"

"But how did Mickey have the fake diamond and the real one?" Tom asked, still trying to piece the sorry tale together.

"I don't know, maybe the replica, or perhaps even two replicas, would have been stored with the real diamond, but he would have had this planned for years," Hershel said. "Never mind that now ... do you agree to bring her to me as soon as you can?"

"Not quite," Tom said, finally finding his voice. He leaned forward and placed the backpack on the old man's lap. "Hershel, I'm giving you the bag. They won't know it's mine when we get there, so I want you to say it's yours. You sign it over to them and then sign it out when you leave. Who knows, they may even send you home with the bag today. As you say, what on earth have they got on you to be able to hold you? And when you do get out, ahead of us, this gives you the time to set up the sale. Hopefully, you'll have done this by the time me and the others have been released."

The old jeweller was speechless for a moment, but the slowing of the van alerted him to the fact they now had very little time left to talk. "You're entrusting me with this diamond?" he whispered. "I'm ... I'm touched, Tom. I won't let you down."

"But there's one more thing I need to ask you."

"Name it."

"You mentioned this morning we could sell it back to its rightful owners, and this is exactly what I want you to do. I fully appreciate the sale would make far less than if you managed to sell it to some underground collector, but I don't want to spend any more time than necessary on the wrong side of the law. Don't get me wrong, I'm as excited as you are at the thought of that sort of money, especially after the nightmare of the past few days. We've been hunted down despite being innocent – well, apart from a few misdemeanours – and I want to be able to live with myself when this is over. I need to be able to justify my actions to the woman I love and not feel I did the wrong thing. Hershel, can I count on you to make sure the Pink Lady is sold back to the Dutch royal family?"

The old man leaned over the backpack that now sat on his lap and placed an old hand on Tom's. "You have my word."

* * *

"Gunfire!"

"I counted six shots," Williamson confirmed.

The DI and his sergeant had just parked their unmarked car outside Peanuts.

"What do we do, sir?" Price asked. "I'm pretty sure they came from inside the club."

"Change of plan. We'll need to call it in and wait for backup. Armed response is earning their money today."

Williamson was about to make the call when his sergeant grabbed his arm. "Sir, wait. Look!"

Donnie Sykes had just exited the front door of his club, and the officers watched as he hastily descended the short flight of steps and march off in the opposite direction of their car. As he did so, they saw him tuck something large and shiny into the back of his belt before pulling his jacket back down.

"That is one big gun. Who the hell carries a revolver these days?"

"Probably to match his old-school cowboy ego, Price. Right, let's get into the club now."

Williamson was already out of the car when Sergeant Price said, "Wait, sir? What happened to the change of plan? I thought we were going to wait for backup."

His DI leaned back into the car. "Sergeant, the plan has changed again. We've just seen Donnie exit the building, and most likely with the weapon that fired those shots. If someone in that club has just been shot and is lucky enough to still be alive, then we simply cannot sit here waiting for backup while they bleed to death. I won't have that on my conscience. Now let's go."

The dutiful Price quickly followed. Williamson tried the handle of the door and, to his surprise, it was unlocked.

"Seems as though Mr Sykes was in a hurry."

They found themselves standing in a foyer with deep red flock wallpaper. There were doorways on either side. To the left was a dance hall with a bar the entire length of one wall and floor-to-ceiling chrome poles on a raised platform running down the centre of the room. The room to the right had a large central bar surrounded by tables for blackjack, roulette and baccarat.

Satisfied that nobody appeared to be present on the ground floor, they carefully ascended a flight of stairs to the first floor. When they reached the top, Williamson sniffed. The unmistakable scent of sulphur lingered in the air.

"I think the shots were fired up here."

Price said nothing but nodded and followed the DI. Long corridors led away in either direction, each one with high walls that were punctuated by a succession of closed doors, many of them with heavy-duty bolts and padlocks on the outside. Towards the end of the hall that led to their right, Williamson saw what appeared to be broken glass on the carpet. As they approached, he realised the pane of glass in an office door had been smashed, and then he saw something else. After stooping to pick the object up, he gasped and said, "Would you look at that!"

In the palm of his hand sat the largest jewel Price had ever seen. The gem had a pink hue and shone brightly, even in the dim light of the corridor.

"I'll wager this is the diamond that's caused all the fuss, Price," he whispered. "God alone knows what something like this must be worth."

"If that's the case, sir, why on earth would Sykes leave it lying here on the floor?"

"Good question. Panic maybe. But he hardly seems the panicking sort."

"Sir!" While the DI mused in the hallway, transfixed by

the sparkling gem, his sergeant had entered the office. "Sir, quickly!"

Williamson joined Price, who was stood staring down at a bloodied body lying on the plush purple carpet in an office that looked like it had been attacked by robbers.

"Commissioner Hawke-Staines ..." the DI whispered. Even in death, the commissioner looked immaculate if you looked past the six holes in his chest.

"But ... b-but this doesn't make any sense?" Price stammered.

Williamson sniffed again: whisky. "Doesn't it, Price? To my mind, he may well be the final missing link between those dots we've been trying to join up."

The pair stood for a few seconds longer, thoughts racing to piece together an explanation for the carnage and the corpse that lay at their feet. The sheer amount of blood that had pooled around the commissioner's body, and the fact that his eyes remained open, stricken with terror, was confirmation that the senior officer had died almost immediately and in fear.

"Sir, look."

Price moved a few strides across the office and bent to pick something up. Turning back to his DI, he held up a shimmering object.

"Another one?" Williamson gasped. He went to Price and raised the gem he had been carrying. "This is extraordinary! They look identical!"

"Another reason to ask why on earth Sykes would have left them here."

"There are only two explanations in my mind. These gems are either both worthless or they are both priceless, and Sykes will be back for them very soon. If I had to hazard a guess, it's beyond doubt he's responsible for the commissioner's death, and he will know that you cannot kill such a high-ranking officer without severe consequences. He may be a murderer, but he'll be smart enough to know the entire police force will not rest until they find the commissioner's killer. He'll need to assemble his most trusted people in order to completely eradicate every single piece of evidence that will lead back to him. We can't assume this will take him long, so we need to move very quickly."

Williamson passed his sergeant the gem he had been holding.

"Put these stones somewhere safe, Price. Then I want you to call in the cavalry and get armed officers here immediately. Also, get an alert out that we have a killer on the loose, armed and dangerous, and last seen heading west from here towards Hanover Square."

Williamson then strode across the office to the remnants of Donnie's desk, above which a tasteless painting of a man on a white horse hung a little too low on the wall. He shuddered. Stooping among the shattered drawers, two broken whisky tumblers and a lamp, he picked up four mobile phones.

"I'm going to call Shelly and get her forensics team here straight away. We're so close to wrapping this case up, Price. We have apprehended the gang. Bizarrely, we have not one but two diamonds. And finally, we have Sykes bang to rights, and it's just a matter of time before we bring him in." Williamson turned the phones over in his hands. "I'm also going to get a trace on these phones. If I was a betting man, I wouldn't be at all surprised to find incriminating evidence of communication between Sykes and the commissioner, and perhaps even the chief. Time will tell just how deep this rabbit hole goes."

"Yes, sir. It will. Let's go."

Both officers glanced toward the commissioner's bloodied body on their way out. Each bowed his head in an automatic gesture of respect, despite what the commissioner had been up to, and then quickly made their way out of the building.

Chapter Thirty-Three

THE MAN WHO MURDERED HIS STAG (AND THE OTHERS)

The verdict of 'guilty' was unanimously called eight times for the following crimes:

(*1.*) The destruction by fire and sinking of a narrowboat.

(*2.*) Killing a fox.

(*3.*) Joyriding a speedboat across a lake to escape marauding antihunt protestors and the hunt.

(*4.*) Stealing a van and wild camping in an unauthorised lay-by.

(*5.*) Discharging a firearm, although no firearms were discovered and seized during the arrests.

(*6.*) Carrying a perceived priceless gem to various locations, although no such gem was discovered or seized upon arrest (and which later turned out to be a worthless piece of coloured glass).

(*7.*) Stealing seven pairs of jeans/cargo pants in assorted colours, including one pair in orange, and seven assorted sweatshirts and sweaters, including one in orange, from the

Covent Garden branch of H&M.

(8.) Wasting police time by evading apprehension through various means, including escape from the scene of a crime by narrowboat, hiding in woodland, stealing a speedboat, and procuring a white Hawk's Nuclear Power van.

In his summary, the judge appeared to be exasperated by the case which, for the most part, when related to the seven men on a stag do on a narrowboat on the Norfolk Broads, he called 'ridiculous', 'absurd' and 'nonsensical'.

Tom Marshall, David Alpar, Gavin Davies, Dennis Slaughter, Sherwin Aitkin, Neville Chambers and Gaston Chevalier were sentenced to custodial sentences of three months each at Her Majesty's pleasure at HMP Hollesley Bay.

Detective Inspector Austin Williamson and Sergeant James Price attended and offered witness statements in favour of the group's compliance under arrest and questioning and spoke of their good standing – with the slight hiccough of Slaughter's previous conviction – in society and genuine confusion and contrition at what a simple stag do had escalated into.

The officer's statements confirmed that forensic evidence for the murder of Colin Sturgeon had proved the killer had been a huge man, now known as Dusan Doković. They also confirmed no diamonds or weapons had been found in the group's possession during the arrests, or when searched in police custody. It was concluded that had the group been in possession of weapons at any point prior to arrest, then they would likely have belonged to Lawson and Doković, as the former, it was discovered, had stashed a gun along with the stolen jewel in some unknown hiding place in London's Soho ten years prior, and the latter had residue on his person which confirmed he had fired the weapon that had been used to kill the probation officer.

The far more serious accusations were of the unlawful deaths of Mickey Lawson, himself a known felon with previous acts of extreme violence, and Dusan Doković, whom it was now established was an assassin and was most likely hired to dispose of Mickey Lawson, including the seven men he had affiliated himself with for reasons only known to his deceased self. Due to corroborative witness statements from Tom and his friends, plus the favourable character assessments from the two officers, all charges of murder and manslaughter were ruled out entirely. It appeared to the judge that the seven men had simply found themselves in the wrong place at the wrong time, with the wrong men and a fake diamond, while attempting to enjoy an innocent few days celebrating Tom's forthcoming marriage.

Williamson received a fast-track promotion to chief superintendent shortly after the trial and apologised to fiancée Shelly Baxter, once again, for needing to delay their own plans to marry while he familiarised himself with his new role. She accepted the apology.

The media scrum that followed the closing of the case resulted in both officers being requested to attend countless official interviews and make numerous formal public statements on behalf of the Metropolitan Police Service.

Hershel Cone

Hershel Cone, who himself gave favourable testimony to the group members' decent character when they visited his shop, was not implicated in any of the cited crimes and was released immediately. He also confirmed the visiting group had brought him a valueless synthetic stone before it was taken at gunpoint and not without significant damage to his property by criminals who had no connection to Tom and his friends.

Donnie Sykes

Donnie Sykes was a man defeated. His brutal reign had come to a sudden and decisive end, his criminal empire demolished. Not only had he lost his dream of capturing the Pink Lady, he had lost everything.

Currently, on remand at HM Prison Wormwood Scrubs, he awaits trial, captured a mere two hours after the discovery of Hawke-Staines's bloodstained body. The list of his crimes grows by the day, and it is inconceivable he will see blue sky as a free man again.

Commissioner Douglas Hawke-Staines

Despite the embarrassment for the force that one of their own had fallen so foul of his obligations, the criminal behaviour of Commissioner Hawke-Staines received little in the way of public interest. Of far more interest, and to Williamson's personal embarrassment, was his own exemplary conduct and that of his sergeant's which seemed to eclipse the wrongdoing of their superior. The speedy capture of Donnie Sykes, one of the UK's most notorious criminals, had seen to that.

Chief Superintendent David Blakney

Although evidence had been found to fully implicate the late commissioner, for Chief Superintendent David Blakney, the evidence had been inconclusive. Perhaps two rotten apples had been considered too much for the service to bear. Although it was deemed that no further action against Blakney would be required, no public exoneration was either given or discussed, and the ageing officer was discreetly pressured to fall on his sword and accept early retirement.

The vacant post was left open for a week or so, and following commendations of meritorious service for both Williamson and Price, the DI gratefully accepted the post. Williamson was the youngest officer to have held the post in the entire history of the Metropolitan Police Service to date. His dutiful and forthright conduct had always ensured he was on his ascendancy.

Prison Governor Stephen Riley

Riley retired shortly after Mickey's release, tired but eager to become a rich man. He never heard from Mickey Lawson again.

EPILOGUE

Tom had been wrong to doubt Jenny. As Hershel had said to him in the back of the police van, "If she loves you, she'll believe you." But more than that, she had forgiven him. She had scolded him, no doubt about that, but she had forgiven him. She had also visited him in prison, a situation that in equal measure humbled, embarrassed and calmed him. She loved him; he knew that now, and it was all he needed to consider himself the happiest man alive.

This is it, Tom, he thought as they hugged in silence on the warm autumn day of his release. *This is it. Our new life didn't start back in Venice; it starts now. And that thing about taking risks? I'm going to tone that right down, but not enough to go back to being old me, just enough to keep me out of handcuffs ...*

A week later, they stood outside a door with blue peeling paint in London's Hatton Garden.

"Here?" Jenny asked.

"Here," Tom said.

He peered inside at the familiar gloom and raised his hand to knock, but the door opened and there stood Hershel, both his smile and his arms wide in welcome.

"Tom!" he exclaimed. "And Jenny!"

Jenny laughed. "Yes, it's me," she said.

"Come in, come in. Both of you."

Tom had called ahead using a private phone number Hershel had made him memorise when they'd been in the police van, but Hershel had refused to tell him the outcome of the sale of the diamond on the phone and in fact, shushed him before the subject was even raised let alone her name mentioned, and Tom was naturally anxious to hear what had happened. Hershel led them through the untidy, dusty shop to his bright, new workshop. "See!" he said. "See what has happened here?"

"Hershel, the cost! It must have been extortionate!"

"Pah! It matters not."

"And look at this door. It looks like a ... erm ... prison door," Tom said.

Hershel laughed. "No intruder will ever get through that!" he said, and then, "How was that? You know ..." he asked, looking at Jenny.

"It's okay," Jenny said. "Tom and I are very open about that *special* time."

"Very funny," Tom said. "It was okay, but not the place for me. I'm glad it's over."

"And the others?"

"They're okay too. Took it on the chin. But I'll always feel guilty. They stood by me. They didn't have to do that."

"This might help." Hershel pointed behind his desk.

Tom looked at Hershel with wide eyes and then back at the row of seven black cases with combination locks. It could only mean one thing.

"Hershel," Tom murmured. "Are you telling me you managed to ..."

"I am. I am indeed."

"And back to its rightful owners?"

"As requested, and as promised."

The three stared at the briefcases.

"How much?" Jenny finally whispered, unable to control her curiosity for a second longer.

"Eight million sterling. There's one million in each case, each with a code, which I shall give you and you must memorise. My fee is tucked away somewhere safe. And gratefully received, I might add."

Hershel reached for one of the cases and laid it on the desk. After putting in the combination, he opened the case and turned it around. Jenny gasped, and Tom exhaled slowly, unable to process the fact this was real, after all these months, after all the aggro and ...

"Should keep you two going for a while," Hershel said with a smile.

"And the Dutch royal family?"

"Tickled pink, Tom," replied the old man, chuckling at his own joke. "They were very happy to get their Lady back. I'm sure they thought they'd never see her again. So, yes, they are incredibly thankful, as you have just seen for yourself."

"I wish I'd seen her," Jenny said. "The Pink Lady."

"She was ..." Tom said. "She was ..."

"Magnificent," Hershel said. "Magnificent." He closed the case and set the lock. "Well, Tom, you'd better bring the car round to the back. Get yourselves out of here and away home."

"With six drops to six shipmates on the way," Tom laughed. "And trust me, they'll all be chipping in for a new narrowboat for Bill!"

"And so they should! And then?"

"We'll have the wedding that should have happened three

months ago," Jenny replied, putting her arm through Tom's. "But with a slight change of location."

"Where?" Hershel asked. "Where will you go?"

"Venice," Tom said. "It seemed right, you know, after everything."

"Oh, it's right, alright. Come on, let's get you gone. Oh, Tom?"

"Yes?"

"What was the gift Jenny bought you, in the secret compartment in the backpack? Did you ever tell him what it was, Jenny?"

"I did. But I'll let Tom tell you."

"Gosh, your memory's good!" Tom said, and the old man tapped the side of his head and laughed. "When she heard it was lost, well, she had another one made. It says this ..."

Tom pulled up his sleeve to reveal a black leather bracelet with a silver band. Inscribed on the band were the words: Decision is a risk rooted in the courage of being free.

"Tillich," Hershel said.

"Tillich," Tom smiled.

LEAVE A REVIEW

We hope you enjoyed this book – if you did we would really appreciate it if you can write a review. Your ratings really make a difference to authors, helping the books you love reach more people.

You can rate this book, or leave a review at Amazon.

HADDOCK
MANOR

Made in the USA
Las Vegas, NV
04 October 2022

56544816R00173